# GOLD ROUND THE EDGES

Louise James

C

CENTURY

LONDON MELBOURNE AUCKLAND JOHANNESBURG

First published in Great Britain in 1987 by
Century Hutchinson Ltd
Brookmount House, 62–65 Chandos Place
London WC2N 4NW

Century Hutchinson South Africa (Pty) Ltd
PO Box 337, Bergvlei, 2012 South Africa

Century Hutchinson Australia Pty Ltd
PO Box 496, 16–22 Church Street,
Hawthorn, Victoria 3122, Australia

Century Hutchinson New Zealand Limited
PO Box 40–086, Glenfield, Auckland 10
New Zealand

ISBN 0 7126 1167 3

Typeset by Inforum Ltd, Portsmouth
Printed in Great Britain by
WBC Print Ltd, Bristol

To Jimmy,
Alastair, and Simon

# Acknowledgements

The history of Britain's fisher-folk is kept alive by our excellent Fisheries Museums. I would like to thank the staffs of the Anstruther and Eyemouth Fisheries Museums for their kind assistance: also Miss Miller of J. Miller & Sons, boat-builders of St Monans, Fife, and the staffs of Anstruther Public Library, Renfrew District Library Services, and the Mitchell Library, Glasgow.

# CHAPTER ONE

Eden Murray arrived in Buckthorne to claim her family on the day the herring boats brought in the best catch of 1873.

Almost every one of the inhabitants of the Scottish east coast village was at the harbour to see the boats come home; there was only a row of horses, waiting on the street with their carts to take the fresh fish inland, to welcome Eden as she stepped from the cart that brought her from Eyemouth.

The carter handed down the straw basket holding all her possessions then clucked to his horse and clattered off over the cobbles, leaving her alone by the door of F. Ross – Ships' Chandler.

Perspiration beaded Eden's smooth forehead and ran down beneath her brown silk bodice. The full-skirted dress and matching pelerine slit-sleeved jacket were far too hot for such a fine July day, and as the outfit had been bought a full year before, when she was sixteen and still a skinny stick of a creature, it was crushing her full breasts. Her feet hurt, too; they were unused to being confined in shoes and stockings, and she longed to stretch and wriggle her toes on the warm cobbles.

But these were her best clothes, and the right thing to wear when she met her father's people. Comfort would have to wait until she found Uncle Caleb Murray.

She picked up her basket and crossed the road, keeping well away from the horses. A broad ramp led down to the harbour; as she paused on it, looking shyly down on the

1

people below, Eden suddenly longed for her mother with an intensity that brought tears to her eyes. She sniffed, and blinked the moisture away with a vigour that made her eyelids ache. Her mother had been in the Eyemouth churchyard for the past week. This was no time to dwell on her memory.

Instead, she concentrated hard on the scene before her. The enclosed water below was thronged with incoming boats, each weighed down with its sea-harvest, and the harbour walls were crowded. A rich buzz of voices rose in the clear summer air to mingle with the screaming of greedy gulls circling overhead, a moving ribbon of grey, black and white.

So many people, and not a single one of them known to Eden. She hesitated, her eyes moving over the crowd. They met the startled and appreciative gaze of a young man who was just scrambling up the last rung of an iron ladder set in the harbour wall.

Tall and tanned, he sprang on to the flagstones and straightened, sea-boots straddled as he adjusted his sense of balance from sea to dry land, his fair head to one side, his mouth curling into a grin as he looked her over.

He began to push his way towards her, but before he had taken three steps someone in the crowd grasped his arm and he was swung away, his broad back towards her.

Eden had stepped to the ramp without thinking, ready to go down to him. He would help her, she knew it with a surge of warm assurance. But when he was waylaid she hesitated shyly.

She didn't realize that she had moved close to one of the horses, and when the animal reached out to nuzzle at her white chip straw bonnet she squeaked, lost her nerve, and fled back to the safety of the buildings on the other side of the street.

The door of F. Ross – Ships' Chandler gave way beneath her hand and she stepped into a large room filled, as far as she could make out in the sudden gloom, with boxes and baskets, shelves piled high, oars leaning against the walls, sacks and coils of ropes.

Eden's neat nose twitched and snuffled at the rich aroma of tar and canvas, grain and new rope. A shaft of light from the window showed her a clear spot on the crowded floor, and she made for it.

Feet shuffled forward from a dark corner in uneven rhythm.

'Aye?' a man's voice asked.

'Could you direct me to Caleb Murray's house, if you please?'

'Caleb Murray?' The man moved forward and the patch of sunlight sparkled in his eyes, which were the colour of a deep green sea. His face was lined, his thick hair well speckled with grey, and there was a wry upward twist to his mouth that she liked.

'Caleb and his family'll be on the harbour. You'll find him by the farlins with the rest of the coopers – '

The door burst open. A wedge of blue sky, pencilled by the top of the boats' masts across the road, formed a background for the young fisherman she had seen at the harbour.

'Father, Coll wants more baskets – '

He stopped, then said slowly, 'So – you weren't a dream after all.'

'The baskets are ready, Lewis.' The man nodded at a pile near the door, ' – and here's someone seeking Caleb Murray.'

'He's back there.' The newcomer jerked his fair head in the direction of the harbour. 'I'll take you to him.'

'I'd be grateful. Can I leave my things here?'

The shopkeeper limped forward and picked up the basket. 'I'll see to it for you.'

'I've no mind of you visiting with the Murrays before,' the fisherman said with open curiosity as Eden tittuped carefully in her confining shoes across the road and down the ramp by his side.

'I never have, but I hope to make my home with them now. Mister Murray's my uncle. I'm Eden Murray.'

'I'm pleased to meet you, Eden Murray,' he said solemnly. 'My name's Lewis – Lewis Ross.' His eyes, she noticed, were of the same clear green as his father's. She felt a flutter of excitement each time she glanced up and met their gaze.

In the past six months Eden had become accustomed to seeing swift appreciation – as often as not mingled with secret lust – in men's eyes. Even in her stepfather's eyes, which was why she had left home soon after her mother's funeral. Men liked her glossy black hair, the dark eyes above upward slanting cheekbones, her smooth tanned skin. But masculine admiration had never stirred her – until now.

'I didn't know old Caleb had a niece.'

Eden swallowed hard. 'I'm not certain he knows it himself.'

Mischief seasoned his grin. 'Then this should be an interesting meeting. Here we are – '

They had reached the farlins, the long shallow wooden troughs where the freshly caught herring were gutted and packed by gangs of chattering fisher-lassies. The sight eased some of Eden's homesickness. She had earned her keep as a fisher-lassie in Eyemouth for the past five years, ever since she was twelve. Her skilled fingers twitched as she watched the gutting knives twinkle among the fish.

'Mister Murray – '

A thickset, balding cooper stopped his hammering and looked up, frowning at the interruption.

'Aye?'

Lewis put the baskets down and linked his thumbs into his belt. 'Here's your niece come to pay her respects.'

'I have no niece,' Caleb Murray said sourly, and bent to his work again without looking in Eden's direction.

She swallowed hard and stepped forward, into the inquisitive stares from the womenfolk and the other coopers.

'Uncle Caleb? I'm Eden – Eden Murray.' The name she had adopted since her mother's death still felt strange on her tongue. 'My mother was Jessie Gray.'

A murmur ran through the crowd. Eden saw the cooper's jaw drop and his small eyes fill with dismay as he looked at her.

'There was never a Jessie Gray married into my family!'

'Mebbe not – but I'm your brother Joshua's daughter all the same,' she said doggedly.

A woman at the farlins leaned forward to peer at her, her fingers never faltering with their work, for fisher-lassies were paid by the barrel and they couldn't afford to waste time.

'She's right, Caleb Murray – the girl's the image of your Joshua, handsome imp of Satan that he was.' Her cackle rang out, attracting more people to the crowd round about. 'Joshua's come back to haunt you, right enough!'

Caleb's gaze travelled slowly down Eden's length, all the way to the neat shoes peeping out from beneath her stylish skirt, then back to her face, before he said shortly. 'And what would Jessie Gray's daughter be wanting here?'

'My mother's dead. I've come home to my father's village to stay with my own folk.'

A tall, gangling man a few years older than Eden left the full barrel he was rolling away from the farlins and pulled at Caleb's sleeve. In spite of the heat of the day Eden felt a shiver run through her as his pale blue eyes slid over her, probing through her best brown silk.

The cooper shrugged the youth's hand away. 'Stay with me? D'you think I'm a rich man, able to feed another mouth with no effort at all?'

'I can earn my keep! I'm a fisher-lassie – and a good one.'

'You see, Caleb?' her escort said easily. 'The girl's going to earn for you – and I've never known Caleb Murray turn his nose up at the prospect of money.'

Someone in the crowd laughed, and the cooper's flush deepened. Then a new voice made itself heard, loud and harsh, and the laughter stopped as though choked.

'Send her back where she came from, Caleb Murray!'

The speaker was a woman working at one end of the farlins. Her gaunt, thin-lipped face and the black shawl wrapped about her head gave her the look of a malevolent crow, a look emphasized by deep-set sharp black eyes.

'You heard her, Mother – she's a fisher-lassie,' Lewis Ross protested. 'And here's you having to work at the farlins yourself because you're a woman short – '

'Mind your own business, Lewis Ross!' she snapped at him. 'I'll decide who works for me and who doesn't!'

'At least give me the chance to show what a good worker I am,' Eden said, then she almost shrank back against her ally as the woman's gaze fixed on her. She had never in her life encountered such hostility from another human being. Her mouth went suddenly dry and her knees trembled, but she managed to hold her ground and repeat, 'Let me show you what I can do.'

The gimlet eyes swept over her. 'You'll spoil your bonny gown, lady,' the woman sneered, and there was some hasty, dutiful chuckling from the crowd.

'Here – hold that – ' Eden tore her bonnet off and thrust it into the young fisherman's hands. Her confining jacket followed, to be looped over his arm.

She pulled her shoes off and there was a gasp from the crowd as she turned away and bent to scoop up her skirt and unfasten her stockings. Her bare feet welcomed the warm cobbles as she spun back to the farlins.

'Now – if I can have your apron and your knife I'll show you how well I can work,' she said boldly.

'Come on, Mother – give the girl a chance to show what she can do,' the young man urged, and there was a faint, very faint, murmur of agreement. Eden sensed that this woman was respected and feared in the village. If she were to stay,

6

Eden must convince her as well as Caleb Murray. She advanced across the scale-jewelled cobbles, one hand outstretched with a confidence she didn't feel.

Her bluff worked; the big canvas apron the woman wore was slowly taken off and given to her. As she tied it about her own slim waist Eden took her place behind the farlins, nodding to the two wide-eyed, startled girls she was to work with. Then she grasped the knife that lay waiting and plunged her hands into the glittering river of fish that had just been poured on to the table.

Her fingers were bare, without the protective cloths she usually wore. But Eden had learned her trade well; the sharp knife in her grip slashed and probed with a speed that defied the naked eye, within a hair's breadth of her free hand but never harming it.

A herring was slit, cleaned, and in the barrel at her side in seconds, to be followed by a second, a third –

Then she forgot that she was on trial and settled into the familiar routine, the stones warm beneath her feet, the sun beating on her uncovered dark head; silvery herring, the sea's harvest, cascading from basket after basket on to the table before her.

The sun reached its highest point in the blue dome overhead then began its afternoon descent. The fisher-lassies' table was never emptied; an inexperienced onlooker might have begun to wonder if the Buckhaven fleet had emptied the North Sea of fish entirely.

The coopers worked as tirelessly as the women to keep up with the demand for more and more barrels. One by one the waiting carts on the road above were filled and went off inland with their cargo of herring. Other barrels were packed with fish, filled with pickle and rolled away to the storage sheds beyond the harbour.

As they worked the fisher-lassies ate a sketchy midday meal. An older woman with a tired face that had once been pretty shyly offered Eden an oatcake and a bottle of cold tea.

The liquid was strong and bitter, but Eden drank thirstily.

'I'm Barbara Murray, Caleb's wife. This is my daughter Charlotte' – the woman nodded to one of the girls working with Eden – 'and my son John's over there.'

With dismay, Eden realized that her cousin John was the gangling young man with the pale slippery eyes. But there was no time to think about him – the hundredth or perhaps the thousandth basket to arrive from the boats emptied its glittering contents on to the table and she wiped the back of her mouth, handed back the bottle, and picked up her knife.

It was late afternoon before the flow of fish slowed, then stopped. The last barrel was filled and trundled away, buckets of water were brought to sluice down the table and the cobbles beneath it.

Suddenly aware of how weary she felt, Eden straightened her back and lifted her sun-warmed face to the sky, now a deeper blue with approaching evening. She looked around for her jacket and bonnet and saw that Lewis Ross had laid them carefully over a nearby pile of lobster pots.

Lewis. She turned his name over in her mind as she wiped her hands on the coarse apron and took it off. She picked up her shoes and looked around for her stockings. They were there – dangling from her cousin John's fingers.

She fought the impulse to step back from him, and held out her hand. 'Give them to me.'

He grinned teasingly. She snatched the toes of the stockings and he let her pull them free, holding them so that they slid slowly, sensuously, through his long fingers. His eyes held hers all the time, as though it were her slender legs that his hands caressed.

'Mistress Ross says you can work the farlins – for the time being,' he said, and one hand seemed to glide like a snake into and out of a leather pouch hung at his waist. 'Here's your wages for the day.'

As she took the coins his fingers curled about hers, warm

and clinging and repellent. She drew her hand back as quickly as she could.

'Charlotte'll take you to the house,' John said, and turned away, leaving her free to rub her hand hastily against her skirt to rid it of his touch.

Charlotte, the stolid, unsmiling girl indicated by her Aunt Barbara Murray, was nowhere to be seen. Presumably she had gone off with the other women while Eden had been collecting her scattered clothes. Most of the people who had thronged the harbour earlier had gone and she stood alone, looking about her, unsure of what to do next.

'So you're to work for my mother?'

Lewis Ross beamed down on her. 'I knew as soon as you picked up the knife that she'd have to take you on. She hates having to work along with the other women. Your bag's still at the store – we'll fetch it and then I'll take you along to the Murrays' cottage.'

He slid a hand beneath her elbow and guided her back along the harbour to the ramp. His mother was in the shop, her face floating in the shadows.

'Lewis, I want to see you up at the house.'

He alone seemed totally unafraid of her, 'Later, Mother. I'm taking the lassie to her uncle's place,' he said cheerfully, and ushered Eden back into the street.

They didn't have far to go, but by the time they got there she had told Lewis about her mother's death and her own decision to leave Eyemouth, where her stepfather was a butcher, and seek out her own blood-kin. She didn't tell him about the romances she had woven around her unknown father, the fisherman who had wooed and won her mother, left his wife to live in sin with her, and drowned a few months after Eden's birth.

Lewis, in turn, supplied a swift description of Caleb Murray and his family.

'He's a sullen sort of man – he's been taken bad with religion.' He made it sound like a disease. 'Watch you don't

9

get dragged into it. Your cousin Charlotte's a lump of a girl with nothing to say for herself, but her mother's a civil soul – when Caleb allows her to open her mouth.'

'And John?' she asked, fearful of the answer but eager to know his views.

'Him? There's something sleekit about that one, but my mother's fond enough of his whining ways. He works for her as a carter, and he helps in the store sometimes. You'll find that most of the folk here work for my mother, including you,' he added casually. 'But don't let her frighten you.'

'I've no mind to let anyone frighten me!'

They were in a narrow lane leading off the main road. He stopped at a low-roofed house and put down her bag, leaning on the whitewashed wall, grinning down at her. 'I can believe that.'

'Do you work for your mother too?'

'Only in the summer months. I'm crewing on the *Rose-Ellen* while I'm at home. She's our boat. The rest of the year I'm reading law at the university in Edinburgh.'

Disappointment welled up in her, and she was sure that it must have showed in her face. 'When do you go away?'

'Not for more than a month. There's still plenty of time.'

'For what?'

Laughter danced in his eyes. Her pulse fluttered as he leaned closer and murmured into her ear, 'For whatever you might have in mind – '

Then the door behind Eden opened and she turned to see Caleb Murray glaring suspiciously at them.

'I've brought your niece home.' Lewis handed the basket containing all Eden's wordly goods to her uncle. Caleb took it automatically as the younger man added to Eden, 'I'll look out for you tomorrow at the harbour – '

Then he nodded to Caleb, eased his shoulder from the wall and strode off down the lane and round the corner.

'Are you going to stand gaping after Lewis Ross all night?' Caleb barked, and she followed him into a small, low-

10

ceilinged kitchen. Charlotte and her mother, both setting food on the table, halted to stare at her. Barbara's eyes, Eden noticed, moved almost at once to her husband's face, as though waiting nervously for his reaction to the new arrival.

John Murray sat at the table in his shirt sleeves; his mouth fell open as Eden appeared, and his heavy lids drooped over his eyes in a way that unnerved her. She wished, with all her heart, that she could have put her hand in Lewis's and gone with him.

'Set another place,' Caleb growled. As Charlotte hurried to obey he dropped Eden's bag on the floor and held out a big calloused hand. 'You can share Charlotte's bed.'

His daughter opened her mouth, shut it again.

'Since you're set on staying you'll pay for your keep like the rest of us.'

She put the money she had earned that day, all of it, into his palm. He counted it carefully then stowed it away in his pocket. She watched with growing dismay.

'I must have some money of my own, Uncle – '

'For what? To throw away as the whim takes you? I'll give you money when I think you deserve it. Sit down, the food's cooling.'

There was little enough of it, and Barbara ladled the lion's share on to Caleb's plate. She herself, Eden noticed, took scarcely any.

Caleb glowered round the table, then clasped his hands and bowed his head.

'Lord, bless this food and cleanse our evil souls of sin, that we may be worthy of a place in your House,' he said heavily. Eden, believing that he was finished, lifted her head and opened her eyes, to find herself looking straight into John's fevered gaze.

A wave of revulsion broke over her and she instinctively ducked her head again, to listen with growing incredulity as Caleb went on, emphasizing each word:

11

'And Lord, I ask you to help me to accept my new burden, the bastard child born in sin to my brother Joshua, whom you have seen fit to send here to me, as my punishment and my Cross.'

# CHAPTER TWO

The door creaked. Eden, dressed only in her petticoat and reaching out a slim arm for the clean blouse on the bed, stopped and listened intently.

For a moment there was nothing to be heard but the sounds her Aunt Barbara made as she moved about the kitchen, clearing up after the silent evening meal. Then the door creaked again.

'Charlotte?'

There was no answer, but the back of her neck prickled and she suddenly felt chilled, though the tiny room she shared with Charlotte was airless and stuffy.

It was the evening of her second day in Buckthorne. As far as she knew everyone but herself and Barbara had gone to a meeting in the little wooden hut where Caleb's sect worshipped.

'John?'

There was no answer, but she didn't need one. The silence had become a waiting thing, a prying, hot-eyed slimy thing that reached for her through the crack between the badly fitting door and the jamb. She snatched up her blue skirt and clutched it to her breasts as she pounced, wrenching the door open wide.

'Get away from here, John Murray!'

He stood his ground, his eyes slipping over her like wet frogs.

'I was just — '

'Keep away from me!' Anger ran like a flame through her, driving back the chill. She was suddenly aware of her loose hair, scarcely curtaining bare shoulders.

'Eden – ' He moved forward swiftly, crowding into the small room with her.

'Leave me be!' she ordered, low-voiced, mindful of her aunt's presence close by, and unwilling to cause trouble.

In answer he moved towards her and she backed, to feel the frame of the bed that almost filled the little room hard against her calves. With rising panic she realized that if he came nearer she would either find herself pressed against him, or she would have to fall back on to the bed, at his mercy.

Thick brows met and dragged down over John's sulky blue eyes. 'Too proud to have anything to do with a carter?' His tongue slipped over his lips. 'I watched you at the farlins today. I saw the way you smiled at Lewis Ross, and the way he hung around, looking at you.'

'I'll – I'll call your mother if you don't get out of here!'

His eyes swarmed over her, and her breasts seemed to cringe against her ribcage under that searching look. John's fingers caught at the material she held protectively, tugging at it.

'You're soft in the rigging if you think you can catch the likes of him – ' He used the local fisherman's phrase contemptuously. 'His mother's got fine plans for him. You'd be better to seek your future among your own kind – '

'With a man like you?' Rage and fear brought a shrill laugh to her lips and his scowl deepened.

'I know about women, Eden. They were put on this earth to tempt men and turn them from the Lord's ways. But I could take your sins to myself and cleanse you. I could tear the devil from your body – '

'John?' his mother said from the doorway, and he whirled guiltily.

'What are you doing here?'

14

'I – was asking Eden to come to the prayer meeting with me.'

'And I was telling him I don't want to go!'

Barbara's gaze flew from her son to her niece, and back again.

'Then you'd best go alone, John. And go now, or you'll be late.'

For a moment he hesitated. With a flutter of fear Eden realized that if he wanted to John could easily push Barbara out and bar the door against her. Then, to her relief, he pushed past his mother and went, crashing the street door behind him.

Barbara's lips fluttered, then firmed and closed. With a final glance at Eden's bare shoulders and unbound hair she retreated, and Eden was alone again. When she had dressed herself she went into the kitchen.

'I'm going for a walk along the shore.'

'Caleb'll be home by nine. Mind and be back before then,' Barbara said without lifting her head from her knitting.

The golden evening welcomed Eden, enfolding her, lifting her spirits with the touch of a pleasantly cool breeze shot through with a mixture of sea salt and the light perfume of flowers from the gardens between her and the shore. She stepped out, stretching legs that were cramped by hours of standing at the farlins that day. Along the lane she went, and turned right into the main street, parallel with the sea.

A few men and women sitting outside their houses to get the benefit of the good weather nodded to her and she smiled back, grateful to them for including her so quickly in their close-knit community. Her uncle's open hostility was chilling, but she had made up her mind during her first meal in his house, after the shock of his plea to his God on her behalf, that she wouldn't let him drive her away from her father's village. Charlotte had scarcely said three words to her, Barbara seemed to be terrified of her husband, and John –

A shudder shook Eden and the evening lost its glow.

15

'Good evening – ' Lewis Ross said at just the right moment, then laughed as she stared at him, startled. 'You're looking at me as though I was the devil himself.'

'No – ' she hastened to assure him. 'I'm just so glad to see you – ' He laughed again as a hand flew to her mouth, too late to stop the foolish words.

'I thought you'd have been nose-deep in your Bible at this moment with the other holy-jennies up on the hill.'

His description of the folk who belonged to the same sect as the Murrays was so accurate that she giggled.

'I went last night – and made up my mind that I wasn't going back.'

'Caleb won't like that.'

'Then he must suffer it.'

He had fallen into step beside her, shortening his stride to match her step. 'I was hoping we might meet, away from the harbour, Eden – ' he used her name casually, easily, as though he had said it a hundred times before.

She recalled John's sneering words. 'Mebbe your mother wouldn't like to see you out walking with an ordinary fisher-lassie.'

'You've got the measure of my mother already, have you? Well – ' he slipped a hand beneath her arm, and his touch warmed her blood. 'Like Caleb, she must suffer what she won't accept. Come in here – '

He steered her through an open wrought-iron gate to an enclosed area where tall trees cast cool shadows on the grass. She looked about at an assortment of headstones, some new and neat, others soft green with moss and slumped wearily into the ground. 'It's a graveyard!'

'It's the story of Buckthorne,' he corrected her. 'See here – ' They walked, close together, between the stones as Lewis pointed out one local name after another. Then he stopped before a small stone and knelt, rubbing the moss away. 'See?'

She lifted her good blue skirt above neat ankles to kneel beside him.

16

'Ohhh – !'

' "To the memory of Joshua Murray, fisherman, born October 1826, drowned August 1856 – " ' Lewis read aloud. 'Your father. His body must have come ashore.'

'Yes. He went overboard just outside the harbour in bad weather. My mother told me.'

'Then it says "And to the memory of his dutiful wife Jean Muir, born January 1827, died June 1860." ' He chuckled. 'You'll note she was dutiful, not loving.'

'No wonder, poor woman – he left her and lived in a house right here in the village with my mother. But she got him back in the end – though it was only to bury him.'

'And it's a cold bed they share now,' Lewis said with scant feelings for the pair who lay in uneasy companionship beneath his feet. He straightened, offered a hand to Eden and pulled her up beside him.

'She must have loved him deeply. And so did my mother, till the day she died, for all that she married someone else after he went. She always told me that I took after him in looks.'

'I can believe that, for there's a strong family likeness with your uncle Gideon, more than with Caleb.'

'Gideon? My father's brother Gideon? But surely he's far away, serving in the navy?'

He raised an eyebrow. 'Did Caleb not tell you? Mebbe not, for there's no love lost between the two of them. Gideon Murray's been home from his travels these ten years back. He's a boat-builder here in Buckthorne. He's building a new skaffie for us, to take over from the *Rose-Ellen* next summer.'

'Where is he?'

'You'll have seen the boatyard at the shallow end of the harbour, where the seabed slopes up out of the water. He lives in the cottage just beyond. I'll take you there if you want.'

But the clock on the church steeple showed that it was almost time to get back to the house if she were to be home

17

before Caleb. 'I'll see him tomorrow. I have to go now – '

'One more thing – ' He drew her away from Joshua's grave, along one side of the graveyard, where the low stone wall had a longer drop on the other side to a small shingly bay. A burn with stepping stones across it ran down through the shingle to the sea, muttering and whispering to itself as it went.

'See – ' Lewis stopped at a fine table monument, a great slab of stone supported on four sturdy pillars. The elaborately carved inscription announced to the world that it sheltered the remains of one Alexander Grant, boat-builder of Buckthorne, and went on to list the names of his wife and his numerous children. Lewis laid an almost loving hand on it.

'One day,' he said, 'I'll lie in this yard, and that's what they'll put on my stone. "Lewis Ross, boat-builder, of Buckthorne." '

'You? You'll be a fine lawyer in Edinburgh!'

He shook his head. 'When I'm finished with my studies I'll work in the city for as long as it takes me to make enough money. Then I'll come back here, whether it pleases my mother or not, and Gideon and I are going to be partners.'

Her heart suddenly, foolishly, lifted.

The evening shadows were long now. Here, beneath the trees, the two of them seemed to be far away from everyone else, in a world of their own.

Lewis stepped close, cupped her face in his hands, and kissed her. Her hands went up to hold his shoulders as she let her mouth melt against his. Then he released her. 'I'll be back,' he said as though he were making a solemn promise.

They walked back to the corner of the lane together, then their ways divided.

'Will you meet me in the graveyard tomorrow night?' he asked, and she nodded, and watched as he turned away, striding up the hill to where his parents' grand house brooded over the village and the sea beyond with heavily curtained eyes.

18

*

The boatyard was an untidy sprawl of timbers and ropes and tar-buckets, with two skaffies, the fishing boats favoured by the Scottish east coast fishermen, lying clumsily on their sides awaiting repair, and the skeleton of a third, half-built, supported on stocks.

Eden picked her way carefully round a great pile of spicy-smelling new planks and found an elderly man on a ladder propped against the stocks. 'Are you Gideon Murray?'

She had to ask the question again, at the top of her voice, before he heard her above the racket of his own hammer. Then he spat a handful of nails into his palm and pointed with the hammer to the little cottage nestled in a corner of the great wall that held the sea at bay. 'You'll find him in there.'

The door was open. She stopped on the threshold to let her eyes grow accustomed to the shadowy interior.

Gideon Murray obviously saw nothing wrong with letting the yard intrude into his home; dirty dishes sat companionably cheek by jowl on the table with hammers, chisels, paint pots, and a few brushes.

At first, fascinated by the clutter of the place, she didn't notice its occupant. Then a drift of pipe-smoke stung her nose and a deep, easy voice said, 'So – you've found your way here, have you?'

She screwed up her sun-dazzled eyes. 'Uncle Gideon?'

He was sitting at the table, pencil clutched in one great fist, a note book open before him; a strikingly handsome man with thick dark curls streaked with pure white, and far-sighted dark eyes dominating a brown face.

'Just Gideon,' he corrected her. 'I'll not be called uncle by anyone, specially those two Caleb spawned.'

'Can I come in?'

'If you promise me you'll not try to put the place to rights as soon as you step over the door. I can't be doing with women who want to clean all the time. If you ask me it wasn't a snake that spoiled things for Adam and Eve – it was a whisk broom.'

'Now I know why my Uncle Caleb didn't tell me about you.' She picked her way to the table, took a box of nails from a chair and sat down, resisting the temptation to dust the seat first. A grin tugged at one corner of Gideon's mouth.

'Has he tried to convert you yet?'

'Tried and failed.'

'That's welcome news. So Jessie Gray's dead? She was a fine-looking woman. But you favour your father.' He studied her with interest. 'Did you ever hear of the Spanish ship that sailed into Ainster after the Armada?'

Her throat constricted with memories. 'My mother told me, time and time again.' It was the sort of romantic story that her mother loved. The galleon had sought refuge in a nearby harbour, and it was said that the local women had played their part in comforting the homesick, battle-weary Spaniards so enthusiastically that their descendants owed their dark looks to the crew of that great Spanish galleon.

'She must have been a grand sight, for all that she was in a sorry state by the time the English and the weather had finished with her,' Gideon reflected, half to himself. 'Joshua was more of a Spaniard that any I met on my travels, and from the look of you, it wasn't a common below-decks seaman our ancestress favoured, but one of the grandees.'

A voice called him outside.

'Don't you tidy anything away,' he warned and went out, ducking his head as he went through the doorway.

Eden sat quite still, hands clasped tightly in her lap to keep them from busying themselves among the mess that strewed every inch of the table, eyes darting round the room. Cluttered as it was, it held more warmth and welcome than Caleb's home. The smell of tar and paint and pipe-tobacco was pleasing and everything about the place seemed to have the same air of solid reliability and confidence that Gideon himself possessed.

'By God, she did as she was told!' he boomed from the doorway behind her. 'There's hope for womankind after all! You can make somé tea, then we'll talk about Joshua - for I'll lay my life on it that you've had no word of him from Caleb.'

'Where are the tea-leaves kept?' Eden rose, turned, and felt a flush warm her cheeks as Gideon stepped into the room and Lewis Ross appeared in the doorway at his back.

'I thought you might be here,' he said.

'The tea's in a wooden box on the sill somewhere,' Gideon said vaguely, knocking his pipe out on the range. 'Sit down, lad. I think Eden and me are going to get on fine.'

Then he looked shrewdly from one young face to the other and added, 'Indeed, I think the three of us'll do well enough together.'

# CHAPTER THREE

Eden walked up the cobbled wynd from the harbour, bare brown toes curling about the uneven stones as she went. A shallow basket containing a dozen plump haddock beneath a cloth was slung from one arm.

The air was still and warm. The skaffies had long since returned from the fishing grounds and their catch had been gutted, packed, and pickled. Some had been whirled inland in the dealers' carts and the rest was stored in the Ross's curing shed, going through the first process of pickling. Below and behind Eden the harbour was half-asleep, the boats scraping each other as an occasional eddy rippled in through the entrance.

The sea itself was on its best behaviour, offering its sparkling, innocent bosom, demurely frilled by small waves, to resting gulls. A group of children, too young as yet to be boxed into the schoolroom on that lovely day, could be heard shouting to each other on the rocks behind the shore-road cottages.

The breeze fluttered the ribbons of Eden's white cap and cooled her rounded arms. She wore a faded green dress, the sleeves rolled up to her elbows, the skirt long enough to be decent but short enough to let fresh air about her ankles.

She stopped for a rest, looking with satisfaction down the hill at the sleepy scene. She had sensed, when she heard her mother's tales about Joshua Murray, that Buckthorne was her real home, and despite Caleb's surly attitude she had no regrets about her return to her birthplace some three weeks earlier.

She opened the Ross's back gate and went across the neat flagged yard, eagerly scanning the house windows. Lewis, however, was not to be seen. He had become one of the reasons why life in Buckthorne was so sweet. She saw him every day, either at the boatyard or by arrangement in the graveyard or on a rocky ledge on the shore. She dreaded the day he would leave the village and go back to his other life in Edinburgh.

Euphemia Ross's maidservant opened the back door and lifted the cloth from Eden's basket.

'Are they good and fresh?'

'Fresh?' Eden said in mock outrage. 'They swam up the hill all by themselves and I just this minute popped them into the bas – ' She stopped as a door at the kitchen opened and Euphemia appeared.

'Eden Murray, I'll have a word with you.' Her voice was harsh. 'You can come through to the parlour. Becky, see to the fish.'

The maid and Eden exchanged swift glances, then Becky stepped back to let Eden in, putting out a hand for the basket. Showing more confidence than she felt, Eden stepped into Lewis's home for the first time.

She hadn't spoken to his mother since their exchange at the harbour the day she arrived in Buckthorne. On a few occasions the woman had come down to watch the fisher-lassies at work, her bony hands clasped round her elbows as though she were chilled, her hard black eyes and thin mouth giving nothing away.

Eden knew that Euphemia Ross had been a fisher-lassie herself, but now she and her husband owned the chandlery, the curing sheds, and the *Rose-Ellen*, the boat Lewis crewed in. They also had financial interests in several other fishing-boats and most of the small businesses in the village. And everyone knew that, whatever it said above the door of the

23

shop, it was Euphemia who made the decisions and held the power, not Frank.

As she followed the woman through the dim hallway Eden's gaze darted here and there. There was little to be seen. A few paintings decorated the walls, a fine wooden staircase led to the upper roms; the impeccable grained surfaces of three closed doors gave no indication as to the rooms that lay beyond them. There was a strong smell of soap and polish about the place, but the air was chill, as though sunshine was never allowed inside.

Euphemia opened one of the doors and Eden was led into the parlour, her bare feet leaving dusty outlines on the polished floor before sinking into a real carpet. The room was crammed with furniture – over-stuffed chairs, a huge ornate sideboard, a towering, heavily carved mantelshelf, a round table supported on thick bowlegs with a white lace cover over it, a leafy plant on its special long-legged stand, thick dark curtains looped back at the window, a tapestry screen before the grate. A ray of sunlight probed through the window panes, landing on what was, to Eden, the most miraculous part of this magnificent room. Propped up in a row on the sideboard were several big china plates, the hand-painted kind prized by east coast folk. The sunbeam showed up the bright reds and blues and greens of the patterns, and reflected off the gold edging on each plate.

Euphemia seated herself in a high-backed chair by the window, hands folded in her lap, her face in shadow. She didn't waste time in niceties.

'Caleb Murray's a hard-working man. It would be foolish of you to make trouble for him.'

For a moment Eden stared, completely taken aback by the woman's words. Then she understood, and felt angry colour surge into her face.

'Are you speaking of my friendship with your son, Mistress Ross?'

'Friendship!' Euphemia almost spat the word out. 'There

can be no friendship between my son and a – a bastard!'

Eden's hands clenched on her skirt. 'Aye, I was born out of wedlock – like many of the folk hereabouts. What's wrong with being a love-child?'

The woman's face twisted as though she had been slapped. 'How dare you talk to me like that!'

'If I have to mind my tongue, why should you be free to say whatever comes into your head?' asked Eden, reckless in her bewilderment and anger at the woman's unwarranted attack. 'I never asked for this meeting, Mistress Ross, and I'll not be miscalled by anyone! As for Lewis – surely it's for him to say who he wants to befriend?'

Euphemia rose, fury making her even more witchlike. For a moment Eden thought that the woman was going to attack her. Then the door opened and she saw Lewis in the hall, Becky peering over his shoulder.

'Eden – ' he said, bewildered. 'Why are you here?'

'Becky – pay this girl and put her out of my house!' his mother thundered.

'Nobody'll put me anywhere, for I'm going of my own free will! And I'll thank you for my money!' Eden pushed past Lewis and scooped up the coins that the maid dumbly held out to her.

'Eden – ' he tried to stop her but she pulled away. In the kitchen she snatched her basket and sped out of the open back door and up the hill, running as though Euphemia Ross were after her, not stopping till she reached the village school and schoolhouse, stolid grey stone buildings on the edge of the village. There, she halted to catch her breath and calm herself before calling on the schoolmaster's sister.

Below her Buckthorne clung limpet-like to the rock that rose from the sea. Above, the rough grassy hillside, with outcrops of stone and clusters of wind-beaten bushes, reached up to an undulating plateau of rich farmland.

The school playground, open to the elements, overlooked a huddle of pantiled cottage roofs, faded from their original red to a soft rose by the wind and the sun and the rain; the harbour entrance was briefly glimpsed before the eye was carried from there to the open sea.

It was fitting that the school should sit on a hill – the young scholars, most of them destined for work as farmhands, fishermen or fisher-lassies, had little need for formal learning. They made their way to its doors five mornings a week, those from the village dragging reluctantly up the hill, then scampering gleefully back down when released at the end of the day by Robert Laird, who combined the duties of schoolmaster and church session clerk to make ends meet.

Reluctant or not, the children were obliged to attend until they reached the age of twelve, though in a village where everyone, from toddlers upwards, contributed in whatever way they could to the local industry, attendances were sketchy on occasion.

The steady chant of multiplication tables wafted soothingly to Eden as she passed the one-roomed building. Her destination was the schoolhouse where Robert Laird and his sister Annabel lived. It stood in the shelter of the school itself, a neat little place with shining windows.

Annabel Laird was baking. Her sharp-chinned face broke into a smile when she opened the back door. The Lairds had once been moneyed folk and Robert, who had never forgotten that fact, did his best to discourage his sister from mixing with the villagers. But she enjoyed company, and she and Eden had become friends, much to the schoolmaster's annoyance.

'The girl's away to Pittenweem to visit her sister's new baby, and I was wearying for somebody to talk to. You've time for a cup of tea?' Annabel began, then she looked closely at her visitor. 'What's amiss? You look as ruffled as a hen in a gale.'

Eden put down her basket. 'Mistress Annabel, why does Euphemia Ross hate me?'

'Because you're young and you've got looks – and because

Phemie's got fine ideas for her Lewis and she doesn't like the way he's smitten with you.'

'Smitten?'

'What warm-blooded young man wouldn't be?' said Annabel crisply. 'And from what I've heard of him in the past, Lewis Ross is as warm-blooded as the next man. But don't let it go to your head, Eden, for he's not nearly ready to settle down yet.'

'Then why is his mother so angry with me?'

Annabel shook her head and a cloud of flour drifted from the red hair that was her finest feature.

'Phemie Ross likes nobody except Lewis,' she announced, shaping dough and putting it into the pan to stand for a few hours. 'Not even that poor man of hers – and him such a gentle creature, too. As I've heard it, Phemie looked after her father's house since she was small. When she was near grown the man married again and fathered a son – that's Coll Galbraith, who skippers the *Rose-Ellen* for Phemie. After Lewis was born her father and his new wife died and she'd to take Coll under her roof. They say he didn't have much of a life, being brought up by his half-sister. Then Frank fell between the harbour wall and his boat and hurt his leg so badly that he had to give up the sea. It was Phemie who scrimped and saved and managed the shop and looked after them all. She's not had an easy life.'

'Even so, she's got no right to look down that long nose of hers just because I'm a fisher-lassie and a' – Eden swallowed – 'a love-child.'

'Did she say that?'

'She put it another way,' Eden admitted, and Annabel tutted sympathetically.

'Pay no heed. For all the airs and graces Phemie puts on now that she's moneyed, you're still more of a lady than she ever could be, and I should know, for I used to live among the gentry in Edinburgh.' Her eyes clouded with memories. 'I very near married one of them. But that was a long time ago,

27

before my father lost his wits and his money.'

Eden felt her face flush at her own daring. 'Mistress Annabel, would you teach me the right way to carry myself, and the right things to say?'

Annabel shook loose flour from the tin, causing another cloud. 'Mercy, Eden, why would you want to learn things like that?'

'Just – in case.'

The older woman looked closely at her. 'I've already warned you not to pin your hopes on Lewis – '

'I'm not. I just – ' Eden sought for the right words. 'Mebbe one day I'll be like Mistress Ross, with a grand house and fine furniture and – and have beautiful plates in my parlour with real gold round the edges. She was a fisher-lassie once, wasn't she? If it could happen for her it could happen for me. I want to show the likes of her that I can be a lady if I put my mind to it. Please?'

'Well – ' Annabel said doubtfully. 'It's been a while since I was called on to behave like a lady.' Then her blue eyes began to sparkle; all at once she wasn't the schoolmaster's spinster sister, but a lively, intelligent young woman again. 'But no doubt it'll come back to me, and I'd enjoy teaching it to you.'

A sudden babble of young voices outside signalled the end of school for the day. Eden got up to go. She knew full well that Robert Laird frowned on his sister's friendship with her, and she kept out of his way.

Annabel took a golden freshly baked pie from the tray and wrapped it deftly in a cloth.

'If you're going to the harbour you can give that to Gideon. I've no doubt he's not eating properly. He'll make himself ill again.'

A year earlier Gideon Murray had gone down with a bad attack of bronchitis and Annabel had taken it on herself to bully him back to health with vigorous nursing and nourishing food. Despite Robert's disapproval she con-

28

tinued to visit the boatyard now and then – the only woman apart from Eden whom the boat-builder considered worthy of a platonic friendship.

Gideon, pipe between his teeth, was leaning on his door frame watching the fishermen prepare to go out on the tide.

'He's not here,' he said, without taking his eyes from the scene.

'Who?'

He removed the pipe and grinned at her. 'Lewis. You've never come to the harbour just to see me.'

She squeezed past him, brandishing the parcel beneath his nose as she went into the cottage. 'I have. And I've brought a present from Miss Annabel.'

He followed her in, unwrapped the pie, and cut himself a thick slice with a knife he disentangled from among a bird's nest of string. Eden watched disapprovingly.

'You're attacking that as if you haven't had a proper meal for weeks.'

'I manage well enough,' said Gideon, a confirmed bachelor.

'Manage!' She looked around the room, then emptied a basin of its collection of nails and filled it with water from the big kettle by the range. Rolling up her sleeves, she began to wash the dishes. She had learned that Gideon didn't object to a little tidying up, provided it wasn't over-done.

'How's my brother?' He cut himself another wedge of pie.

'As bad-tempered as ever. I wish I lived with you instead of – '

'I don't, and I've told you that before,' he interrupted. 'It would get in the way of my pleasures if you lived here.'

'There's some say you're getting far too old for your pleasures.' She scrubbed hard at a greasy plate.

'Aye?' he asked easily. 'You mean Caleb, no doubt. Just because he's taken to the Bible it doesn't mean that I should

29

be a saint. When I'm too old to enjoy life you've my permission to take me out with the fleet and feed me to the fishes, for there'll be no more use in living.'

Gideon had two passions – boat-building and womanizing. According to coastline gossip he was well skilled at both.

'I wonder that any woman can bear to set foot in this place,' Eden sniffed.

'They can stay away if they choose, but somehow they never notice the mess. Mind you, Phemie Ross is different. She wouldn't even put her arse on a chair when she was in this morning for fear she'd catch a bad dose of dust.' He chuckled at the memory but Eden's hands stilled on the pot she was scrubbing.

'What did she want with you?'

'Ach, she was on at me again to let her and Frank help me out, as she puts it, with a loan.'

'You'd not let her do that, would you?'

He turned and spat out of the open doorway. 'Not while there's breath in my body. I've seen the way Phemie works. She lends a man money, then she suddenly wants it back just when he can least afford to pay her. So instead she takes on a share of his boat or his shop, or whatever the poor fool owns. And before he can turn round he's working for her or out on his ear. That's how she got the *Rose-Ellen*. Oh, I'd have no objection to Frank, for he's an honest soul. But that wife of his is like a starving dog – give her a morsel and she'll not rest till she gets the whole larder.'

Then amusement crept into his voice. 'You've got a visitor, Eden. I'll just away and have a word with Coll – '

She snatched up a cloth and began to dry her hands as she heard Gideon go out and someone else come in. Her face flamed with embarrassment, and she couldn't turn to face him.

'I thought I'd find you here,' Lewis said, then his hands were on her shoulders, turning her round. 'Eden – '

'I'm not sorry about the way I spoke to your mother.

30

There's no sense in pretending I am,' she blurted.

'Sorry?' he asked in surprise. 'I'm proud of you! Oh, Eden – ' Then the cloth she was holding dropped to the floor among some wood shavings as he scooped her into his arms. 'I've wanted to do this properly since the first day I set eyes on you – ' said Lewis, low-voiced, and bent to kiss her.

They were light, hurried kisses at first, then a deeper, tongue-teasing embrace, more serious than anything she had ever experienced before, that fired her blood and set her trembling. Finally, reluctantly, he released her.

'Will you meet me along the shore tomorrow night?'

'Not till tomorrow?'

He kissed the tip of her nose. 'I'm off to the fishing grounds just now. Walk with me to the boat.'

'Mister Ross!' she teased. 'What would your mother say?'

He slipped an arm about her shoulders and hugged her. 'That doesn't bother me.'

'Or me,' Eden said contentedly.

'I'll see you tomorrow night?' he asked when they reached the ladder down to the water.

She nodded. 'Take care, Lewis.'

'I'm good at doing that,' he said cheerfully, then he was gone, slipping down the ladder like an eel, jumping from deck to deck until he had reached the *Rose-Ellen*, turning to wave to her.

Then she saw his chin tilt defiantly and his arm sketch a more formal salute to someone on the road above.

Eden turned and saw Euphemia Ross on the street above, watching her.

For a long moment they locked eyes, then Coll Galbraith asked from just behind Eden, 'Have you seen Lewis?'

'He's on the boat.' She stepped aside to let him go down the ladder. He hesitated, glanced up at his half-sister and back at Eden, began to speak, thought better of it and swung over the edge of the harbour. She watched as he went down sure-footed, the box containing his food and personal belongings swinging from its rope handle and bumping against his broad back with each step as he reached the first boat and jumped from deck to deck with as much ease as he'd have shown crossing the road.

Eden turned back to find Euphemia still there, still watching her. As their eyes met again the woman turned and walked away, back straight.

A cloud from nowhere had drifted over the sun, darkening the colours of the boats, giving the water a steely appearance. Eden let her breath out in a long sigh. She could almost believe that Lewis's mother had the evil eye.

She went back to Gideon's house and exorcized Euphemia from her mind by scrubbing the dirty dishes with such vigour that water flew everywhere and the plates were in danger of losing their patterns.

Gideon peered in, and decided to retire to the comfort of the local tavern. He hoped that Eden would be out of his house before that night's 'pleasure' came tapping at the door under cover of darkness. Gideon was never short of company on the nights the fishermen were out at sea.

One by one the boats were rowed through the harbour entrance. Once outside, they had to negotiate a jagged reef lurking just beneath the surface of the sea, then they reached deeper water, raised their big dark brown dipping lugsails and set off towards the May Isle lighthouse, which beckoned to them from the horizon.

# CHAPTER FOUR

Coll Galbraith was in a bad mood by the time the *Rose-Ellen*
shot her nets that night. Three times he had had to bellow at
Lewis for almost snarling the warp that carried the great
drift nets overboard, and as every fisherman knew, once the
warp and nets were tangled a boat might as well turn for
home for all the fishing it would achieve.

It was a relief to him when they completed their wide
circle, dropped the nets safely and came head to wind to wait
out the hours until the nets could be brought inboard again.
The dipping sail that had sped them to the fishing grounds
was folded neatly and the great foremast lowered. The small
aft mizzen was set to keep the boat's head to the wind, then
the crew were free to talk, eat, or fish with hand-lines as they
whiled away the waiting time.

It was a clear night; each time the *Rose-Ellen* lifted on a
wave other boats could be glimpsed, their masthead lamps
twinkling in the dark night as far as the eye could see. There
were about a hundred boats in Buckthorne's fleet, and at
least two hundred more from neighbouring villages spread
over miles of fishing grounds.

Galbraith's hand absently caressed the lowered foremast.
The *Rose-Ellen* was twelve years old and her life was coming
to an end. She had weathered countless storms on that wild
coast, had towed stricken ships home and saved their crews;
she had carried the sea-harvest back to shore by the ton – but
her day was almost over.

She was a skaffie, the design most favoured by the fisher-men on that part of the coast. A short-keeled, nimble boat, sixty feet in length, she possessed the characteristic rounded bow of her class, designed to reduce damage if she should run over her own nets while they were over the side.

Skaffies were tricky to handle in rough seas, but Galbraith had sailed in the *Rose-Ellen* for most of her twelve years and he could have taken her confidently through the worst storm ever devised, if necessary. He loved her more than he loved anything else; more, even, than he had loved his wife, the girl who had given her name to the skaffie.

He had first sailed on the boat as a young crewman and had found a close friend in old John MacFee, her owner, and a second home, infinitely warmer and happier than the home he was used to, with John and his delicate daughter. On his twentieth birthday Coll Galbraith had married Rose-Ellen MacFee and gone to live with her in her father's cottage on Shore Street. Six months later, content in the knowledge that his daughter had found security, old John MacFee died. Within another six months, numbly trying to grasp the realization that he had only been permitted to borrow happiness, not own it, Coll followed his young wife's coffin to the churchyard by the sea and gave her back to her father. He remembered her now as a pale, shadowy girl, so frail that he had been afraid each time he touched her that his big hands and strong body might shatter her like a delicate china bowl.

He had inherited the cottage but he didn't become the *Rose-Ellen*'s new owner. His father-in-law had died in debt to Euphemia Ross, who took over the boat in payment and made Galbraith her employee.

It made little difference to him who owned the *Rose-Ellen* as long as he was still with her. But now the boat's useful days were coming to an end.

The other four crewmen were in the stern, talking amongst themselves.

Sure-footed, Galbraith went over the deck of his boat to where Lewis sat forrard, away from the other men.

'I'd have been as well bringing the schoolmaster's sister on this trip as bringing you,' he said bluntly. 'Have you lost heart for the fishing?'

'I've something on my mind.' Lewis's voice was sharp and Galbraith knew that his half-sister's son was ashamed of his clumsiness.

'Then you've no business to be here. A fisherman has to keep his thoughts on the sea and nowhere else.' He sat on a coil of rope. 'Your mother was watching you and Eden Murray together before we sailed, d'you know that?'

'I'm not bothered.'

'Phemie'll not stand for any fisher-lassie claiming you.'

Lewis glared. 'Nobody's claiming me!'

'I hope you're right. You'd be daft to let any woman take over your life.'

They had been raised together, more like brothers than uncle and nephew, and Coll Galbraith could get away with saying things that the younger man wouldn't have taken from anyone else. Their eyes locked and held, and it was Lewis who looked away first.

'Mebbe you've the right way of it,' he admitted. 'I'll tend to what I'm supposed to be doing and put Eden out of my mind for the time being.'

Galbraith stood up, balancing himself easily to the movement of the boat. 'It's either that or you'll feel the weight of my fist, never mind my tongue, if you make one more wrong move on this trip,' he promised, and Lewis knew that he spoke the truth.

Dawn came, a pencil-line of grey along the horizon, a dimming of stars and a lightening of the sky from black to dark blue, then to pearl grey brushed with stretches of palest blue. The other boats appeared one by one from the shadows, the lamps were extinguished.

Muscle and sinew was needed to drag the heavy nets

inboard. The men struggled and cursed, seawater mingling with sweat on their faces.

The boat heeled hard over, but they were confident in the knowledge that she had been built for this task and there was no danger of her capsizing although big waves broke into her as she dipped.

The nets were almost in when one of the men yelled and jumped back. Galbraith roared at them all to keep pulling, then he too stopped as he saw the dark shape wallowing just below him, surrounded by fish, with a pale gleam in the dawnlight where there had once been a recognizable face.

'D'you know him?' someone asked. The sodden shapeless jersey and big sea-boots showed that once this had been a fisherman, probably from their own coastline, but the body had been in the water for too long to be easily identified and nobody was of a mind to study the face too closely.

The *Rose-Ellen*'s nets had scooped bodies from the deep before, but even so there was a shocked, superstitious silence as each man stared down at the thing lying among the fish. Then Coll Galbraith ordered harshly, 'Don't stand about gawping – let him go!' and Lewis managed to dislodge the bundle from the net with one of the long sweeps used for rowing in and out of the harbour.

With a sullen splash it disappeared. Perhaps some wife or mother would have been grateful for a corpse to mourn over, a grave to visit, but the fishermen firmly believed that once the sea took a man it had the right to keep him, unless it chose of its own free will to throw him back on to the shore. It was unlucky to bring a body on board a fishing boat.

'The boots looked good. I could have done with them,' muttered one of the men, and Galbraith pushed him with such force that he almost toppled into the leaping mass of silvery fish in the net still suspended from the skaffie's side.

'Hold your tongue and get those damned nets in!' he bellowed.

It was a poor catch. August was nearing its end and the

36

herring were beginning to swim south. Soon the season would be over and the boats preparing to follow the fish to their winter feeding grounds off the English coast.

Coll Galbraith's heart was heavy as the crew went about the business of turning over the catch with wooden shovels and salting it well to keep it fresh, stowing nets, raising foremast and lugsail for the trip back to harbour.

It seemed to him that by electing to get caught up in their nets instead of staying where he now belonged, the drowned fisherman had added the final touch to a trip that had begun badly, cursed by the look on Euphemia's face as she looked at her son and Eden Murray together.

# CHAPTER FIVE

Eden scrambled along the shore, over weed-slippery slopes and jagged prongs of stone, until she reached the broad ledge that had become a special meeting place for her and Lewis. As afternoon gave way to evening a bank of grey cloud had covered the sky and the breeze became a chill wind. The tide was almost in and water sucked and gurgled some three feet below where she stood.

Behind her, rocks hid the nearby houses from sight and provided privacy; before her the sea was slate-grey, its sparkle replaced by cold white foam as the waves danced skittishly, nervously, to the shore.

The slow passage of time and the relentless sea's pounding had eroded the rock beneath the ledge; Eden could hear water splashing and echoing beneath her feet. Time and time again the waves drew back then launched themselves into the attack once more. At the tide's height the water would rise over the spot where she stood; then it would retire, revealing jagged clusters of rock cunningly hidden beneath its surface at the moment. And eventually it would return – restless, hungry, never content to be in one place for any length of time.

The wind tugged at her skirt, pulling it against her legs. She stood firm, pitting her strength against it, her toes on the very edge of the rock. When Lewis called her name she spun round and might have overbalanced into the foam below if he hadn't caught hold of her.

'Are you mad?' He held her close and she felt the throb of his heart against her body.

She ignored the question, smothering him with kisses until she had bewitched him into forgetting everything else as they sank down on to the ledge, locked in each other's arms.

He drew the shawl from about her head and shoulders then gently tugged at the knot of her hair until it loosened and streamed night-black in the wind. Then his fingers moved to her throat, stroking the smooth skin there before warming it with his lips. She twined her fingers through his thick hair and held him close, her own long tresses making a blanket about them both.

'Eden – ' he said, his voice thick and pleading. She knew what he asked, and she wanted him to take her, wanted it so badly that her body burned and ached with need; but she shook her head when he began to unbutton her blouse, drawing away.

'No, Lewis. No man's going to have his fill of me then leave me.'

'If you cared – ' he said almost sulkily, twisting a strand of her hair about his fingers. She laughed.

'Many a girl's heard that before!'

'You're like nobody I've ever met before. You're a witch, Eden Murray – '

He kissed her again and she felt her resistance weakening. She let him lower her to the ledge, reached her arms up to him – then a gust of wind slammed into their niche and Lewis only just caught Eden's shawl as it was whisked away, almost over the edge. A wave broke not far below and baptized them both with spray.

'Let me up, Lewis – we'll be blown into the sea – ' She struggled against his restraining hands.

'We're fine here - if we go over the edge I'll hold you close and never let you go.' Laughter danced in his eyes. 'We'd be together for always – just you and me and the fishes!'

She shivered at the thought and broke free. 'I have to be home before long.'

He let her get up, and stood himself. 'I'm off back to Edinburgh in another ten days, don't forget that. You'll not let me go so far away without a farewell gift to remember you by?' he asked meaningfully.

She felt her heart turn over at the thought of being without him. Only ten more days! 'When'll you be home again?'

'Not till the New Year.' He took her hand, helped her carefully over rocks she could have climbed blindfold with ease. 'I've to escort my mother there in the morning. She's visiting her cousin, the one I lodge with. But we'll be home in the late afternoon.' He caught her and kissed her hard before they rounded the last rock and came into view of the shore houses. 'Meet me in the old graveyard tomorrow night – '

'If I don't find someone better first,' she teased to cover her dismay at the thought of his going.

They walked back together along the main street. Night had fallen early. The local people usually went to bed with the dark and rose with the dawn, so most of the houses were unlit. Only the tavern was bright and lively.

At the harbour they parted, Lewis to go uphill to his home, Eden to walk along a few more yards to her uncle's cottage.

As her hand touched the latch someone moved in the shadows under the eaves. She jumped, choking back a scream.

'Where have you been?' John Murray asked suspiciously.

'Walking by the sea.'

'On your lone?'

'That's my concern.' She reached again for the latch then snatched her fingers back as she realized that his hand already covered it.

'Have you sinned, Eden?' he asked unexpectedly.

'Sinned?' she asked, confused; then flinched as one of his hands touched her cheek. 'Let me by, John, I want to get to my bed.'

'We all have impurity in us, and we have to seek it out and

40

destroy it – ' His fingers brushed her neck. This time he was too quick for her; as she pulled back his hand curved about the nape, drawing her towards him. His thumb moved against her throat.

'Let me draw the sin from you,' he said huskily, then his mouth was on hers, hot and moist, sucking at her lips as the sea had sucked at the rocks. His free arm clamped about her, defeating her struggles.

Panic flared in her before his mouth at last eased its pressure, allowing her to breathe again. Suddenly aware of the cry speeding through her throat he clapped a hand over her lips, too late.

The door opened and the light from a taper fell on the planes and hollows of his face as he turned. Thus sharply shadowed, his thin intense features looked demonic to Eden. He released her abruptly and she had to grasp the door-frame to keep herself from falling.

'John?' Barbara Murray asked. 'Eden? What's amiss?'

'Nothing. We met at the door,' he said swiftly, brushing past her into the house, his face averted.

Barbara raised the candle, peering closely at Eden. Behind her, in the curtained wall-bed, Caleb Murray grumbled about the noise and ordered his wife to come to bed at once.

'We – met at the door.' Eden had no wish to bring Caleb's anger down on her. In her turn she hurried past her aunt, into the short passageway beyond the kitchen, past the door of the room she and Charlotte shared, past John's closed door, out into the little yard at the back. There she rinsed her face under the pump, scrubbing her mouth to cleanse herself of her cousin's touch.

Charlotte was asleep, lying on her back and snoring softly. She mumbled something, but didn't waken as Eden undressed and got into bed. She lay in the darkness, deliberately blocking the memory of John's fumbling caresses and concentrating her thoughts on Lewis instead.

In ten more days he was going off to his other life, leaving

41

her behind. For the first time since she had arrived in Buckthorne Lewis wouldn't be there. She tossed on to one side and then the other, her body aching for him.

'Never give yourself to a man unless you're wearing his ring,' her faded, once-pretty mother had told her again and again. 'Loving a man who doesn't belong to you brings shame and trouble and' – the greatest pain of all twisted her face – 'and the knowing that you can't even bury him if he should die. Promise me, Eden!'

Eden had given her word, but that was before Lewis came into her life. Perhaps he was right, perhaps she should let him know how much she cared for him.

Perhaps – perhaps – she drifted into sleep at last, thinking of her next meeting with him and what it might bring.


In the stone house on the hill Euphemia Ross, a shawl thrown about her nightclothes, waited in the parlour for her son.

Fear and anger had driven her from her bed. Fear for Lewis, and burning rage over Frank's mulish behaviour earlier. He was usually biddable and easy to bully. But he had defied her when she tried to make him dismiss Eden Murray from the farlins.

'She's a good worker, and pleasant enough,' he had said in that very parlour not two hours earlier. 'There's no reason why she should be turned away, Phemie.'

'She's impudent!'

'I've seen no signs of it. What's she done that you hate her so much?' Frank asked, bewildered. 'She's only been in Buckthorne a few weeks.'

'And since the day she put foot in the place she's set her cap at our Lewis. Are you blind, that you don't see it?'

Understanding dawned in the green eyes that were like his son's, though dimmed now with disillusionment. 'Ach, Phemie! Lewis likes a pretty face, that's all there is to it.'

42

Her contempt for him almost choked her. 'Have you no sense? It's more than a kiss or two she's after – and my son's not for the likes of her!'

'What's wrong with having a fisher-lassie in the family? I was happy to marry one myself,' he said ingratiatingly, and knew, when crimson blotched her sallow cheeks, that he had said the wrong thing.

'My Lewis isn't a common fisherman to drink himself into the harbour,' she said crushingly and Frank wilted, as he always did. He hadn't touched a drop since the night of his accident, but Euphemia never let him forget that he was a drunkard and a fool.

'You've a cruel tongue, Phemie,' he said, then limped upstairs to the small room where he slept alone.

Euphemia's sharp ears heard the kitchen door closing softly. She opened the parlour door and Lewis, tiptoeing through the hall, lamp in hand, blinked at her.

'Come in here.' She beckoned him into the room. 'You've been with that Murray girl, haven't you?'

He hadn't seen his mother with her hair loose since he was a small child. It hung in a straight dull sheet of grey-black from the crown of her head to her hips and gave her stern face a younger, softer look. Her long white gown, covering her decently from throat to ankles, was a startling contrast to her usual black dayclothes.

The slow, dull warmth of honest anger grew in him. 'That's my concern, not yours.'

'You're a fool!'

His face tightened. 'Don't treat me as if I was still a child!'

The warning in his voice got through to Euphemia. She was in danger of losing her son, and she must go carefully.

'Lewis – ' She made herself speak softly. 'It's my blood that beats in your veins, and I know you better than you know yourself.'

Her fingers touched his sleeve and he allowed her to draw him to the sofa.

43

'If I'm vexed it's because I know you're full of the heat of youth. It's natural that you should want to enjoy her. I'm not denying that – I'd be a fool if I did.'

'As long as I don't lose my head entirely,' he mocked, drawing away, standing up.

Anger flared in Euphemia. She got to her feet and her hands caught at his jacket, holding him fast.

'Lewis, listen to me – !'

'I'm going to bed,' he said, moving back.

'No – Lewis – !'

It was a cry from the heart. Her hands moved to his shoulders, caught at them, held him in what seemed to be the prelude to a lover's embrace. She saw surprise, alarm, then embarrassment blossom in his clear green eyes before he tore himself free and almost ran from the room, stumbling up the dark stairs.

Euphemia was left alone, arms outstretched. A deep shudder racked her and she wrapped her arms closely about her body, shivering, as shocked as Lewis had been by her unexpected passion.

Of all the people in Euphemia's life she loved only Lewis – but not until that moment had she realized that her obsession for him was shot through with something other than purely maternal feelings.

She had only once before loved deeply and helplessly. That painful memory had been banished from her mind – until the day Eden Murray had walked into Buckthorne and Euphemia had looked at her young features and saw superimposed on them another face – dark, handsome, adored.

'Joshua!' She whispered his name aloud and her middle-aged body burned with sudden need for him.

Nobody had ever known, and nobody ever would know, of her affair with Joshua Murray. Frank had gone to England with the fishing fleet and Euphemia was left at home tending to Lewis, then months old. With the hunting instincts of a sensual man Joshua had taken it upon himself to waken the

44

slumbering passions lying so deep within her thin body that she herself knew nothing of them.

Their coupling had been swift and torrid. Shame shivered through her even now when she recalled the way she had behaved in Joshua's arms during that insane time, and with the shame came a longing to know such passion again.

All too soon Frank had returned home and the affair was over. Euphemia would gladly have left Frank for Joshua, but her lover had no thought, at that time, of deserting his barren wife. She nursed the secret hope that he would come back to her when the boats next went south, but before then Joshua had turned his attention to Jessie Gray, a fisher-lassie.

When he left his wife and moved to another cottage with Jessie, blithely ignoring the scandal that rocked Buckthorne, Euphemia's anger had almost been too much to bear. The thought of the other woman carrying his baby tortured her day and night and she hadn't been able to tolerate her husband's touch from that moment.

Then came Frank's accident, and she had plunged herself into nursing him, raising Lewis and her half-brother Coll, and earning a living for them all. Within another year Joshua was drowned, Jessie Gray found a man from Eyemouth willing to marry her and took herself and her child far from Buckthorne, and a long time after that Euphemia succeeded in banishing bitter memories – until the day Joshua's love-child came to Buckthorne, her dark eyes and glossy hair and high cheekbones all taunting reminders of the man who had shown Euphemia heaven and then hell.

She set her teeth in her lip so hard that the skin split and blood beaded her chin, unnoticed. For her own sake as much as for his she must get Lewis back to Edinburgh as soon as possible.

Euphemia sat by the grate, planning, not even noticing that the fire had gone out and the room had taken on an icy chill.

45

Early on the following morning Euphemia sent for Caleb Murray. She was dressed for her visit to Edinburgh when she received him in her parlour.

'I'd be grateful, Mister Murray, if you'd stay in Buckthorne instead of going down to Yarmouth with the herring boats when the season starts. I've need of a good man here.' She had long since dropped the habit of saying 'we' as though she were passing on decisions shared with her husband. 'John can go south and keep an eye on the lassies. The Lord only knows they've need of close watching.'

She drew on her gloves with careful precision. 'How's your niece settling in?'

He coloured and shuffled his feet uncomfortably. 'Well enough.'

Euphemia's mouth writhed. 'She's fortunate to find shelter under a God-fearing roof. Far too many young women walk the wrong path these days. Indeed, I feel it's only right I should tell you I've heard gossip already, and the girl only here a matter of weeks. It would never do, Mister Murray' – her cold black eyes held his – 'to let her foolishness give you and your family a bad name, would it?'

As understanding and apprehension showed in his eyes she added, 'It's our duty, is it not, to guide the young?'

'Our God-given duty – and I'd not swerve from it!' he hurried to assure her, and she nodded, a cold smile touching her lips.

'Raising children can be a thankless task. I worry a great deal about my own son's future. We must do what we can to teach the young proper humility and an acceptance of their place in life. I think I hear the carriage. Good day to you, Mister Murray.'

Well satisfied with her work, she watched him retreat along the passageway to the kitchen, then made her own way out by the front door to where Lewis, handsome in his best clothes, waited for her beside the hired carriage.

*

That day passed slowly for Eden, but at last the family were at their evening meal.

'You look fair pleased with yourself,' Caleb said sourly across the table.

'Mebbe she's thinking about who she's going to meet later,' Charlotte dared to suggest, malice in her voice.

'She's meeting nobody without my permission!' her father rapped out.

'That's for me to say, not you,' Eden said at once, and his knife clattered on to the table.

'You're under my roof and you'll do as I say! We're all employed by Mistress Ross and I'll not have you making a fool of yourself, chasing after her son!'

'So – ' she said through lips stiff with anger. 'Euphemia Ross has been giving you your orders? You're surely not going to let her make a pet monkey out of you!'

Charlotte and her mother gasped and John's mouth hung open slackly as he watched his father. Caleb's face gleamed bone-white with rage in the room's dim light and his fist crashed on to the table.

'You dare to speak to me like that – '

'You don't own me, and neither does Lewis's mother.' Eden rose, then caught her breath as her uncle's hand snaked out and caught her wrist, forcing her back down to her seat.

'I do own you, my lady, just as I own everyone and everything under this roof.' His eyes glittered at her, his fingers crushed the soft flesh and fragile bones of her wrist until she felt sick with pain. 'You'll do as I say! Stay away from Lewis Ross!'

'Caleb – ' Barbara put a hand on his arm. John's eyes, hot now with excitement, flickered between his father's face and Eden's. Caleb gave a final twist to the imprisoned wrist and Eden bit on the skin inside her lower lip as pain seared up to her elbow. Despite her efforts to hide her suffering, a whimper escaped from her, and as though waiting for that signal, that sign of submission, her uncle released her abruptly and strode out, slamming the door behind him.

She sat with bent head, nursing her arm, refusing to let the others, John in particular, see the tears of pain that scalded her eyes. The outer door opened and closed a second time, and she looked up to see, through a rainbowed mist, that she was alone with the two women.

'Let me look – ' Barbara took the injured wrist gently, examining the red, swollen flesh. 'Charlotte, fetch me some water and a rag. Eden, you should know better than to anger your uncle!'

'If she knew better she'd never have taken up with Lewis Ross,' Charlotte said spitefully.

'Do as I tell you! As for you, Eden, you can think yourself fortunate this is all he did to you for bringing Mistress Ross's anger down on this house.'

'Fortunate!' Eden began, then swallowed her words. There was no sense in antagonizing the entire family. Meekly she let Barbara bathe her wrist, then she went into the tiny bedroom and got ready for her meeting with Lewis, giving her hair an extra hard brushing and putting on the flowered white petticoat her mother had made for her only months before, with the scarlet frill. Over it went her grey gown with little mother-of-pearl buttons on the bodice and pink ribbon knots above the hem.

Caleb Murray's womenfolk looked at her then at each other when she went back into the kitchen, but said nothing as she went out.

Eden took a deep breath when she heard the street door thump behind her, then she began to run. She was free, for the moment, of that loveless, unhappy house. Her pulses skipped in time with the patter of her feet on the cobbled street. She was going to see Lewis – she was going to be with him. She was going, she decided, to do whatever he asked of her. At that moment, nothing else mattered but being with him, being happy. The future could look after itself.

She was halfway to the graveyard when Coll Galbraith's sturdy figure blocked her way.

'If you're going to meet Lewis you needn't hurry,' he said bluntly. 'Phemie's home from Edinburgh, and she's alone. Lewis is staying on there. He's not coming back until the New Year.'

# CHAPTER SIX

The week after Lewis went was a bitter interlude for Eden. She put a brave face on her misery, shrugging off the sly sniggering remarks from the other fisher-lassies, chattering brightly as she worked at the farlins, keeping a smile pinned on her face when she went round the doors with her wares, making certain that nobody knew about the hours she lay awake each night or the tears she allowed herself to weep in the privacy of the rocky ledge she and Lewis had used as a secret meeting place.

His first letter, silently handed to her by Coll Galbraith within days of Lewis's return to Edinburgh, was angry and frustrated. His kinsman in the city, a merchant, had been ailing for some time and Euphemia had smoothly suggested that Lewis might help the family by staying on and looking after the man's store for him until he went back to his classes. Furious though he was at being duped, he could do nothing but accept the situation and stay behind in the city.

At least the sweeps and whorls of ink on paper represented contact with him; Eden realized that she must be satisfied with letters until the end of the year brought him back to her.

Coll Galbraith became a reluctant messenger, delivering Lewis's notes to her, addressing her replies in his steady, rounded script in case the Edinburgh cousins were spying for Euphemia.

Eden was more determined than ever to continue the lessons she had begun with Annabel.

50

'One day I'll get the chance to show her that I can be just as much of a lady as she is. Some day I'll have a parlour of my own, and painted china plates, then she'll see – '

She moved with easy grace across the Lairds' parlour carpet, two large volumes balanced on her head. 'I can do this easily. Should you not add another book?'

Annabel studied the girl's straight back, long proud neck, and poised chin. 'I needn't bother, for you've got a fine natural carriage any lady would give money to possess.'

She watched enviously as Eden's rounded arms swept up to lift the books off her head.

'It's carrying barrels that does it,' her pupil said blithely. 'Now – tell me if I'm sitting down the right way.'


Gideon was working on the plan of a new skaffie, painstakingly listing measurements in the battered old notebook that was always to hand despite the cottage's clutter, and estimating the amount of timber he would require.

'The timber merchants have started being pernickety. They're looking for payment before they'll deliver; they know as well as I do that no fisherman has that much silver to hand,' he grumbled.

Eden knew it was normal practice for the fishermen to make payments regularly as the building of their boats progressed, and the suppliers were given their money once the boat was launched.

'Why should they want to change their ways?' she wanted to know, and her uncle shot a look at her from under thick dark brows.

'I'll lay my life on it that it's Phemie's doing. The woman's got everyone in her pocket, buttoned in tight. She's trying to force me to turn to her and Frank for the extra money I need. Ach – damn the thing!'

In his anger he had leaned so hard on the pencil that the point broke. Gideon threw it across the room and reached for

51

his tobacco pouch. Eden searched among the chaos on the window ledge, found another pencil, and drew the notebook towards her, noting the size of the skaffie to be built, leafing through the book to find out from details of similar craft what materials would be needed.

'I will not –' said Gideon from between his teeth '– let that woman take my yard! I'll burn it down first!'

Eden moved the notebook into a patch of sunlight. 'There's a lot of old boats in the fleet. Surely they're due to be replaced?'

Gideon, at the door, gazed morosely over the yard. 'Oh, there's plenty would like new boats, but they can't afford them. This year's fishing hasn't been all that grand.'

'Oregon pine –' Eden wrote carefully and clearly. 'Oak – Scottish larch –' Aloud she said, 'Could they not put their money together and pay you to build their boats one at a time?'

'Whoever had his boat built first would never rest easy for worrying about whether the others might think he was out to cheat them.' Gideon shook his head. 'Women don't understand the way of it –' He suddenly noticed what she was doing and pounced on his precious notebook. 'Here – leave that alone!'

Eden let him snatch it from under her hands. He cast an anxious look over the page she had completed, then his eyebrows almost vanished into his thick hair.

'You got it right!'

'I know,' she said serenely. 'And I've got it right about the boat-building too, if you'd only think about it.'

He shook his head, putting the precious book away, out of her reach. 'You don't understand our way of doing things.'

Let them work out their own salvation, she told herself as she went back to Caleb's loveless house. But a part of her mind began to probe for a solution to Gideon's dilemma.

*

As September wore on the herring turned away from the cooling waters off Scotland, and the boats prepared to follow them south for the winter season. The high wooden 'gallowses' by the harbour and in the back yards blossomed with great brown wings as the canvas lugsails were cutched — dipped in huge copper vats bubbling with a thick brown liquid that strengthened and protected the material.

The nets, too, had to be dipped and dried, and for a week or so most of the men and women in the village had hands and arms stained dark brown from the task. The smell of tar and boiling cutch hung in the air on dry days. Gideon's fortunes changed for the better; he and his men were kept busy renewing timbers, repairing boats and replacing old caulking with new oakum.

Vessels lay beached in the harbour shallows, their round green barnacled hulls, normally hidden below the waterline, almost indecently displayed to public gaze while they were scraped, re-caulked, tarred, and made seaworthy again. The air rang with the busy clatter of hammers and chisels. Although scarcely any herring were being brought ashore now there was plenty to keep the fisher-lassies busy. They helped with the cutching, baited lines for the boats that went after the whitefish, and mended nets. Euphemia Ross, determined to get her money's worth from her employees, set the girls to knitting stockings and heavy jerseys for the men who were to go south, or making oilskins by painting canvas with ochre then rubbing in layer upon layer of linseed oil with a cloth pad.

'I'm to go to Yarmouth with the rest of them, though I thought your mother might have found some way to stop me,' Eden wrote to Lewis. 'I've never been to Yarmouth before. Mistress Annabel has been helping me to renovate my brown silk dress. We turned it and made a frill bound with black velvet, and put a row of black velvet ribbon round the skirt. Soon after I come back from Yarmouth it will be the end of the year and you'll be home — '

She lifted her head. Voices murmured in the kitchen, one deep, the other light and tremulous. Eden was in the tiny room she shared with Charlotte, taking advantage of an hour alone in the cottage to write her letter. Hurriedly, she slipped it under the clothes she kept in a tin trunk and went along the short passageway to the kitchen. When Caleb was at home he liked to see the womenfolk busying themselves, not sitting idly, inviting Satan to take over their weak souls.

Charlotte's head-shawl lay on the floor where it had fallen. John had a tight hold of his sister's arms, his fingers biting into the plump flesh. His back was to Eden. When she spoke Charlotte's name he whirled round, startled, then released his sister and pushed past Eden into the passageway and to his own small room.

'What's amiss, Charlotte? You shouldn't let him bully you –'

But Charlotte snatched up her shawl and went out of the street door without answering. Eden hesitated for a moment then followed, taking her own shawl from the nail behind the door.

She had no wish to be left alone in the house with her cousin.

The boats left harbour in early October, jostling their way one by one from the narrow entrance. The crews took the long sweeps inboard once the rocks had been negotiated, raised the lugsails, and the boats turned towards the May Isle on the horizon like a cluster of tawny butterflies.

The deeply superstitious fishermen wouldn't allow women on board their boats, so the fisher-lassies travelled to England by train.

The people left behind – mothers and children, the old and the sick, the men who made their living catching whitefish by line, or who, like Caleb Murray, had enough work to do in Buckthorne, prepared for winter. Euphemia Ross nagged at

54

her husband, who had been caught gazing hungrily in the direction taken by the boats; Annabel Laird sighed for the excitement she was sure must wait in Great Yarmouth for those fortunte enough to travel there, then got on with checking the bed linen and turning sheets end-to-middle; Gideon reflected contentedly on the number of women who would look to him for comfort while their menfolk were fishing English waters.

Eden hugged her basket in her arms and stared, round-eyed, at the neat little station and the steam train waiting to take her on the first lap of the journey south. Most of the women had travelled by rail before, and laughed at her startled jump when an engine hooted shrilly.

She was enchanted by the small carriages, each with its double row of slatted wooden seats, jolting along at an incredible speed with the countryside whirling past the windows.

The skinniest girls began to shift uncomfortably after a few hours spent bouncing on the hard seats, but Eden, her rounded bottom comfortably padded, had nothing to complain about. She exclaimed and enthused over everything – the cows and sheep in the fields, the houses, the stations they stopped at, the people who halted in their work and waved as the train flashed by them.

It wasn't until hunger broke through her excitement and she delved into her bag to ferret out bread and cheese that she became aware of Charlotte's misery.

'Here – ' she handed her cousin two thick slices of bread bracketing a wedge of cheese, but the other girl waved it away. Eden looked at her properly and saw that Charlotte's face was waxy, her eyes shadowed.

'What's amiss?'

Charlotte's hands clutched her ribcage. 'I wish the damned thing would stop,' she said fretfully.

'We've got a way to go yet, haven't we?' Eden appealed to the others.

'We have that. You'd be as well to put something into your belly, lassie,' an older woman advised Charlotte, and the girl turned pale green and clapped a hand over her mouth.

'Sit here by the window – ' Eden urged generously, sorry to be losing her fine view, but upset on her cousin's behalf. Charlotte changed places without a word and slumped miserably in her corner. By the time the journey was over she was looking worse than ever. She had to be helped from the train, and sank on to a box on the station platform, shivering miserably.

Eden rubbed her clammy, cold hands. 'It'll soon be over,' she kept promising her cousin.

One of the women laughed. 'If you're lucky, Charlotte. If not – '

'Hold your tongue!' Charlotte wailed peevishly, and turned her head away from them all.

They spent the night in lodgings, and she was considerably improved by the morning, when they had to leave early to catch another train. She sat by the window again, staring out, refusing to speak to anyone, and the other women left her in peace. Eden, finding her friendship repulsed, gave up and went back to the pleasure of the journey.

It was over all too soon for her; she followed the others out of the station to waiting wagons that trundled them down along earthen roads until they reached Great Yarmouth harbour. The English fishing port covered a great flat stretch of land. All the streets were level, unlike the climbing, twisting wynds Eden was used to. They were just as narrow as wynds, crowded on both sides with tall houses that seemed to lean over to peer curiously at the people passing below.

The streets were crammed with horses and carts and wagons. Dialects of all sorts exploded against Eden's ears; it seemed that no sooner had she begun to unravel one than another took its place. There were fishermen, bronzed and rolling along with the gait that spoke of men used to balancing against the sea's rhythm; fishwives and ladies and domestics with baskets over their arms; children running barefoot; hawkers trundling barrels or pushing carts and screaming their wares — mackerel, live soles, crabs and lobsters, mussels, turnips, oranges, nuts, cabbages and plums and cherries — the list was endless.

There were knife-grinders and beggars, coffee shops and bakeries and eating houses spilling their own rich aromas into the air to tantalize and confuse her nose. She loved everything about the place.

The Buckthorne fisher-lassies shared a large upper room, formerly a sail-loft, in an old house near the harbour. It was respectable enough but tradition demanded that they scrub it out before settling their belongings in, to mark it as their own home for the next six weeks.

After that Eden was glad to crawl into bed and fall into a sleep that was continuously disturbed by the feeling that she was still on the train, her body rocked and jolted by its motion.

Once she thought she heard a faint sobbing from the next cot, where Charlotte lay, but when she lifted her head there was silence apart from broken snores from further down the room, and Eden was glad to let her head drop on to the pillow again and sink back into sleep.


They were reunited with their menfolk the next day when they started work at the farlins. The harbour water was hidden by a tight crush of boats, their masts an impenetrable forest of timbers and ropes. The quay itself seemed to stretch for miles, with almost every inch taken up by farlins, crans, creels, boxes, and, above all, barrels. They were stacked in great mountains, strung like gigantic bead necklaces, piled in triangles and squares, hundreds and thousands of them.

And still the coopers beavered away, making more.

It was hard to believe that the sea could hold enough fish to fill all those barrels. But it did, and during that season alone the vast united fleet would bring in catches to fill all the barrels and thousands more. Beyond the farlins lay sheds and warehouses where the sail-makers and shipwrights and chandlers worked, and where the dealers struck their bargains. The area swarmed with people – coopers, fisher-lassies and curious onlookers, dealers and carters and fisher-men. Their voices mingled with the ring of hammers and the screech of gulls to make a continuous din that deafened Eden at first, but ceased to bother her once she got used to it.

The work was hard, for boats were in and out of the harbour all the time and the girls were kept busy ten and twelve hours at a stretch; but the sheer exhilaration of the place, the bustle and the coming together of people from all over Britain gave Eden a sense of vitality she had never experienced before. Word of the Scottish fisher-lassies' skill travelled before them and there were always people gathered about them as they worked.

In the evenings, when the last fish was gutted and packed, the girls went back to their lodgings to eat, wash and mend their clothes and above all, to see to their hands.

They all bound rags about their fingers to protect them from the knives, but the autumn winds and the salt and pickle they worked with often caused cuts and hacks which had to be treated with ointments they made themselves from sugar and soap, or paraffin and treacle.

Duties over, they usually went out, more often than not to the little mission in a nearby street, where they attended prayer meetings and social soirees with equal enthusiasm. They worked hard and they enjoyed the chance to socialize in their free time. Sleep was for the old and infirm.

Whenever Eden found herself with spare time during daylight hours she walked round the streets gazing, enthral-led, into the shop windows. She had never seen such treasures as those crowded on to the shelves behind glass panes. Here were the brightly painted plates and cups and saucers and bowls she had seen on display in kitchens at home, brought back by the men and women who followed the herring south. She feasted her eyes on them, going from shop to shop, street to street. And then she found the most beautiful plate ever made – a plate that was every bit as grand as those on Euphemia Ross's sideboard.

It was large, almost covered with a harvest of scarlet poppies, blue cornflowers and clusters of deep red mouth-watering berries. Bright green leaves and tendrils wove their way in and out through the fruit and flowers, and in the centre of the plate, in curling gold script, the artist had lettered 'A Present from Great Yarmouth'. But most important of all, the same shining gold lay in a thick band all round the edge of the plate.

Eden went back again and again to gaze at the plate. It was positioned right in the centre of the window, jostled by lesser pottery, figurines, cheap jewellery, wooden dolls, painted toy soldiers, tops and hoops, cups and balls and skittles. She saw nothing but the plate.

John Murray, representing Euphemia as usual, paid the women at the end of each day, holding back an amount for their lodgings. As far as Eden and Charlotte were concerned, he also represented his father, and the girls were allowed to keep only a few pence a day to spend as they pleased. Most of it had to go on paraffin and soap to treat their hands, but Eden's angry objections were ignored. John looked at her from under thick pale eyelids, and said nothing.

The need to buy the plate before someone else got it became a craving. She managed to scrape together half the cost, then struck a bargain with Janet, one of the other women, whereby Janet advanced the rest of the money and Eden pledged to take on her share of the housework and laundry for the rest of their time in Yarmouth.

The bargain cut deeply into her own leisure time, but it

was worth it to hold the plate in her hands, to see the light dazzle from its gold lettering and edging, and to know that she had taken the first step towards becoming more than a mere fisher-lassie.

When the first glow of ownership had abated, she told herself that she should give the plate as a gift to her Aunt Barbara. But Caleb Murray scorned possessions, especially frippery. He would probably throw it out. Having reasoned her way to this conclusion, Eden decided with a clear conscience that she was entitled to keep the plate for herself. She would hide it deep in the locked tin box under the bed at Buckthorne, and one day it would become the centrepiece in her own home.

She could already visualize the kitchen she would have – a hand-made rug before the range, everything clean and shining and welcoming, the plate on a shelf, perhaps flanked in time by other ornaments.

She didn't go so far as to make a definite decision on the man who would share this spotless kitchen with her, but somehow he seemed to be tall and lean, with sea-green eyes and soft fair hair. And outside the window there was a cobbled yard, tidier than the bird's nest of planks and ropes Gideon had, with the finest boat yet built on the east coast taking shape on the stocks.


Charlotte was the only one who stayed away from the soirees, claiming that they were sinful. But she attended every prayer meeting, fingers clasped so tightly together that the knuckles gleamed white; her face, which still held a waxy sheen that gave its usual tan an unpleasantly greenish tinge, uplifted to the beamed ceiling.

John watched his sister suspiciously whenever he happened to be in her vicinity. Eden saw that Charlotte always ducked her head when he appeared, or drew her shawl forward as though trying to hide from him.

The girl still looked far from well, but she worked like a demon. They worked in gangs of three, two gutting, one packing. Charlotte was the packer in Eden's gang, rolling heavy barrels aside when they were filled, dragging fresh barrels into place single-handed, even helping the coopers to stack them in tiers of three when they were ready for shipment, as though determined to prove that she was fit for any sort of work.

'Come out with me,' Eden coaxed one day when they found themselves alone in the lodgings. Charlotte, crouched on her bed and staring into space, shook her head listlessly. Eden hesitated by the door, gnawing at her underlip.

'Charlotte—if you're sick you should mebbe go back home—'

Her cousin's head was suddenly thrown back and the girl's small brown eyes, so like her father's, blazed at her.

'Home? You're a fool!' Charlotte said contemptuously, and suddenly it all fell into place for Eden. The pallor, the continued sickness, the remarks made by the other woman – 'You'll be right enough come the summer, Charlotte – pleasure always has its cost – '

'A bairn! Oh Charlotte – why did you not tell me?'

'Tell you? Have you not listened to the rest of them going on at me?' The other girl indicated the large, empty loft. 'They all knew on the train – no doubt some of them knew before then. That lot have eyes like needles.' Her voice rose to a wail, her hands clutched at her belly. 'It'll not shift! I'd hoped the train journey might put me right, or lifting the barrels. But I'm cursed, for nothing'll take it away from me!'

'You mustn't let anything happen to it!' Eden caught the clawed fingers, pulling them away from Charlotte's body. 'Charlotte – no! It would be wrong to kill it!'

There was hatred in the eyes that gleamed at her through strands of lank, uncared-for hair.

'D'you not realize what my father'll do to me if he finds out?'

'The man who – will he not wed you?'

61

Charlotte's laugh was an unpleasant sound. 'Of course not!'

'I'd stand by you, Charlotte – I'd face your father with you – '

'No!' Charlotte came off the bed as though operated by a hidden spring. She caught Eden's shoulders in a painful grip, her eyes suddenly hot with fear. 'I swear I'll kill you if you tell him or John about this. Don't say a word to John, for if he knew of it – '

'I'll say nothing,' Eden hurried to assure her, and the agonizing hold on her shoulders eased. Then tears welled up in Charlotte's eyes and she turned away, wrapping her arms about herself, rocking, wailing, a helpless, terrified child.

'Eden – what am I do? What is there to do?'

'Ssshhh – ' Awkwardly, Eden took her cousin's unwieldy body in her arms, feeling Charlotte's hot tears on her neck. 'I promise I'll help you, whatever happens.'

Charlotte drew back, scrubbing at her wet face, suspicion in her eyes again.

'No you won't,' she said sulkily. 'Not when you know who the man is.'

'You're wrong! Tell me, then you'll see that it makes no difference – '

'You don't know what you're saying,' Charlotte said, with an almost sly look on her pale face. 'You'd turn from me sure enough – '

And all at once, in a burst of heart-stopping agony, Eden knew.

'Lewis – ?' It came out in a painful whisper, her lips shaping his name clumsily.

Charlotte's eyes flickered, then steadied on Eden's face. 'Yes – Lewis,' she said in a high brittle voice. 'Did you think you were the only one he favoured? Are you so soft in the rigging that you never thought he could have his choice of the local girls?' The words flowed from her like dammed water freed from its confining banks. 'Or did you think Lewis

Ross wouldn't be interested in the likes of me? He's made sport of the village girls for years – you're just one of them – '

Eden stumbled to the door, opened it, went down the narrow wooden stairs, bumping clumsily into the walls. Charlotte stood in the doorway above, her voice pursuing Eden step by step.

'Try telling that to my father! Tell him that your fine sweetheart's the one that sinned with me – and see what happens to him then!'

# CHAPTER SEVEN

It was easy enough in a town the size of Yarmouth to find women who earned their money by saving their own sex from itself – and Charlotte, Eden soon discovered, was determined.

The first pains struck in the late afternoon two days later while the women were knitting and gossiping in the lee of a shed, waiting for the next load of fish to come ashore. Charlotte gasped and dropped her knitting wires, then clutched at her back, her face twisted with pain.

'The bairn?' someone asked at once. 'Best get back to the lodgings and get on with it.'

Charlotte released her pent-up breath in a long sigh and let her body relax, bending to pick up the wool from the ground. 'And put the whole crew out of wages? I'll stay where I am.'

Janet, the third member of their crew, shrugged and commented, 'Well, it'll not be the first time a bairn's arrived at the farlins.'

Then they were called back to work, and Eden only had time to grab Charlotte's arm and hiss, 'For your own sake, if not for the bairn's, let me take you back to the lodgings now!'

'And have John coming to ask what's amiss with me? I'll stay where I am – leave me be, Eden!'

The next pain came as Charlotte bent over a barrel, packing the gutted fish in layers. She gripped the rim and only Eden, close by, saw that she was doubled up a little too long, or heard the faint groan as the pain gripped.

By the time their work was over the girl's eyes were bright in a flushed face and her pains were coming more and more frequently. The women, even those who had little time for the Murrays, supported one of their own number in times of trouble. They clustered together for the walk back, so that nobody saw how Charlotte had to be helped along in their midst.

When they reached the lodgings she was lifted bodily in their strong arms and carried up to the loft where she was laid on her bed, free at last to groan and whimper as the others worked over her.

'The bairn that's not wanted fights hardest to come into the world,' Janet remarked cheerfully as she tied a length of rope to a strong hook embedded in the wall. 'Pull on that when it gets too bad to bear. You'll find out soon enough that it's a sight easier to come by them than get rid of them.'

They made her as comfortable as they could then went about their own work, casting an eye occasionally on the girl who writhed on the bed, her chin flecked with blood from bitten lips. Eden sat by her, wiping perspiration from her forehead, letting Charlotte grip her hands, then guiding the other girl's fingers, when they threatened to tear and bruise her skin, to the rope tied to the hook.

The night lengthened and most of the other women crawled into their cots.

'Surely this can't go on for much longer?' Eden asked Janet in despair.

'There's no knowing with a first. Never fear — she'll survive. It's a mercy it's the Sabbath the morn, for it looks as if we'll have to stay away from the farlins.' The woman sighed and shook her head. 'I could be doing fine with the extra money, too.'

Because the Scottish boats didn't go out on the Sabbath their fisher-lassies had less to do, though they could work for the English boats if they wished.

As the night wore on Charlotte lapsed into semi-consciousness, coming fully to her surroundings only when summoned by pain. Janet, yawning over her knitting, was unperturbed.

'She'll face worse before she's done, I've no doubt,' she said serenely.

Charlotte's eyes rolled in her head, showing the whites. 'I've been wicked – I've broken the Commandments,' she said feverishly. 'It's a punishment on me – '

'That it is, lassie,' agreed Janet, scratching her head with one of her wires. 'We should know better but we never learn, more's the pity.'

The climax came with little warning shortly after midnight. Charlotte gave a shrill scream that ripped through the room and woke all those who had managed to fall asleep. Her body convulsed, fighting against Janet's restraining hands, and Eden was showered with thick warm blood. Then Charlotte fell back, her breath rasping in her throat, and Eden stared in the lamplight at the child that had slipped smoothly into her two hands. It was over.

Roused from their rest, the women saw deftly to Charlotte, who almost immediately fell into an exhausted sleep. Eden's motionless burden was taken from her by Janet who, expressionless, rolled it in rags and spirited it away. She was handed a bundle of bloody sheets and ordered to wash them, then at last she was free to fall into bed where she slept a deep sleep that was like the end of the world.

She woke the next morning to a grey, rainswept day. She felt empty and exhausted, as though she were the one who had struggled throughout the night then lost a child.

Charlotte slept for most of the day. She only once came to life, when one of the others reported that John was on his way along the street.

'He's looking for me!' She clutched at Eden in a panic. 'Don't let him in, Eden, don't let him find me like this or he'll know – ' Her fear was pitiful to see.

Eden threw a shawl about her shoulders and got downstairs in time to meet John at the street door.

'Where's our Charlotte?' He made as though to push past her, and scowled when she blocked his way.

'She's out.'

'Where? She wasn't at the service this morning. And neither were you. What's amiss?'

Her mouth was dry. She was sure that he could see the guilt in her eyes.

'I had - a toothache during the night and Charlotte sat up with me. We slept on this morning.'

'That's no reason to miss a prayer meeting.' His eyes probed the small hallway behind her. 'Where is she?'

'I told you, she's gone out!'

His scowl deepened and for a moment she thought that he was going to push her aside. She took a gamble, stepping back, indicating the stairs. 'Go on and look, if you don't believe me.'

He hesitated, then shrugged and turned away, clumping down the street without another word, leaving her weak with relief.

She couldn't go back upstairs to where Charlotte lay, lumpish and seemingly indifferent to what had happened in the night hours. Instead she watched from the doorway until she saw John round a corner, then she went in the opposite direction.

As she was passing the small house where Coll Galbraith lodged, only a few doors along from the fisher-lassies' loft, he stepped out and hailed her.

'A letter from Lewis.' Then, as she drew back, staring at the small parcel in his hand, he added irritably, 'D'you not want it?'

Reluctantly she took it, and at the sight of the familiar script, shaping out her name in Lewis's clear hand, she felt a rush of tears choke her throat then fill her eyes.

'Eden?' Galbraith asked from above her. He put a hand on

67

her arm and she twisted away from him and almost ran down the street, knowing that his blue eyes were probably watching her in bewilderment. Her feet slowed to a walk as she reached the town's outskirts and started over the great flat open stretch of sand. When she finally stopped and looked back the town was an erratic jumble of roofs and spires on the horizon, the boats in the vast harbour a squiggle of masts and ropes.

She sat on the upturned keel of an old abandoned rowing boat and opened Lewis's letter. Somehow she had expected it to be different from usual, heavy with guilt and shame. But it was as Lewis's letters always were: short, giving a swift report on his studies, a mention of the weather, a description of some social occasion he and his great friend Tom Lamont had attended. He was not an imaginative letter-writer. At the end he wrote that he missed her and longed to see her again.

Eden scanned the final words twice then tore the paper into tiny pieces and threw them away. The breeze caught them, then almost at once lost interest and released them. They fluttered to the sands a few yards from where she sat.

She began to walk back to the town, suddenly determined to write to him at once, to tell him of Charlotte's suffering, of the tiny, motionless body she still seemed to feel in her hands, to pour out her bitterness and anger over his deception. Then her feet slowed, stopped, and turned to take her back to the upturned hulk.

Charlotte's dead baby had been well-formed, she recalled. It had been conceived before she herself arrived at Buckthorne. In any case, she had no claim over Lewis Ross, no right to judge or condemn him. They had given each other no pledge of marriage, and any secret thoughts and hopes Eden might have had of a future with him were her own doing. Hadn't she, she asked herself bitterly, refused him when he wanted to make love to her, to possess her as his own?

At that moment, she didn't know whether she had done the right thing or whether she envied Charlotte in spite of her pain and fear and loss. She felt more lonely than she had ever been before, even after her mother's death. She was beginning to learn that it was wrong to expect another person to help her to achieve happiness in life. That when all was said and done, she could only be sure of herself, nobody else.

And the learning was a sharp pain deep within her.

# CHAPTER EIGHT

Normally Lewis Ross strode through Edinburgh's streets without noticing the cold winds harassing the city from the North Sea. Well clad and tingling with the confidence of youthful good health, he paid little attention to the climate.

But on this dreary November night he shivered and hunched his shoulders against the knifing cold as he let himself out of his lodgings. He had had a long and exhausting day at the university, and should have been working hard over his books at that moment – but he was gripped with a restlessness, a longing to be out of the city and back home within sight and sound of the sea.

He plunged into the shadows beyond the lamplight, walked briskly through a small square, turned a corner and hurried up some steps to a big door, its brass fittings gleaming in the light from the street's gas lamps. His work could wait until early morning – now he needed cheerful company, the bustle of the crowded taverns to be found in the lively old streets near the castle, the warm sting of whisky in his throat.

The door swung open.

'Good evening, Elizabeth. Tell Tom that we're going out tonight – '

'Tom's already gone out, and Mother and Father – and oh, Lewis, I'm so glad to see you!'

Tom's younger sister Elizabeth positively dragged him in

and shut the door against the night. 'Take your coat off – come into the withdrawing room – '

She chattered on as she edged him across the hall and into the warm room where books and papers were scattered across the thick rug before the fire.

'They all went to the theatre and left me here alone.' She sneezed loudly, then her grey eyes, tearful after the massive sneeze, surveyed him over the lacy edge of her handkerchief.

'I have a cold,' she informed him unnecessarily. 'It's almost better, but Mother wouldn't hear of me going out. I've been so bored!'

She dragged the last word out, and Lewis groaned inwardly. He considered his friend's sister, when he bothered to consider her at all, to be an empty-headed child with an annoying tendency to giggle.

'If Tom's out I might as well go home – '

Elizabeth caught his arm again, and the scent of fresh flowers wafted to his nose.

'But I've nothing to do but read those silly papers. I'll pour out a drink – or would you prefer tea? Please, Lewis – please stay,' she begged.

He hesitated for a moment, then shrugged. He had nothing else to do and the room was comfortable on such a raw night. 'Perhaps just for a moment – '

'Good! Now, shall it be Madeira, or whisky – ?' she busied herself over her father's decanters while Lewis watched with amusement, and finally brought him a glass well filled with excellent whisky. Then she settled on a low stool, almost at his feet.

'Tell me about yourself,' she said, and he laughed.

'There's little enough to tell.'

Elizabeth shook her head and dabbed at her nose, which was neat enough but, for the moment, a trifle pink. 'That can't be true. Tom wouldn't bother with you if you were dull. Just begin at the beginning. Tell me about your home.'

She possessed an amazingly quick mind, and he was

surprised to find that his reminiscences of Buckthorne and the sea interested her.

'I like hearing about other people – though I must confess that I could never live in a place like that. It would be too quiet for me,' she said decisively, scrambling up to refill his glass.

'It's where I'll settle, one day.' He watched her in the soft light, part of his mind idly appreciating the grace in her child-woman body as she moved. She returned, holding the glass carefully.

'Lewis – may I try a sip?' Her eyes sparkled with mischief. 'It looks delicious, and father and Tom would never let me try – '

He laughed, but nodded indulgently. She tasted the whisky and immediately her small face grimaced under its fringe of soft brown hair. He laughed again as she thrust the glass at him. 'It's horrible! How can men bear to drink it?'

'Very easily.' He swallowed a mouthful of the golden liquid and grinned at her. He had never realized before what a charming and pretty girl his friend's young sister was. She was going to turn heads one day – when she was older, Lewis thought indulgently.

She settled herself on the stool again, hugging her knees with her arms. Her hair, a little darker than his own, was spun gold in the fireglow. Her fashionable pale blue dress left her throat bare, and there was a pearly sheen to the exposed skin.

'Do you have a sweetheart back home in your village?'

The question took him by surprise.

'I – why do you ask that?'

'I'm sure you must have.'

He thought of Eden, and his heart twinged with sick longing.

'Poor Lewis. Did she treat you badly?'

'I don't know what you mean.'

Elizabeth touched his hand. 'You look unhappy.'

'Content yourself with your dolls and your books,' he

mocked, suddenly angry with this child who had tricked him into remembering home, and Eden, and his own exile.

'My dolls?' she said with amusement, slipping from the stool to kneel before him. 'I'm seventeen. Perhaps as old as – whoever you've left behind in your village by the sea.'

He looked down at her with eyes sharpened by shock. She had always been Tom's sheltered, silly young sister. Now he saw the sweet rounded upper breasts peeping above the neck of her gown and realized that she was indeed a woman – a woman with tenderness curving her sweet soft mouth and the scent of flowers on her skin –

He stood up. 'I must go – '

But Elizabeth's hand took his before he could turn away. Her full skirts rustled as she rose with graceful ease, standing very close to him.

'Stay for a little longer, Lewis. They won't be home for hours yet.'

There was an invitation in her face and in her voice. He wondered why he had ever thought of her as a mere child. 'The maid – '

Elizabeth's mouth curved and the impish gleam reappeared for a second in her gaze.

'She was sent for urgently to visit her sick brother just after Mother and Father left,' she said, low-voiced, retaining his hand in hers. 'It was most improper of me to invite you in, but I'm glad I did. Aren't you, Lewis?'

He should have turned at that moment and fled from the house. But Elizabeth Lamont was very lovely, and he suddenly found himself wanting her as much as she wanted him.

With a groan that was half-despairing, half yearning, Lewis gathered her into his arms and kissed her. Her hands came up to bury themselves in his hair, her lips opened willingly beneath his.

Unlike Eden, she made no protest when his mouth and hands roamed across her creamy throat, edging the warm silk of her neckline lower to free her young breasts.

73

Gently, Lewis lowered her to the fire-warmed rug.

An hour later she gave him one last lingering kiss in the hall
then stepped back as he opened the front door. He hesitated,
looking at her. She seemed as childish and virginal in her
blue dress as she had been when she opened that same door
to him a scant hour earlier.

'Elizabeth – '

Her smile was radiant. 'Don't fuss so, Lewis, I'm glad that
you came to call on Tom,' she said with all the charm of a
hostess. Then a faint frown puckered her smooth forehead.

'I only hope,' she added considerately, 'that you haven't
caught my cold.'

Going back across the little square and through the streets
he was aware of a warm ease in his loins, replacing the
tingling frustration he had fully determined to satisfy when
he was next in Buckthorne and alone with Eden.

Back in the little room allotted to him at the top of his
cousin's tall house, he applied himself to his studies and
worked easily through the papers that had baffled him
earlier. Just before dawn he fell into bed and slept, dreaming
of a woman with Elizabeth's willingness and Eden's dark
beauty.

# CHAPTER NINE

Although Charlotte never once referred to her ordeal it changed her subtly. She kept close to Eden as though dumbly seeking her protection; with good reason, for John continued to eye her suspiciously. He took to calling often at their lodgings and shadowing his sister when she was out in the streets with the others.

Eden wrote to Lewis, telling him something of her work at Yarmouth, emphasizing the social life the Scottish girls enjoyed when they weren't working. Let him see, she thought, that she, too, could find her pleasures elsewhere.

There was very little privacy for any of the girls, working together and living in one large room. Although Eden enjoyed the meetings and dances, she liked to stay behind in the loft now and again, washing her clothes, sewing, or reading a book borrowed from the local library; cherishing a few quiet moments alone.

A week after Charlotte's miscarriage she stayed in the loft to do Janet's share of the housework while the others went to a meeting. She scrubbed and swept diligently, and when the big room looked as neat as it could ever be and her own and Janet's clothes were washed and hanging on a line she washed her hair and pinned it on top of her head, laid out clean clothes and dragged the tin bath into the centre of the room by the stove. Laboriously she filled it with hot water then brought out a precious piece of scented soap, and stripped.

She soaped and rinsed herself slowly, revelling in the silence after the continual din at the harbour, then stepped from the tub and scrubbed her smooth firm body hard with a rough towel until the blood raced in her veins and she glowed from head to foot. She felt deliciously fresh and alive.

Slowly, sensually, revelling in the freedom of movement nudity gave her, she stretched out a hand to her clean shift, just as the latch clicked and John Murray walked into the room.

They both froze. She hadn't heard a thing – he must have crept up the stairs like a mouse, she thought wildly. She could see, almost feel, his eyes moving over her uncovered breasts, her flat belly and rounded hips, down to her buttocks, following the curve of her thighs and calves and ankles, even staring greedily at her slender feet.

She wanted to move, to snatch up her clothes, but sheer shock held her where she was. Then as his gaze returned to her face and she saw the look in his eyes, fear gave her mobility again. She snatched up the towel she had just dropped and clutched it tightly before her.

'Get out of here!'

His eyes fixed on the square of cloth that only just covered her. 'I've come for Charlotte.'

'She's at the meeting.'

He said nothing, but she saw the gleam of saliva as the tip of his tongue ran along his lower lip.

'Charlotte's not here!'

He ignored her, taking a step into the room. Eden's grip tightened on the towel. John was between her and the door. Her mind twisted and turned like a caged animal frantically seeking freedom.

'You knew fine that she wasn't here! You knew I was alone. Why else would you creep up the stairs like a criminal?'

His eyes flickered up to her face. 'What makes you think I did that?'

'I know you, John Murray! You've been spying around me and Charlotte ever since – ' she broke off.

'Ever since what?' he asked swiftly. 'What's our Charlotte been telling you? What have the two of you been plotting together?'

'Why should we plot anything? You're havering! Now get out of here and let me get to the meeting!'

'We can go there together, you and me – later,' he said huskily and she shook her head, backing away from the long, strong fingers he held out towards her.

'Get out of my sight!'

Anger suddenly leapt into his eyes, and she realized that she had been foolish.

'Don't speak to me like that! Don't look at me as though I'm worth nothing!' His voice began to rise. A worn floorboard creaked as he moved towards her. 'Behaving as if I should beg favours from you. Me – your own kin!'

Fear trickled cold fingers down her spine. His voice ran on as though he couldn't hold back the words that had been festering in his brain.

'Tempting, always tempting me – I will not be tempted!' he shouted at her, then his voice dropped suddenly, eerily, to a low groan that chilled her blood. 'I will wrestle with the devil and cleanse you – I can save you, Eden – I can! As I saved Charlotte – '

'Charlotte?' The name broke through the haze of terror that had begun to paralyse her mind.

Charlotte – and John! Not Lewis – Lewis was a name that she herself had offered Charlotte, a straw that the desperate, terrified girl had clutched at. Anything, Eden realized, rather than let it be known that her own brother had fathered her child. She remembered, with sick revulsion, the scene she had witnessed in the kitchen at home – John clutching Charlotte's arms, not in a frenzy of anger, as she had thought, but one of passion.

She cringed back as his hand clawed out for her. His nails

caught in the cloth and tore it away, but Eden was still free, scrambling to put the table between them, trying without success to shield herself from his burning eyes.

'Harlot! Jezebel! Tainting the immortal souls of men with fleshly desires – '

The words spewed from his twisting mouth, defiling her with their filth and venom. Spittle glistened on his lips, his eyes blazed hatred.

'Leave me be!' she screamed at him, covering her ears with her hands, closing her eyes against the sight of him.

It was a mistake. In one move he had rounded the table and his hands were on her shoulders. As she tried to twist away his mouth fastened on hers, clamping down until she thought she was going to suffocate.

She sucked in air when he finally lifted his head from hers, then felt his fingers fumbling at her breasts, her hips and thighs, and fought back as hard as she could, clawing and biting.

Her knee jammed hard into his belly and he grunted and let her go. She whirled, moving blindly, obsessed with the need to get out of reach of his hands, then pain burned through her scalp as he caught a handful of her thick hair and dragged her back against his solid body. He spun her about, his breath hot against her face.

'Whore!' he panted at her. 'Daughter of evil!'

His hands crushed and bruised her soft skin. Her head was forced back and pain crunched into the nape of her neck. One of his heavy shoes mashed her toes and burning waves of agony ran through her leg. His face seemed to fragment before her eyes and she tasted blood, hot and salty.

Confident that he had gained complete control John gave her a sharp push, opening his fingers to let her stagger back helplessly, arms windmilling, fingers reaching out for support. The big table caught her painfully across the buttocks and she collapsed across it. She was aware of John lunging forward, looming over her, tugging impatiently at the belt around his waist. Above the gasping, grunting sound he made she could hear a choked whimpering from her own throat. Then his weight pinned her down, his hands tore at her body, his voice panted triumphantly in her ear. 'I'll drive the devil from you, Eden – I'll purify you – '

Bile surged into her throat as she felt his half-naked body grind against hers. As he raised himself above her she saw that his face had changed in its intensity, become a slack-jawed, almost unrecognizable parody of itself. With a burst of strength culled from somewhere deep inside she tried to eel out from beneath him but he caught her wrists and slammed them hard on the wooden table beyond her head with one hand.

She cried out as he tore his way into her, and he muffled the sound with his mouth, biting at her lips, gagging her with his tongue.

She was quite certain, at that point, that she was going to die. The pain and fear went on and on mercilessly; black waves washed over her, threatening her with unconsciousness.

Then at last the pulsing, crushing, disgusting burden lifted from her body and she was left alone, spreadeagled on the table, choking and whimpering. A hand caught at her chin and jerked her face round roughly. John stood by the table, sweat coursing down his chest, looking at her with fastidious, contemptuous eyes. She tried to draw herself into a ball, to protect her bruised, violated body from this final humiliation.

'Dress yourself, woman,' he said, his voice clotted with disgust. 'Cover your nakedness, then pray with me for forgiveness for your sins!' He picked up her shift and threw it at her, turning away to reach for his own clothes, strewn about the floor.

She half-fell from the table, keeping it between herself and John. She was sore and stiff all over; her hair was a tangled mess about her face.

'Cover yourself!' he repeated, turning his back on her as

she let go of the table and reeled over to lean against the wall. Her groping fingers curled thankfully round the edge of a small shelf, then brushed against a familiar object – the handle of her razor-sharp gutting knife, put away in readiness for the next day's work.

It seemed to slip naturally into her fingers of its own accord. She stared at it, dazed; then looked up again at her tormentor, her betrayer, her enemy. Lurching drunkenly, the knife's handle hard against her palm, she moved forward, her arm raised then sweeping down to strike at his back.

She thought that John would fall when the knife sank into him. Instead, the blade hit him then stopped with a suddenness that sent a shock jarring through her wrist and up the full length of her arm. The knife twisted like a live thing in her fingers then clattered to the floor as John arched backwards, gave a thin high scream, and half-turned.

Eden fled to the other side of the room, convinced that he was going to catch hold of her again, but instead he clutched at the table then sank to his knees. To her horror he didn't lie still, but twisted and writhed like a fish caught in a net. One hand clamped on to the rim of the tub she had bathed in; in his struggles he managed to overturn it, so that he flopped in a pool of water.

She stood huddled against the wall, watching him, hands crushed to her mouth. He rolled over and she saw his face, grimacing and inhuman, his naked chest and belly gleaming dully in the lamp's light, then he writhed again and turned with his face to the floor, fingers clawing and slipping on the wet, bloodied planks.

And all the time he screamed – thin high animal-like screams that tore into her skull like the keening of the demons of hell.

'John – ' she whimpered, and forced herself to go to him, trying to take his head in her hands, to quiet him in some way, but he wouldn't be quietened. He continued to writhe about, his body thumping soggily again and again in the puddle of reddish water.

All she wanted was for him to be quiet. Had the knife still been in her hand she might have used it again, just to put an end to the unbearable nightmare they were locked in together. But the knife was somewhere on the floor, out of sight. John twisted violently and an outflung arm hit her legs and almost pulled her over to join him in the bloody water. Terrified, she jumped back. She had to get out of the loft, away from John and his terrible dying.

Shaking, crying, she pulled on the clothes she had laid out so carefully an hour earlier then snatched at her shawl and wrapped it over her tangled hair.

John was still trying to pull himself to his feet, but each time he failed and slid back to the damp floor.

Eden scarcely felt the latch beneath her fingers. She managed to wrench the door open, then she was through it, and it had mercifully closed against the sight of John trying to crawl after her.

Stumbling and slipping, she somehow got down the stairs without falling headlong, then the street door was open and she was outside.

The night was dark and cold, the street empty. Eden leaned against the wall and realized that she was whimpering Lewis's name over and over again. The chill wind helped to bring some order to her thoughts.

Lewis could be of no help to her at that moment, however much she longed to be safe in his arms. She could go to the meeting and bring the women back with her, or she could go straight to the police office –

So many choices! She almost gave way to an impulse to sit down on the cobbles, huddled against the wall, and let sleep take her – then she thought that she heard a thumping, slithering sound from the other side of the door as though John was making his way down the stairs, trailing a bloody spoor behind him.

Panic-stricken, her breath ragged in her throat, she began to run. Her feet, apparently acting on their own initiative, carried her straight to the door of the house where Coll Galbraith lodged.

A plump, fair-haired young woman opened the door in answer to Eden's frantic hammering.

'What do you want?' her easy Norfolk drawl sharpened as she peered out into the night. Then she called over her shoulder, 'Coll – ?' He appeared behind her, shirt open at the throat, the sleeves rolled up, a toddler riding comfortably astride his hip. For a moment, as the three of them stared at her from the cosy lighted doorway, Eden thought that she had gone to the wrong house and disturbed a local couple enjoying a quiet evening with their family. Then Galbraith spoke her name, thrust the child into the young woman's arms, and caught Eden as her knees finally buckled and she began to slide to the ground.

He carried her into a small lamplit room and set her down in a chair by the open fire. Only then did he ask, 'What happened?'

Her teeth were chattering so badly that she could scarcely speak. 'J – John. I've k – killed Jo – ohn!'

He drew in a hissing breath. 'Dear Lord!' the woman said over the baby's head then, as Eden moved and her shawl fell away, she added 'Look at the poor soul's arm, Coll – '

Galbraith's dark blue eyes were already on the purpling bruises that flowered on Eden's skin. 'Where is John?'

'At the lodg – lodgings – '

He reached for his jacket, which lay over the back of the other fireside chair. 'See to her, Louisa – ' he said tersely, and went out.

In the three hours before his return Louisa bathed Eden's aching body, exclaiming over her wounds, and helped her to dress again. She put the baby to bed and made some of the

82

black strong tea that fisherfolk the length of the British coast thrived on.

'If you did kill this John it seems to me it's no more than he deserves.' She settled herself in a chair on the other side of the fireplace.

'I doubt if the constables'll think so.' Eden gripped her cup tightly. The small, low-ceilinged room was warm and airless, but she couldn't stop shivering.

'Men shouldn't be allowed to use their strength to prey on women.' Louisa leaned across the home-made rag rug before the fire and put a comforting hand on her knee. 'Don't worry, girl, Coll'll see to it for you – ' she said, her soft drawl giving a new dimension to his name. 'And mind this – you're not the first to fall victim to a man, nor you won't be the last. You'll be all right. Now – best get you to bed.'

Once she was in the little bed in the wall-recess Eden's mind and body clamoured for rest and oblivion, but her eyelids refused to close. She was still wide awake when the street door opened.

Louisa, sewing quietly by the fire, got up at once and went into the passageway. Eden strained her ears but she could only hear the low murmur of two voices. After a moment Coll Galbraith came in alone.

She sat up in bed. 'Is he – did I – ?'

'It'll take a lot more than a frightened girl with a gutting knife to finish off John Murray,' he said abruptly, taking his sea-going box from the table and checking through its contents as he spoke. 'It was nothing but a scratch. I saw to it then got him back to his lodgings.'

'What about the constables?'

'It's not their concern. I managed to put the room to rights before the women came back. As long as you're at the farlins in good time tomorrow nobody'll say anything. As for John Murray – ' a grim note crept into his voice when he said the name. 'He'll have the sense to hold his tongue, and Louisa'll say nothing. Best get some sleep. She'll see to you in the morning.'

He delivered the speech, the longest she had ever heard Coll Galbraith make, without once looking at her. Then he picked up the sea-kist and moved to cup his hand over the funnel of the lamp.

'Where are you going?'

'To the harbour,' he said in the same matter-of-fact voice. 'The Sabbath finishes in another ten minutes and the boats'll be going out on the stroke of midnight. Get some sleep while you can.'

He blew out the lamp. The room door and then the street door opened and closed. The rattle of his studded sea-boots on the stones outside was the last sound she heard before she fell into a deep dark sleep.

Louisa woke her early in the morning.

'You'd best get back to your room and get ready for work.' She watched sympathetically as Eden eased herself out of bed, wincing. 'You'll feel better once you start moving about.'

As she dressed Eden looked around the little room. It was furnished with a sailor's tin trunk, a shabby table, two stools, two armchairs that looked home-made, and the rag rug; but it was spotlessly clean, the baby looked contented, and Louisa herself was a cheerful young woman.

'Your husband's not here just now? she asked curiously, and the young woman looked at her with clear, honest grey eyes. 'He died before the wee one was born,' she said without a trace of self-pity.

'How do you manage?'

Louisa's gaze didn't waver. 'There are always ways. Mind what I said last night – a woman can get over anything if she makes up her mind to it. And don't be afraid to put your trust in Coll Galbraith – he's a good man.'

\*

84

Eden had to put up with a lot of sly remarks from the other women, particularly when they saw her bruised face and arms, but none of them pried; they were all convinced that they knew how she had spent her night.

John was at work as usual, holding himself stiffly and letting others carry the barrels. His face was deathly white and his eyes never once met hers, much to her relief. When the Scottish fleet came back into harbour and Coll Galbraith brought the *Rose-Ellen*'s catch to the farlins he paid no attention to her. The matter was over and done with.

It was bitterly ironic, she reflected during that long diffi-cult day, that she had denied Lewis and then been robbed by John. Her mother was wrong – it was better to be taken in love, ring or no ring, than to be taken in cold-blooded lust.

She was tormented by the knowledge that she had let Charlotte delude her into thinking that Lewis was her lover. No; she had assumed it, and Charlotte had merely seized the opportunity to shield her brother and herself.

Eden's mind shied away every time it touched on the subject of Charlotte and John. It was something that could never be told to anyone; a terrible black secret that must be buried in the depths of her mind for ever.

# CHAPTER TEN

The rest of the English fishing season passed uneventfully.
John left on one of the first Buckthorne boats to head for Fife.
As each turn of the train's wheels carried the women nearer
home Eden and Charlotte grew more uneasy; Eden because
she couldn't bear the thought of being under the same roof as
John, Charlotte because she was convinced that her father
had found out about the baby.

'But none of us would tell him,' Eden argued as the two of
them walked from the station to the house. 'And nobody else
knows. How could he find out?'

'He knows everything. He always knew every single sin I
committed – ' Charlotte whimpered pathetically. 'Oh,
Eden!'

'If he finds out – and he won't – I'll stand by you,' Eden
promised. The girl had never shown her any kindness or
friendship, but she was pitiful in her terror. Eden squeezed
her cousin's arm comfortingly as they reached the cottage,
but her own heart was fluttering as she followed Charlotte in
through the low doorway.

Before she was properly in Charlotte stopped short and
Eden, right at her back, felt the solid body tense.

Something was wrong. There was a black, brooding
atmosphere about the kitchen, open fear in Barbara's red-
dened eyes. She hovered by the range, twisting her knobbly,
work-worn hands round and round in her apron. Caleb stood
like a bull beside the table, feet planted apart, balding head

lowered on its thick short neck so that it was hunched between his shoulders, small black eyes glowering at the girls from under menacing brows.

John sat in a corner, face slack with anticipation, his eyes darting from Eden to his father and back again in a ceaseless dance.

'So – you're back?'

Eden squeezed past her cousin. 'Were you not expecting us, Uncle?' She could feel Charlotte beginning to shake, and reached out to curl her fingers reassuringly round the girl's unresponsive hand.

Barbara moved forward. 'Caleb – '

'Hold your tongue!' he snarled.

'Come on, Charlotte – we'd best get our aprons on – ' Convinced that the girl was on the point of fainting with sheer terror, Eden pulled her across the kitchen. Caleb stepped aside to let them go into the passageway.

'He knows – ' Charlotte whispered. 'Eden – he knows! Oh God, what am I to do? He'll kill me – !'

Eden jerked savagely on the hand she held. 'Wheesht! He doesn't know. I'll look after – '

The words died on her lips as she opened the bedroom door. The bed she shared with Charlotte was strewn with the ripped, shredded remnants of her precious clothes. Eden looked with disbelief at the brown silk dress Annabel Laird had helped her to renovate with black velvet, her best hat, a cream straw with little artificial flowers on it, the white petticoat with red bows that her mother had made for her just before her death. They had all been viciously torn to pieces. The tin box they had been packed in lay beside them, its lock wrenched open. The pages had been wrenched out of the only two books her mother had ever possessed, a novelette and a collection of romantic poetry, and lay scattered over the mound of ruined clothing.

Her first reaction was relief that she had had the sense to take Lewis's letters to Great Yarmouth with her instead of leaving them in the box; then crimson rage swept over her. She pushed past Charlotte, who was staring at the mess as though mesmerized, and stormed into the kitchen.

'Who touched my things?' Her voice shook with fury. Caleb's chin jutted belligerently.

'I did – with a gutting knife.' He put heavy emphasis on the last word. 'You're not the only one who's handy with a knife, lady.'

'So he told you.' She didn't even look at John.

'You might have killed the lad, Eden – ' Barbara's thin voice was drowned out by Caleb.

'Murderess! Satan's handmaiden! Is this how you reward me for taking you under my roof? Is this – '

'Did he tell you everything?' Eden raised her voice to make herself heard. 'Did he tell you what he did to me?'

Veins stood out on Caleb's temples and in his neck. 'Hold your lying tongue!'

'Ask him why he didn't fetch the constables to me. It was because he couldn't – because they'd have known by looking at me – known what your son had done – '

'Be quiet!' Caleb roared.

'He's been at me from the first day I came into this house! Aunt Barbara, you know! Tell him – '

Barbara's face was frozen with fear. 'I – I know nothing,' she babbled, her hands knotted into the apron now. 'John's never looked near you – you've caused us nothing but trouble– '

'Charlotte – ' Eden rounded on her cousin and her heart sank as she saw the girl's grey, stony face, and realized that although she had promised to stand by her cousin, Charlotte had no intention of standing by her.

'Well, Charlotte?' her father asked softly, 'what have you got to say about this business?' The girl's head wagged frantically back and forth, as though someone was gripping her by the neck and shaking her violently.

'There's no – nothing to t – tell – '

'But you – ' Eden began, then stopped. Nothing would

make Caleb believe ill of his son; there was no sense in dragging Barbara and Charlotte into the sorry mess.

Caleb lunged. Charlotte let out a high thin scream of animal terror and threw herself sideways into the doubtful safety of her mother's thin arms. Eden braced her body for an attack, but he pushed her aside and barrelled into the bedroom to reappear a moment later with his arms full of the remnants of her clothes. He kicked the street door open and hurled his burden outside.

'Get out of my house, whore!' he ordered, his voice vibrating with fury. 'And you needn't think you'll go on earning your living at the farlins, for I'll see to it that you don't. Get out of Buckthorne!'

She picked up the straw basket she had brought with her from Great Yarmouth and which now contained everything she had in the world, and walked out, head high. The door slammed hard behind her.

It had begun to rain. The rags Caleb had thrown out were already darkening with water; the torn pages of the books flapped aimlessly about like wounded birds. Inquisitive faces appeared at some windows and across the narrow lane a door opened and a woman stood staring at her.

Without another glance at the pile of rags and paper Eden walked down the wynd towards the harbour. The Murrays' door opened again and something crashed and clanged on to the cobbles, then rattled into silence. It was her tin box, she realized, but she didn't look back.

The harbour was crowded with boats newly returned from England. They nudged and grumbled at each other as the rain sluiced across their decks. The sea beyond the harbour wall was a cold grey, blending in with the sky to obliterate the horizon. The May Isle had disappeared completely into the greyness, and the main street was almost deserted.

Gideon Murray's yard was deserted, the cottage door closed against the cold wet day. It opened easily under Eden's hand.

A good fire burned in the range and the cluttered room was warm and fuggy, pipe-smoke coiling in the lamplight. Gideon sat in the more comfortable of his two chairs, his pipe in his mouth, a book in his hand, his feet resting on the range. He looked supremely contented in that moment before he registered that the door had opened, and looked up.

'Uncle Gideon, I've come to live with you,' Eden said with cool dignity, then ruined it by bursting into tears.

The pipe dropped from a mouth that had fallen open in dismay.

'Oh – dear Lord!' said Gideon Murray.

# CHAPTER ELEVEN

Five days after his niece moved into the cottage by the boatyard Gideon Murray climbed the hill and paid his first ever visit to the schoolhouse.

'I hear your maidservant's marrying a farmhand by Kilrenny way,' he said, perched on an upright chair in the parlour, a glass of ale in his big fist. 'Would you consider taking Eden on in her place?'

Annabel raised an eyebrow. 'I thought she was well settled with you.'

'Settled?' he exploded, then modified his voice as the porcelain in the corner cabinet tinkled softly. 'You'd be nearer the mark if you said she'd taken over. My work-book's not mine any more, and she's never away from the yard. As for questions – '

'You mean she's sticking her nose in where it isn't wanted,' Annabel said briskly. 'And you'd sooner see her pester me as pester you.'

'It's not that at all! I'll admit that the girl's got a good head on her shoulders. My work-book's been brought up to date, and she writes a neat hand. And now that the boats are back from England and the men paid she's been round them all and collected money that's been owing to me for long enough. For years, some of it. I don't know how she managed that. It's just that – hell, Annabel,' said Gideon, forgetting where he was, 'I can't call my life my own. I'm sleeping on two chairs to let her have my bed and I'm bent in two when I try to rise in the mornings. I'm not master in my own home. Anyway' – he changed to a wheedling note – 'a young woman needs to learn about household things, not about ballast and keels and the difference between oak and larch. Even with the best will in the world – which I feel towards nobody, even Eden – I'm getting desperate, Annabel!'

He drained his glass while she pursed her lips thoughtfully. Then she said, 'As it happens, I'd been wondering how I could best help the girl now that Phemie and Caleb between them have managed to take her livelihood from her. I think she might suit me very well. I'll come down to the yard this afternoon and have a word with her.'

'Annabel Laird,' Gideon breathed, 'I never knew angels came with carroty curls before!'

She shot him a blue-eyed glance. 'Oh, we angels manage all sorts of disguises. You'd be surprised,' she said enigmatically, going to the store cupboard and bringing out a jar of home-made gooseberry preserve. 'Here – take this home with you.'

'Teach Eden how to make that,' said Gideon earnestly, 'and you'll have done more for her than anyone else could!'


Robert Laird scowled when he heard the news that evening.

'A fisher-lassie? Coming into my service?'

Annabel's frizzy hair seemed to stiffen. 'She wants to better herself. Surely a schoolmaster should encourage that.'

'There's a tale going about that she went after John Murray with a gutting knife.'

His sister's eyes, normally so mild, took on the hard brilliance of sapphires. 'Now, Robert, you're the one who's for ever telling me not to listen to gossip.'

'If you find me one day with a knife in my back, the blame's at your door!'

'As I heard it, John Murray asked for what he got. So if I

do happen to find Eden's gutting knife in you, Robert, I'll know what you were up to.'

The newspaper was thrown aside as the schoolmaster exploded out of his chair and stood over his sister. 'This is my house! The girl doesn't set foot in here without my permission!'

Annabel continued to knit her way serenely along a row. 'We agreed when we set up house together, Robert, that the running of it was my concern. If you'd prefer it I can always get a wee place of my own then you can choose your own housekeeper.'

There was a short silence, broken only by the crackle of the fire and the click of knitting needles. Robert had tried on several occasions to gain control of the money Annabel had inherited from an aunt, but she had always resisted him. She found that her little nest-egg made a useful weapon on occasion.

Sulkily he threw himself back into his chair and picked up the newspaper. He was a pompous man with, at times, a moodiness that would have been more suited to the youngest child in his schoolroom.

'Have it your own way – but I say you'll live to regret the day you decided to hire Eden Murray. Eden! Tchah! It's an outlandish name to give a girl.'

'It's biblical. And I believe her poor mother was of a romantic turn of mind,' Annabel said calmly, and Robert, well aware that he had lost the battle entirely, retired behind his paper and said no more.


A few days later Eden carried her straw basket up the hill and moved into the schoolhouse.

'It's not very big – ' Annabel showed her into the little room set aside for the maidservant, tucked under the house eaves with a view of the village and the sea.

'It's much better than the room I shared with Charlotte. And it's all mine! It's beautiful!'

Annabel flushed with pleasure. 'The first thing we'll have to do is make some new clothes to take the place of the things Caleb Murray spoiled. I've no doubt we'll suit each other very well.'

They did. Annabel was a born homemaker, and Eden an apt and willing pupil. Even Robert had to admit, grudgingly, that the new maid was quiet and deft.

Annabel showed her how to take apart the brown dresses and white aprons that had fitted her stout predecessor and alter them to fit her own slender figure. She gave Eden dresses of her own that were no longer used, and delved into her vast store of bottles and jars to make up an ointment that Eden religiously applied night and morning to her hands, which soon began to lose the roughness that working at the farlins had brought.

'Mistress Annabel knows more than I could ever learn,' she wrote to Lewis. 'She has such lovely things in her house. The schoolmaster scarce says a word, but when he's out of the house our tongues never stop. I've learned how to improve oilcloth and polish silver.'

She handed Coll Galbraith a letter once every week, though sometimes Lewis's letters were less frequent, and they were always shorter than Eden's. She altered a blue-and-white-striped dress given to her by Annabel in readiness for his return at the New Year, and set herself to learning all that she could so that he would be impressed when they next met.

If she encountered Caleb or any of his family in the village they studiously ignored her, and she quickly learned not to let it worry her. The only one with the power to frighten her was John. Although his blue eyes always slid aside swiftly the very knowledge that he was nearby made her skin creep and chilled the blood in her veins.

John was now 'walking out' with the daughter of the lay preacher who led the sect where father and son worshipped. Frank Ross was ill with bronchitis all through December, and John spent most of his time in the shop. Annabel, with a

94

perception that Eden appreciated, took it upon herself to see to the purchases they needed from the Ross's chandlery so that her new maidservant needn't ever go into that particular shop.

Anxious to show how much she appreciated all that the schoolmaster's sister was doing for her, Eden presented her with the precious hand-painted plate she had bought in Yarmouth.

'But – you should keep it for your own home, when you get one!' Annabel protested when she had unwrapped the gift.

'I can get more when the time comes. I'm going to have a whole shelf of them one day.' Eden's forefinger, now smooth and well kept, traced the gilt rim. 'Isn't it just beautiful?'

'Beautiful,' Annabel agreed, imagining Robert's expression if he were to come in and see the Present from Great Yarmouth nestling among the delicate china and porcelain that had been handed down through generations of Lairds. 'In fact – I like it so much that I think I'm going to keep it in my bedroom where I can see it as soon as I waken each morning.'


It was a bitter disappointment to Eden when Lewis wrote to say that he wasn't coming home at New Year after all.

'He says he's vexed at not seeing me, but he'll be home all summer for sure,' she told Annabel, her head bent over the scrawled page so that the older woman wouldn't see the tears she was blinking away.

'But he should be home.' Annabel looked concerned. 'Frank's far from well and there's some say that Phemie should have sent for Lewis before this.'

The tears had been forced back and Eden was able to make out the writing again. 'He doesn't say anything about his father, just that his cousin's arranged some social evenings and she expects Lewis to attend them.'

'If you ask me,' Annabel said darkly, 'Phemie's got a hand

in this somewhere. That boy should be home with his father, not gallivanting round Edinburgh.'

Frank Ross suffered from bronchitis every winter, but he had never before been confined to his bed for so long. John became a permanent fixture in the chandlery, and Euphemia discouraged visitors to the sickroom, telling the many people who inquired after him that he was as well as could be expected, and must get as much rest as he could.


For Gideon and his men 1874 came in with a flurry of activity, finishing off repairs in time for the start of the winter herring fishing. Eden, watching from the road as the boats butted their way back into harbour with their first catch on a bitterly cold day, was thankful she was no longer down at the farlins with the other women, gutting and packing with chilled hands stung by the salt and pickle needed for the fish.

Annabel was watching from the window when she came round the side of the school, and met her at the door.

'I thought you'd never come back! There's a letter for you.'

'For me? But Coll Galbraith's just come in from a night's fishing. He's still at the harbour.'

'This one was delivered by the proper letter-carrier. No, in here – ' Annabel almost pulled her into the parlour, where the letter lay in stately splendour on the big polished table. Eden picked it up, studying the elaborate curling script that spelled out her name.

'Who but Lewis would want to write to me?'

'You'll not know that until you open it!' Annabel brought the ornate paper knife Robert Laird used to open his correspondence. 'Go on, girl. Here – let me – ' she added as Eden's fingers, still chilled from the wind in spite of her mittens, fumbled with the knife.

In a moment the packet was open and the stiff single page within unfolded and thrust into Eden's hand. She scanned it, then looked up.

'My stepfather's died.'

'Poor man, may the Lord have mercy on his soul,' Annabel said rapidly, automatically. 'You'll be sent for to attend the funeral. My black would do you, with a quick stitch here and there.'

'I don't want to go to his funeral.'

'Of course you do. Wasn't the man a second father to you? You've still a duty to him.'

'The last time I saw him, just after my mother was laid to rest, he said the self-same thing. He wanted me to show my gratitude by sharing his bed. That's why I came to Buckthorne.'

'Was that the way of it?' Annabel tutted, her eyes still on the letter. 'Men can be difficult to contend with at times, right enough. But Eden – this is from a lawyer. You'll have to go, the man wants to talk to you. He's even arranged lodgings for you. Mr Oliver Lindsay.' She rolled the name around her tongue. 'It has a good solid sound to it. A moneyed sort of ring. Now – we'll see to the black dress – '

On the following morning Eden waved from the train window to Annabel, a rapidly-shrinking figure as the platform was left behind. Then the train racketed round a bend, and Annabel and Buckthorne vanished.

# CHAPTER TWELVE

Eden's trip to Great Yarmouth stood her in good stead. She coped with the train journey, the arrival, the transfer of her luggage to the address Mr Oliver Lindsay had given in his letter.

Nothing had changed, she was surprised to see, quite forgetting that she hadn't been gone from Eyemouth for more than six months. The streets and shops and houses were just the same, but she herself had changed. She was no longer a fisher-lassie, but in service. She had learned a great deal – and now Lewis was part of her life, even though he was far away in Edinburgh.

At the funeral she was glad of the black dress she and Annabel had managed to alter the previous day. Her step-father had been well-known in Eyemouth, and there was a large gathering of people to see him laid in his last resting place. The eyes that raked Eden were at first curious, then approving, especially when they saw her tears. They weren't to know that she wept for her mother, who lay beneath the mound adjacent to the open grave.

' – a good citizen, a faithful husband and loving father – ' the minister intoned, and Eden suddenly realized that he was right. James Ferguson might have been an insensitive, unimaginative man, he might have behaved badly towards her when he became a widower, but he had provided well for his wife and her daughter. All at once she was glad that she had made the journey to be there, if only to represent her mother.

Oliver Lindsay was benign and middle-aged, a little corpulent, as befitted a successful man, with an anglified drawl to his speech, adopted during several years spent in London. He took Eden's arm as the mourners left the graveyard.

'I have a carriage waiting, my dear. We can go to my office.'

His office was in High Street, not far from the butcher's shop owned by James Ferguson. Mr Lindsay settled Eden carefully into a chair then took his place behind a large, paper-covered desk. In an instant he stopped looking fatherly and became formal and businesslike, rattling briskly over the terms of his client's last will and testament, slipping his trained tongue round words that baffled Eden.

When he finally finished he put the will down and gazed at her as though awaiting her approval.

'Now then – what do you say to that?'

'To what?' she asked, bewildered, and he chuckled.

'I forgot – young ladies don't have to trouble their pretty heads with legal problems. To put it in a nutshell, my dear, my friend James Ferguson, your father – '

'My stepfather.'

'Just so. Though I know he always thought of himself as your flesh-and-blood father,' said Mr Lindsay, who knew nothing of that ridiculous chase round the kitchen table right after James Ferguson had buried his wife. 'Your stepfather, then, has left everything to you. Everything.'

Eden felt as though the high ornate ceiling had fallen down on her.

'But – he can't have!' she said at last, then, as Mr Lindsay just nodded. 'Why me?'

'You are his only relative, apart from cousins in the colonies somewhere.' He busied himself with his papers again. 'The shop and the house above it were rented, but the shop's contents and goodwill should fetch a fair sum. I already have a prospective client, and you can be assured that I will represent your best interests. In actual money terms your fa – stepfather was worth two hundred pounds, which will now go straight to you, of course. My dear child –' he came round the desk, reverting at once to a plump, fatherly figure, and took one of her hands in his. 'You look quite pale. Shall I tell my clerk to fetch some brandy?'

'No –' Eden got to her feet. 'I was just – I think I'd like to go out and walk about for a while.'

'Of course. I realize that it must come as a shock to find all at once that you are a fairly wealthy young lady.' Mr Lindsay's eyes studied her as she stood up. 'Yes. Perhaps you would do me the pleasure of being my guest for supper this evening?'

'It's very kind of you and your wife, thank you.' Eden matched his formality, blessing Annabel Laird and her training.

'I'm a bachelor, I'm afraid, but Siddon's Hotel do an excellent supper and I often entertain clients there. Shall we say seven o'clock?'

He bowed her out and she walked in a daze to the long narrow harbour, its entrance dominated by Gunsgreen House with its massive, distinctive chimney stacks. Like Buckthorne, Eyemouth harbour had its shipyard; this yard, though, had its own cut leading down the side of the harbour to the sea. There was a boat on the stocks, and Eden, who had learned a lot from her short stay with Gideon, studied it with interest.

Most of the men working on the boats in the harbour were known to her; they nodded, their eyes bright with curiosity, and she knew that they were watching her as she walked on.

She called on the girl who had been her best friend at the farlins, and saw the same inquisitive look in Hannah's eyes.

'They're saying James Ferguson left you all his money – is that right?' Hannah demanded to know almost as soon as Eden went in. 'They're saying he'd a sight more hidden away than ever any of us thought – is that so, now? And what

100

are you going to do, now that you're one of the gentry – ?'

Appalled, Eden parried the questions and made an excuse to get out of the house as soon as she could. She hurried back to her lodgings, where she shut herself in her room until it was time to dine with the lawyer. She had had no idea that the news of her inheritance would be known to everyone so soon. She thanked Providence that her stepfather hadn't died earlier, while she was under Caleb's roof, and decided that when she got back to Buckthorne nobody except Gideon and the Lairds was going to find out about her two hundred pounds.

On the stroke of seven o'clock she presented herself at Siddon's Hotel, and was escorted to a comfortably furnished private room where Oliver Lindsay waited to greet her.

She removed her feathered bonnet and let him relieve her of the velvet mantle Annabel had loaned her for the trip.

'And take one other decent dress and a little phial of my rosewater, for you never know if you'll find yourself in company or not,' the older woman had urged.

Eden knew, by the open approval in the lawyer's eyes and the smile bestowed on her by the waiter as he held her chair for her, that she looked right in her blue and white dress with the white chemisette, her hair put up and fastened with a blue ribbon.

She had never seen so much food on one table before. There was fresh herring served with herbs and sour cream; roast lamb and roast beef with green peas, stewed giblets, tongue, boiled fowl, and tarts. The table linen was snowy and the glass and silverware gleamed discreetly in the light from a silver candelabra. It was difficult to remember that she was only a short walk from her old home over the butcher's shop in one direction, and the harbour where she had worked in the other.

Oliver Lindsay ate his way steadily through dish after dish and drank a great deal of wine. Eden sipped at her glass, but shook her head when the attentive waiter made to refill it.

The sight of so much food made her feel quite ill, and it was a relief when Oliver finally wiped his mouth with a napkin, fluffed up his soft white side-whiskers, and suggested that they make themselves comfortable before the fire.

The table was still well-stocked, she saw with disapproval as they left it. It was a terrible waste of food; she noted that the man who had attended them was on the thin side and hoped that he might be allowed to eat his fill of the remains.

The lawyer settled her in one corner of the vast red plush sofa and sat down at the other. The waiter put a bowl of fruit on a small table within reach, and Oliver immediately selected the largest apple and began to peel it with a silver fruit knife which had been placed by the bowl.

'And now, my dear, tell me what you've been doing with yourself since you left Buckthorne.'

He had a disconcerting habit of staring at her mouth while she talked, and she was quite sure that he was watching the words instead of hearing them. He let the long curling strip of peel fall on to a plate that had been left for it, cut off a slice of the firm white flesh, and offered it to her in his plump, manicured fingers as though she were a pet dog. Embarrassed, Eden shook her head, and he popped the apple slice into his own mouth. The table was cleared, the door closed with a soft thump behind the servants. As the lawyer leaned towards her, shifting along the sofa slightly, his balding head, fringed with fluffy white hair, shone in the candlelight as voluptuously as the silver and glass had earlier.

'And what d'you plan to do with your inheritance?'

'I haven't had time to think – I still can't believe that my stepfather left it to me.'

A fatherly hand patted hers, and lingered. 'Indeed he did.'

'But – it's as much as would buy three fishing boats!'

He laughed. 'I'm well aware of that, for I was recently involved in advising some fishermen on how to form a joint-stock company so that they could invest in new boats. But matters of business are best left to men. They're not for young women to bother their pretty heads over – '

His well-rounded rump hoisted itself further along the sofa towards her. 'No, no – a lady has other things to occupy her little head,' said Oliver Lindsay, suddenly starting to look and sound like a pampered, purring white fluffy cat. 'Pretty gowns, jewellery – you have neat little lobes, my dear, they'd be well set off with pearls – '

One finger gently flicked her ear. The lawyer was close enough for her to smell a pot-pourri of scent from his clean pink skin. Eden sat still, aware of his nearness, of the hand lying on hers, the fingers beginning to caress her earlobe.

She realized what his intentions were and the shock on top of the other shocks she had had that day was almost too much to bear. She contemplated a loud scream that would bring people running from all over the hotel, but rejected the move as being even more embarrassing than her present predicament. She concentrated her mind on the problem, then beamed on the lawyer as the solution suddenly came to her.

'I think I will have an apple after all – ' she leaned forward, so that Oliver Lindsay's hands had no option but to fall away from her, and took up an apple in one hand and the fruit knife in the other.

'It seems strange to talk about pearls and new gowns when only a few weeks ago I was down in Great Yarmouth, at the farlins – ' she chattered, wielding the knife so skilfully that his eyes were drawn to its flash and glitter.

'I mind while we were there, a fisherman tried to take advantage of one of our girls.'

'These days are past – ' the lawyer stretched out his hand again, then withdrew it hastily as the fruit knife was pointed at him for emphasis.

'She'd her gutting knife at hand. He should have known better – poor man.'

He drew back slightly. 'What happened to him?'

The peel was discarded, the knife retained. Eden beamed

103

at him. 'Just what you'd expect, rest his soul. I'm sure the men down at the harbour could tell you it's never wise to take advantage of a fisher-lassie, Mr Lindsay.'

'Indeed?' Oliver Lindsay got up, went to the door, opened it, and looked out nervously, as though assuring himself that help was close by if needed. Then, leaving the door ajar, he came back to sit in an armchair by the fire, mopping his pink head with a silk handkerchief. 'It's warm in here, is it not?'

Eden settled herself more comfortably in the corner of the big sofa and bit into the apple with relish.

'I hadn't noticed. Now, Mr Lindsay, I'd like to ask a service of you.'

He watched her warily. 'Anything, Miss Murray.'

'Tell me about joint-stock shares,' Eden invited.

# CHAPTER THIRTEEN

While Eden sipped cautiously at her wine in the Eyemouth hotel room Coll Galbraith was striding up the cobbled wynd to his half-sister's house in Buckthorne, the thin ice over the puddles crackling beneath his boots.

He skirted the low-walled front garden and went in by the back gate. The maid jumped up from her fireside chair when he pushed open the kitchen door.

'Coll, I'm that glad to see you! I didn't know what else to do but send for you – '

He closed the door against the sharp black cold of the night. 'Is it Frank?'

She nodded, twisting her fingers together. 'He's worse – I'm sure he's worse. But the mistress says no, and I've been at my wit's end with worry. She'll not even let me see to him – she's taken on all the nursing herself.'

'When was the doctor here last?'

'This morning. He's coming back tomorrow and she'll not hear of me sending for him before then.'

'Where is she?'

'In the parlour with John Murray, going over the accounts. She says they mustn't be disturbed. Coll – ' she clutched at his sleeve as he went towards the door leading to the hall. 'It's more than my position's worth to let her know it was me sent for you. You'll tell her you just dropped in to see the man – ?'

'Don't fret yourself, Becky.' Grim-faced, Galbraith picked

up a lit lamp from the dresser and went into the hallway and up the stairs without glancing at the closed parlour door.

The two big rooms to the front of the house belonged to Euphemia and Lewis; the small back bedrooms were given over to the maid and Frank.

As he stepped into his brother-in-law's room Galbraith's nose wrinkled at the fetid smell. The room was dark and chill, with a strange stillness about it.

The fire in the small grate was just a dim glow and the lamplight showed that the candle in a holder by the bed had burned out. The small table within the sick man's reach was cluttered with a medicine bottle, a sticky spoon, a cup half-filled with strong cold tea, a newspaper and Frank's pipe and matches.

Galbraith cleared a space for the lamp and set it down carefully before turning his attention to the man in the bed.

'Frank? I've come to see how you're – '

Then he realized why there had been a strange stillness in the room. For the past five weeks Frank Ross's lungs had pumped with a laboured, wheezy sound, but now there was only silence. He lay among a twisted mass of sheets and blankets, the single pillow crushed against the iron bedstead as if pushed out of the way, Frank himself on his stomach, the top half of his body almost out of the bed, his outstretched hand brushing the floor. It looked as though he had been trying to get out of bed when death took him.

'Och – Frank,' Coll Galbraith said softly, reproachfully. He scooped up his half-sister's husband, turned him over and held him close with one arm while he arranged the pillow with the other hand. Then he laid Frank back gently and tidied the sheets over him, leaving his shoulders and head exposed.

Frank's brown leathery skin, result of a lifetime out of doors and, Coll had once heard, the gallons of strong tea the local fishermen drank incessantly, was hard and cold to the touch: his clear green eyes, bereft now of the soul that had

106

looked out through them for forty-eight years, were like glass splinters beneath the half-closed lids. Gently, Galbraith closed them, then, leaving the lamp where it was, he felt his way downstairs and opened the parlour door.

A fire crackled in the grate and the room was well lit and cosy. John Murray sat at the desk, writing in a big ledger. Euphemia stood behind him, studying the book, one hand resting lightly on his shoulder. They both looked up, startled, as Galbraith walked in.

'I ordered Becky – ' Euphemia began coldly.

Coll ignored her. 'Get out,' he told John, indicating the doorway with a jerk of his dark head.

Euphemia whitened to the lips. 'How dare you behave like that in my house!'

Galbraith didn't take his gaze away from John. 'Get out, I said!'

The other man got to his feet, pale blue eyes flickering uneasily between Euphemia and Coll.

'John, you'll stay where you are until our business is finished. My half-brother' – Euphemia emphasized the relationship icily – 'will be the one to leave.'

'I've things to say to you, Phemie – and they're not for the likes of him to hear.'

John's sallow face flushed an angry, blotchy red, then the colour faded as Galbraith added, 'If you refuse to go on your own two feet I can easily pick you up and throw you – '

'Mistress Ross, mebbe I'd – ' John licked his dry lips nervously and reached for his coat, over the back of a chair.

'You may go, Mr Murray.' Euphemia's face was stony and the look in her eyes would have frightened a lesser man than Coll Galbraith. 'I'll see you in the shop in the morning.'

Coll could almost taste John's hatred as the other man slid past him in that boneless way of his and out of the door. Euphemia waited until they were alone before she spoke.

'John Murray was invited into this house. You weren't!'

'I came to see your husband.'

'He's upstairs. You'd no call to come bursting in here with your – your gutter manners!'

'Tell me this, Phemie – when did you last go up to see how Frank was?'

She shrugged. 'An hour since, mebbe.'

'But not since your visitor came to claim all your attention.'

Her mouth twisted viciously. 'I've a business and a house to see to. I've more to do than run up and down stairs seeing to Frank every five minutes. He's looked after well enough!'

'Have you let Lewis know yet that his father's ill?'

Euphemia's black eyes blazed at him. 'Lewis has his studying to think of. I'll not have him taking time off to traipse down here just because of a wee bit of bronchitis. Now – if you're quite finished poking your nose in where it's not wanted I'll thank you to get out of my parlour and out of my house!'

'Oh, I'm going. But I've one more piece of advice for you, Phemie, and you'd best take it if you don't want to damn yourself altogether in the eyes of the whole village. Send for Lewis – tonight. Mebbe the lad never got the chance to say goodbye to his father, but at least let him attend the funeral.'

He threw open the door, then as she stayed where she was, in the middle of the parlour, he added brutally, 'Mebbe it's time you went up and had a look at your husband. He's dead, Phemie. Frank's lying dead up there while you're down here counting your shillings and pence, all cosy with John Murray!'

There was a gasp, but it came from the shadows in the hall, not from Euphemia Ross.

'Go and fetch the doctor, Becky,' Galbraith said to the maid, who had been drawn into the hall by the sound of their raised voices.

'Wait!' His half-sister's voice stopped him as he was on his way out. She walked back to the desk and closed the ledger, her fingers lingering on the leather binding. Then she looked up at him.

108

'You're no longer in my employ. I want you to get your possessions off the *Rose-Ellen* now – tonight. And don't you ever set foot on her again.' Each word was honed by cold rage to a needle point. Coll Galbraith took them without flinching.

'I expected no more than that from you. Goodnight to you, Phemie,' he said, and walked out of the house, leaving the front door open to the cold, cruel January night.

# CHAPTER FOURTEEN

Eden came home from one funeral to find Annabel Laird preparing for another.

'That poor man – they're saying in the village that Phemie was sitting in her parlour as comfortable as you please, not knowing or caring that Frank was lying dead upstairs. Well, mebbe he'll be happier where he is now – '

Eden could think of only one thing. 'That means Lewis'll be coming home!'

'And not before time either. He should have been sent for before this, when the bronchitis settled into Frank's chest – ' Annabel glanced at her maidservant's radiant face. 'Keep in mind that the lad's coming here to see his poor father buried, not to keep a tryst with you.'

'I know, but surely I'll see him. Oh, Mistress Annabel, I've such news for him!'

Annabel's blue eyes sharpened. 'Is it only for Lewis, or can I hear it?'

Shock and then dismay raced across her face when she heard about the inheritance. 'Well! I'm pleased for you lassie, but vexed for myself, having to look for another maidservant just when we'd settled so well together.'

'Why should you do that?'

'Mercy, you're surely not staying here in service when you can afford to go off to Edinburgh to live?'

'But this is my home now. I'd no thought of leaving!'

Annabel looked both surprised and gratified. 'You mean you'd stay on here?'

'If you let me.'

'I'd be glad to let you, it's not a question of wanting you to go.'

'And I'd as soon not let anyone know about the money just now other than Uncle Gideon and yourself – and Lewis, of course. I was wondering if you could tell Mr Laird, and ask his advice about what to do with the money for the moment.'

Mischief shone in Annabel's face, giving more than a glimpse of the vivid, pretty girl she had once been.

'Oh, I'd like fine to be the one to tell Robert he has a maid who's better off than he is!' she chirruped, adding, 'Just promise me one thing – you'll not let him take over the money for you.'

Eden looked at her with a level gaze. 'Mistress Annabel, nobody's going to take it over, I can tell you that!'

Frank Ross was buried on a bitterly cold January day. An easterly wind knifed through the mourners in the churchyard, bringing with it handfuls of icy rain to mingle with the spray thrown over the wall each time a big wave broke on the rocks below.

Both the Lairds attended the funeral, leaving Eden in the snug schoolhouse kitchen to bake scones and see to the soup for the evening meal. Robert Laird came home first, red-nosed and glad to go straight to the fire that crackled cheerfully in the parlour grate.

Eden followed, waiting as he stripped off his hat, coat, and gloves. She took them, together with his cane, put them tidily away in the hall cupboard, and was about to go back to the kitchen when he beckoned from the doorway.

Surprised, for Robert Laird never spoke to her unless he had to and always kept out of her way if they were alone in the house, she followed him back into the parlour and waited, hands clasped demurely on her snowy apron.

'I'll be honest with you, Eden' – he even used her given name for the first time – 'I didn't think you'd the makings of

111

a good domestic servant. But you've done very well since you came here. Very well,' he emphasized.

'Thank you, Mr Laird.' No point in telling him, for he wouldn't understand, what pleasure it gave her to live and work among the lovely things in the schoolhouse – the polished wood, the collection of fine china, the good carpets, the few pieces of silver. Nor would he understand how much she loved learning how to care for such a house.

'Very well,' he repeated, taking up a stance before the fireplace. 'Sit down, Eden.'

She pretended not to notice his gesture towards a fireside chair, and went instead to a high-backed chair by the wall.

'Now – my sister tells me that your stepfather's left you a small inheritance – '

'Two hundred pounds,' Eden confirmed, and heard him swallow convulsively. One of his stubby-fingered hands fidgeted with the white linen at his other wrist.

'Two hundred. Aye. Two hundred,' he said as though mesmerized by the number. 'Have you thought of what you want to do with this money?'

'Not yet. I thought you might advise me on how best to put it away safely.'

'Very wise,' said Robert Laird expansively. 'Investment, my girl – investment is the answer. Let your money earn dividends and you can become a wealthy young woman – if you've the sense to take advice from a sensible, experienced man of the world. Women have no knowledge of financial matters – and why should they, why should they?'

For the first time she saw him smile, an awkward grimace stiff with disuse.

'I'd be happy to give you such advice, to guide your inexperienced little feet along the right road, to protect you and your investments – '

Suddenly she noticed how like Oliver Lindsay he sounded. 'Dear God,' thought Eden behind her fixed polite smile, 'does money do this to every man, or only to the old ones?'

112

She cast around in her mind for some excuse to escape to the safety of the kitchen but Robert, hands tucked under the tails of his black morning coat, was in full flow.

'Now, the best way to go about it is – ' he had started, when the parlour door opened.

'There you are, Eden,' Annabel said, surprised. 'You've a visitor, waiting in the kitchen for you.'

Eden was up from the chair and out of the room before Robert had time to do more than glare at his sister.

'Is it – ?' She didn't dare to hope.

'Aye, it's Lewis. He walked up the hill with me. Now Eden – ' Annabel began, but Eden didn't wait to hear any more. She swept into the kitchen then stopped, suddenly shy, as she looked at the tall, elegant young man standing by the table.

Lewis wore a dark blue frock-coat and waistcoat over a white shirt. His trousers were mid-brown, and there was a mourning band of black material about one arm. His fair hair was as thick and soft as she remembered it, but he had grown a moustache since their last meeting. It gave him the look of a stranger.

He was just as taken aback by her appearance as she was by his; she could see that in the way his green eyes flared and a faint flush rose under his fair skin.

'Eden?' His eyes travelled over her neat red-and-white-striped blouse, brown skirt almost covered by a white apron, and the snowy lace cap over her shining black hair.

'Eden – I'd forgotten you were so lovely,' he said slowly, and his voice released her from her shyness and sent her running across the room to him. 'Oh – Lewis!'

His arms came up automatically to hold her. 'Eden – ' he began to say, but she interrupted him.

'I've missed you! And I've such news for you – you'd never think what it is, not if you guessed until the end of the year. But it's going to make everything all right for you. You'll be able to come home and build your boats and we'll be together – '

113

As she babbled happily into his chest she knew that that was what she had intended to do with her inheritance from the first moment she heard of it – give it all to Lewis so that his dream of being a boat-builder could come true right away. In her pleasure at being able to tell him so she didn't even realize that his arms were loosening about her, that he was drawing back.

'Hush, Eden!'

She stopped, instantly repentant. 'Listen to me, chattering on about my own business when you've just buried your father. Lewis, I'm sorry about him dying – '

He turned away from her and went to lean against the stone sink. The tap was dripping as usual and he tightened it absent-mindedly. Part of Eden's mind registered that she would probably have to use both hands to get the tap on again; the other part was just beginning to realize that Lewis's handsome face was as solemn as it must have been at his father's graveside, his eyes carefully avoiding hers.

'What's wrong?' Her hands linked together, gripping tightly.

'You have to understand, Eden, that living here and then in Edinburgh's like – like being two different people, in two different worlds.'

Her lips were dry; she moistened them with the tip of her tongue. 'And I belong to the wrong world?'

He shook his head. 'No! But you weren't in the other one with me. If you had been, mebbe – '

'Mebbe what?' she prompted when he stopped and gave the tap another unnecessary bone-cracking wrench.

'Eden, I'm – I'm to be married next week.'

'Married? But you can't be!'

'I can and I must.' He turned to look full at her, ramming his hands into his jacket pockets. 'Damn it, Eden, try to understand! Elizabeth's – she's expecting a child. My child.'

There was a silence. She stared down at her linked fingers, wanting to scream and rave at him, to demand shrilly that he

114

tell her that it wasn't true; but she knew that he wouldn't make up such a cruel story, that this unknown, pregnant Elizabeth was real and waiting for Lewis in Edinburgh.

'Can you not shout at me or something?' he asked wretchedly.

'Would it make any difference?' She looked up, and his eyes immediately swung away from hers. 'Is that why you didn't come home at the New Year?'

'I was lonely in Edinburgh,' he suddenly burst out, as though she had indeed bawled and wept and accused him of betraying her. 'If you'd really cared for me, Eden, you'd have let me make love to you properly. Then we'd have had some sort of understanding. But you refused me and – '

'And Elizabeth didn't.' His future wife's name was like a stone in her mouth. The irony of it all hurt her unbearably. She had refused Lewis because at the time she saw it as the right thing to do. Then John had taken her by force and Lewis had turned to someone who had been willing and eager to show how much she cared about him.

She laughed at the stupidity of it all, and looked up to see Lewis staring at her, bewildered.

'I don't see anything amusing in all this.'

Eden got up. 'Neither do I, Lewis.' She went to the back door and opened it, oblivious to the bitter wind that flapped at her apron. 'Thank you for coming to tell me yourself. I wish you well in your marriage.'

He lifted his top hat from the table, came towards her, hesitated.

'Eden – '

'Goodbye, Lewis,' she said briskly, suddenly aware of his nearness and the danger that she might throw herself into his arms and beg him to forsake Elizabeth and stay with her. Now, when it was too late, she knew that she loved Lewis Ross and that every thought, every hope, since she had first known him had centred round a future with him.

There was nothing more for him to say. He went, and she

closed the door, then wrinkled her nose, and ran to snatch up a cloth before opening the oven door.

Annabel came into the kitchen as Eden was putting the tray of blackened, rock-hard scones on the table.

'Mistress Annabel, I've ruined them!' she said in vexed tones. 'Now I'll have to make more!'

'Did Lewis tell you about – ?'

'Yes.' Eden dumped the tray and its contents into the sink then fetched the baking bowl and the crock of flour. 'I'm sorry about the scones, but first Mr Laird wanted to talk to me, then – '

'For goodness' sake, lassie,' her employer said, 'a few burned scones don't matter!'

'But they do,' Eden contradicted her fiercely, 'they do!'

Then she burst into tears.


She met Lewis once more before he and his mother left for Edinburgh. She had gone down to the harbour, taking a freshly baked cake for Gideon. The cottage was empty, and after clearing a space on the table for her gift she took up his work-book and a pencil and sat down to bring the records up to date, a task she had continued after she went to work for the Lairds.

'Hasn't Thomas Fulton paid – ' she began when the door opened, then looked up to see Lewis standing there.

She got to her feet, gripping the edge of the table tightly. 'My uncle's out.'

'It's you I've come to see.' He had on the same smart city clothes he had worn on the funeral day, and the mourning band was still about his arm. He looked drawn and tired. 'I saw you come here, and I knew Gideon wasn't in.'

'I've to get back to the schoolhouse.'

He put a hand on her arm as she tried to go past him. 'Can't we even speak together?'

'There's nothing left to say.'

116

'There is,' he insisted. 'I've treated you badly, but you don't know how lonely life can be in a city, and what it's like to have to study books night after night. It addles a man's head. As God's my judge, Eden, I knew as soon as I saw you yesterday that I'd made such a mess of everything. God, I wish I could turn back the hands of the clock!'

'Nobody can do that. Let me by – '

His hand tightened slightly on her arm. 'It doesn't need to be over, not altogether. I can come and see my mother often, and mebbe you could travel to Edinburgh sometimes. We could still see each other somehow – '

Then he stepped back abruptly, releasing her, one side of his face fiery with the marks of her fingers. The sharp sound of the blow rang in the air between them. Eden's hand throbbed.

'Goodbye, Lewis,' she said steadily, for the second and last time, and went out without looking back.

He and his mother left the following morning. Eden heard that Euphemia, as she travelled away from a funeral and towards a wedding, displayed an unaccustomed air of vigour and well-being. But Lewis, she was given to understand, looked quite haggard.

'It seems he's taken Frank's death worse than anyone thought he would,' said the woman delivering eggs at the kitchen door. 'It's as well one of them does.'

She took her payment and went off to the next customer.

The easterly wind was still about; a gust caught the door, whisked it from Eden's hand, and slammed it shut just as a door had slammed on her past the day before.

Now, she had only the future, and she must decide what use to make of it.

# CHAPTER FIFTEEN

When Euphemia returned from her son's wedding her first move was to send for Gideon Murray and cancel the new skaffie that was to take the place of the *Rose-Ellen*.

'But she can't do that!' Eden protested when she heard the news. Her uncle shrugged, his handsome face grim and drawn with worry.

'Phemie Ross can do anything she pleases in this village.'

'But after all the work you've put in – you had a contract –!'

'She claims the contract was with Frank,' he said wryly. 'Now he's gone, so who's to say she's lying? You'll have heard that Coll's not working for her any longer?'

She had. Coll Galbraith was now crewing for other skippers wherever he was needed.

'Phemie's got together a crew for the *Rose-Ellen*. She'll get one more season out of the boat and that'll do her. She has other irons in the fire.'

Eden's quick mind recalled the page given over in the work-book to the Ross boat. 'But she's paid four instalments already.'

'Aye – and she wants her money back.' Gideon bit savagely on the stem of his unlit pipe. 'That's the worry of it. She knows the money's been long spent – and of course she's willing to give me time to pay, or even to forget about it, on condition that I give her a share in the yard. I'd as soon close down as do that!'

It was unheard of for anyone to go back on an agreement.

But Euphemia had the power and the ruthlessness to do as she pleased. Eden knew that only too well.

'There's one way out. Let me buy into the yard instead of her.'

'Don't be a fool. You take your inheritance and use it for a fresh start elsewhere,' Gideon told her bluntly.

'But I got advice on joint-stock trading from the lawyer in Eyemouth – '

'No!' her uncle thundered, a great fist crashing on to the table and sending a box of nails all over the place. 'I'll not take your silver!'

'Why d'you have to be so thrawn?' Eden wanted to know, scrambling after the nails. 'Listen – it's not just you that would benefit. There's the men that need new boats.'

'Go and talk to them, then.'

'They wouldn't heed me.'

'Quite right too.'

'Listen to me!' she insisted. 'How many need new boats?'

Gideon admitted that at least three men were trying to raise the first instalment, a tenth of the overall cost, which had to be paid when they contracted their boats from the yard.

'And now there's Coll Galbraith, of course – though Phemie paid him so little he couldn't contract a new skaffie just now. He's going round the coast in the hope of finding a stranded boat.'

A boat that had gone aground was considered to be unlucky, but a man from another village could take it over without fear of ill fortune.

Eden's mind raced ahead of her tongue. 'If I was to buy the unfinished skaffie and pay you the full price for it you'd have enough money to pay Phemie Ross and finish the boat – and start another,' she pointed out.

'You? What would a lassie do with a fishing boat? Or are you planning to take it to the fishing grounds yourself?'

She flushed at the sarcasm in his voice. 'I'll hire a crew to

119

work her. Anyway, she'd not be mine – she'd be ours, if you'd only stop being so stubborn and let me come in as your partner. She could be our first joint-stock boat – my money and your work. Surely it's only right for each of us to contribute what we can?'

Gideon scratched his head thoughtfully, 'You've got your father's persuasive tongue right enough. You're beginning to make sense to me.'

'Then tell the others what I'm telling you. We'll pledge a share of the new skaffie's takings to the joint-stock company, and if those who need new boats put what money they've got together and pledge a share of their takings as well, there'll be enough coming in to start a third boat. They could draw lots to see who's to get each boat as it's finished.'

'Hold on! You're going too fast for me. I'm a builder, Eden – I've no head for business!'

'But I have, and I've taken advice on it, I tell you. You and me can each claim a share of the catch from the Ross skaffie. You'll see – that way you'd have money to work with, and I've no doubt I'll earn more in the long run.'

She saw his fingers begin to drum out a silent tattoo on his knee, and recognized the sign. It meant that he was interested.

But he hadn't finished putting obstacles in her way. 'What about the catches? Phemie owns the farlins and pays the fisher-lassies – she'll not allow them to work our fish.'

'We off-load our catches in another harbour. Phemie Ross might hold half of Buckthorne in her fist but she doesn't own the entire Fife coast – and she doesn't own us.'

'By God, you're right!' said Gideon, the light of battle back in his dark eyes. Then he pursed his lips shrewdly. 'This skaffie that you're so keen to buy – what crew have you in mind?'

'I've not thought about that. I'm sure there are men looking for work on a good boat.'

'There are. You'll want the best skipper you can find. And

120

just such a man's looking for work right now. Coll Galbraith.' He chuckled. 'It would fair annoy Phemie if we put the man she turned off in charge of the boat she refused. And it was meant to be his boat in the first place. He had a hand in the designing of it.'

'Then ask him if he'd take on the job.'

Gideon shook his greying head. 'Oh, no. Since you're so eager to be a partner in this company you can take on your share of the responsibility. I'll talk with the other men – you can see to Coll. When all's said and done, it's your boat, not mine.'

Her next battle was with Robert Laird. Eden had allowed the schoolmaster to put her inheritance in the bank but had managed, through a subtle blend of assumed naïveté and sheer evasion, to avoid getting involved in any further private conversations with him.

There was a stormy scene in the parlour when he found out what she intended to do with her money.

'Are you out of your mind altogether, lassie? You're throwing good silver after bad!'

'You advised me to invest.'

'Not in Gideon Murray's yard. Eden' – he tried a coaxing tone which sat ill on his tongue – 'put yourself in my hands.'

The very thought made her shiver.

'I'd as soon keep to the arrangement I've already made with my uncle,' she said politely but firmly. 'I've been to the lawyer in Ainster. He'll draw up the papers for us. Besides, it's just part of my money that's to be used. I'll keep a tight grip on the rest.'

Then, as he opened his mouth to speak, she added hastily, 'I think the broth might be burning – ' and escaped to the kitchen.

'The lassie seems to have her head screwed on the right way, Robert,' said Annabel, who had been sitting in on the

121

discussion and keeping her tongue firmly between her teeth. 'Gideon's a sensible man where business is concerned. I'm sure things'll work out for the best.'

Her brother glared down at her, fleshy lower lip protruding in a way she knew well.

'Why is it,' he asked bitterly 'that money always goes to folk that have no appreciation of its value?'


Once Gideon made up his mind to fall in with his niece's plans he set to work with renewed enthusiasm on the new skaffie and on the skippers who, he knew, were anxious to replace their ageing boats.

'You're not the only one with the gift of persuasion,' he reported smugly to his new partner the next time she went to the boatyard.

'I knew you had it too, though until now you've only used it on the women of the village.'

'Aye – well – ' he said, a trifle disconcerted. 'You can tell your lawyer mannie to go ahead and draw up the papers for signing – and it's time you went to see Coll.'

'When do you want Mistress Ross's money?'

Gideon winked. 'She's kept me waiting for money often enough. Let her wait until she's worked up a good sweat about it. Have you seen to your new skipper yet?'

Eden had no desire to confront Coll Galbraith. She had an uncomfortable feeling that he wouldn't take kindly to being offered work by a mere girl.

'I've still got my work to do up at the schoolhouse, don't forget. You have a word with Coll when he's next at the yard.'

But Gideon was adamant. 'You're the one with the head for business,' he reminded her. 'And mebbe by the time Coll drops by the yard he'll have found work on another boat. You'd best see to it as soon as you can.'

Then his brown face broke into a broad grin. 'I'm looking

forward to hearing what he says when he finds out who's going to take over that skaffie.'

Coll Galbraith, Eden told herself as she walked from the harbour to his cottage, was just a good fisherman in need of a boat. It was foolish to think of him as a link with Lewis. Those days were over.

All the same, it took a lot of courage to knock at the door. It opened almost immediately.

'Aye, I'm ready – ' said Coll, pushing one arm through the sleeve of his jacket; then he stopped, staring down at her in open surprise. 'What d'you want?'

Eden dug her nails into her palms beneath the shelter of her shawl.

'Can I have a word with you?'

He cast a swift glance over her head at the street, then stepped back to let her in.

'Aye, if you make it quick. I'm crewing on the *Heather Bell* and we've to go out with the tide.'

His cottage was sparsely furnished but spotlessly clean. She had assumed that a man on his own would be a handless creature, but Coll Galbraith's range had been black-leaded until it shone, the little window facing the street was clean, and the floor was freshly swept.

He nodded at one of the two wooden fireside chairs and she sat on its faded patchwork cushion. Coll himself, obviously anxious to be off, stayed on his feet, ducking now and then to peer out of the window. The light from the street caught a rich chestnut gleam here and there in his unruly dark brown hair.

'Well?' he asked, a trifle impatiently.

'I've come to offer you work.'

'You? What sort of work could you offer a fisherman?'

Eden felt an angry, embarrassed flush warm her high cheekbones.

123

'You'll have heard that Mistress Ross has decided not to take the new skaffie?'

Bitterness crept into his deep voice. 'Aye – I heard.'

'I'm buying it in her stead.'

All at once he lost interest in the road outside. He came to sit on the chair opposite, and for the first time she realized that Coll Galbraith's eyes had the same translucent quality as his late brother-in-law's and his nephew's. Coll's were blue, not green, but they had that same clear, far-sighted look. They fastened on her, and she felt as though they could see right through into her mind.

'You – buying the skaffie?' he asked with total bewilderment. 'But how can a – a lassie like you find the money for a boat?'

She took a deep breath, mindful of the tide and the *Heather Bell*, due to leave the harbour soon, and plunged straight into the tale about her inheritance, the new joint-stock company, the plan to use the Ross skaffie to start off a new fleet.

When she had talked herself to a standstill he asked crisply, 'Why could Gideon not have asked me himself?'

Eden felt her back stiffen. 'Because it's me that's buying the skaffie,' she snapped. 'Were you not listening?'

He stood up, went back to the window. 'Oh, I listened,' he told her coolly. 'But I can't believe you'd want to put money into boat-building instead of spending it on fripperies and fineries.'

'How I use my own money's my business! All I'm asking you to do is find a crew and take over the skaffie when she's ready, in another month. I'll provision her and you'll take a share of each catch.'

He stood looking at her, one hand thoughtfully stroking his jaw. Booted feet clattered along the street, coming towards the house.

'No,' Coll Galbraith said simply, and picked up the jacket he had taken off when she came in.

'But –' she found herself stammering. It was as though the

124

ground had been whipped from under her feet. 'D'you not want regular work on a fine new boat?'

'I do. I'd like it fine.' He shrugged his other arm into the jacket unhurriedly. 'But I've already worked for a woman, and look where it got me. Women aren't to be trusted.'

'That's not fair!' she stormed at him, on her feet now. 'Just because your sister's a thrawn, twisted woman it doesn't mean you can't trust me!'

The other crewmen were nearly at the door now. Coll picked up his sealskin cap and reached for his kist, the box that carried his food for the trip.

'You're young yet, Eden Murray. Not much more than a child. Who's to say you won't tire of this new ploy and decide to take your money elsewhere and spend it? Then what happens to me? I've no wish to be turned off again.'

'I told you – it would be a joint-stock company – '

'With too much of the control in your hands,' he interrupted. A fist banged on the door, and he raised his voice. 'Aye – I'll be down at your back.' Then he turned, hand on the latch.

'I'd need more than a promise. I'd need to be sure of my position. And the only way I can be sure is if you're willing to seal the contract by marrying me.'

Eden felt her mouth drop open with sheer shock. At that moment the ceiling could have fallen in and she wouldn't have noticed.

'Marry?' she said at last, faintly. 'Are you soft in the rigging?'

Coll's face was expressionless. 'As your husband I'd have control over your actions and my own future. We're both free to make such a contract. These are my terms. You can take time to think about it if you want.'

He opened the door, waited for her to go through it.

'Time? I don't need time. I've never heard such a – such a – ' she floundered, searching for words that were withering enough.

'Then find yourself another skipper,' Coll said with maddening indifference.

'I will!' she flared, swept past, and marched down the street with her head held high and her cheeks burning.

She hoped to get past the boatyard undetected, but Gideon saw her and called her over.

'Well? Did you get a chance to speak to Coll?'

'Aye. He doesn't want to work for us,' she said shortly, and his brows rose.

'I thought he'd have been pleased to skipper a new boat.' Then he peered at her. 'Was it the way you put the proposal that made him refuse?'

The word was unfortunate. 'It was not! I put the offer fair and square and he turned it down. There's no more to be said. We can find someone else easily enough.'

'I hope so. But Coll was the best man for the job.'

'If you ask me,' Eden said with an edge to her voice, 'we can manage very well without the likes of Coll Galbraith.'

A week later, dressed in her good blue and white gown, a warm black shawl and a white bonnet with blue ribbons down the back, Eden walked down the hill from the schoolhouse. She went past Euphemia Ross's back gate, rounded the corner, went in at the front gate and up the path.

Becky opened the door, her eyes widening as she saw who the caller was.

'Good afternoon, Becky. I've come to call on Mistress Ross – on a matter of business,' Eden added firmly as the maid glanced nervously over her shoulder.

'The mistress is in the kitchen – '

'Then I'll wait in here for her.' Eden eased past the girl and went into the parlour, closing the door in Becky's astonished face.

The room was just as chilly and formal as she remembered it; the row of hand-painted gold-edged plates on the side-

126

board gave the only colour. They fascinated Eden as much as they had done the first time she saw them. She was studying them closely when Euphemia Ross spoke from the doorway.

'The girl says you claim to be here on a matter of business. I've no business dealings with you,' she said contemptuously.

'But you have, Mistress Ross,' Eden said as evenly as she could, taking a chair uninvited, hearing the older woman's breath catch at her impertinence in making herself at home. There was a pause, then Euphemia made her way to the chair she had sat in the last time.

As she watched, Eden reminded herself that circumstances had changed a lot since the last time she was in this room. She was no longer a mere fisher-lassie, easily bullied. Gideon was right – she had to face Euphemia, had to prove to herself that the woman had no hold over her now, no ability to frighten her.

'It's about the skaffie in the boatyard – ' she began, and was interrupted.

'If Gideon Murray wants to talk to me about the boat he must come here himself,' Euphemia rapped out.

'It's my place to come here, not his. I've bought the boat. I have your money here – ' She opened her purse and took out a bundle of notes.

Euphemia's nostrils flared and two spots of colour blotched her cheekbones. 'You? So it's true what they've been saying!'

Eden counted the notes out one by one and laid them on the highly polished table.

'I have no idea what they're saying, Mistress Ross. I prefer not to listen to village gossip,' she said with a dignity that had been well learned from Annabel Laird. 'Twenty-one pounds, Mistress Ross.' She closed her bag and got to her feet. 'And now I believe our business is completed.'

'So – you think you've done well for yourself, my lady?'

Euphemia's voice was vicious. 'When all's said and done you're only a fisher-lassie – and don't you forget it!'

Eden stood looking down on the woman. 'That's all you were, Mistress Ross,' she said evenly. 'I don't forget that either.'

Euphemia's hands clutched at the carved arms of her chair, the knuckles gleaming bone-white.

'Oh aye, you're pleased with yourself' – in her anger she resorted to the lilting accent of her youth – 'but there's one thing you'll never get your hands on now. You'd have liked fine to get yourself into my son's bed, wouldn't you? Into my family.' She got out of her chair, tugged fiercely at the bell-pull by the fire. 'But you'll never marry my flesh and blood now. I've seen to that!'

It took all Eden's courage to stand where she was. The woman's loathing was so intense that each word was like a blow. She felt the blood drain from her very heart.

The door opened. 'Becky, show this – this person out,' said Euphemia Ross.

Eden walked, straight-backed, past the maid, then turned and managed to smile sweetly at Lewis's mother.

'Thank you for your offer of tea, Mistress Ross,' she said clearly. 'Unfortunately, I have a most important engagement elsewhere.'

Down the path she went, out of the gate and along the road, certain that Euphemia Ross was watching her from behind the heavy velvet parlour curtains. Once she was safely round the corner she stopped and leaned against a wall, hands pressed against her lips as she fought to still the tremor that came from deep inside and threatened to take over her entire body.

Euphemia's words echoed in her ears. 'You'll never marry my flesh and blood – never – never – !'

Never – ?

The trembling eased, to be replaced by a sudden sense of purpose. She straightened, and went back down the hill to

128

the harbour. There was work to be done at the schoolhouse, but she had something else to see to first, and it couldn't wait.

It was unusual to see a villager dressed up during a normal working day. Men busy with their nets stared when Eden appeared at the top of the ramp leading to the harbour, but she ignored them, her eyes searching for one face. It wasn't there.

'Where are you going with all tap's'l's set?' Gideon wanted to know as they met on the shore road.

'I'm going to get a skipper for my boat,' she threw the words at him over her shoulder as she went past without stopping.

When Coll Galbraith answered the door she said at once, 'I'll marry you – if you'll take on the boat.'

His brows narrowed as the blue eyes beneath them swept over her finery. 'You've dressed in style to tell me.'

She waved the words away impatiently with a gloved hand. 'Will you take on the skaffie?'

'The marriage must come before the boat's launched.'

'Yes.'

'We have an agreement, then.'

'A business agreement,' she emphasized, and he nodded.

'Aye. I'll see about getting the banns called in the church. Then I'll start getting my crew together.'

She held out her hand and after a moment he took it in his. For better or worse, the contract was made.

# CHAPTER SIXTEEN

'I'm not certain I'm doing the right thing – !' Eden said in a sudden flurry of fright on her wedding morning.

Annabel, down on her knees putting the final stitches into the hem of the wedding dress, a full-skirted rose muslin sprigged with pale grey flowers, tutted as well as she could round a mouthful of pins.

'Nonsense – Coll Galbraith's a fine man.'

'But he's too old for me!'

Annabel spat the pins out into her hand. 'Away with you, lassie! He's only twenty-eight – two years younger than me. And I can assure you I'm nowhere near old!' She took a final stitch, bit the thread off, and got to her feet. 'There. Oh, you look bonny, Eden. I just wish you could have married from this house, but Robert's a difficult man at times.'

'Marrying in the manse is fine, and Coll's house'll do for the wedding party.'

'Your house too, after today. It seems as if you've hardly settled in here – and now you're away.' Annabel shook her head sadly. 'I had a feeling that you'd not stay long. Though I thought it would be Lewis and not Coll that would take you away – '

'We never know what's ahead of us,' Eden said abruptly. She wanted no more talk of Lewis, not on her wedding day. He belonged to last summer, when she had been young and carefree. She felt years older now.

'You've got a good man, anyway. Everything's going to go

130

well for you. And it'll be nice for you to have a home of your own at last.'

Her clothes and possessions had been moved that morning to the cottage, but in the bustle of marriage plans and the excitement of seeing the skaffie reach completion she hadn't had time to think of the cottage as her future home, and Coll Galbraith as her husband.

For a moment panic almost claimed her, then she overcame it and smiled at Annabel. 'You're right – everything'll be fine.'

It would be fine because it had to be. She would make everything work. But as she and Coll, like a handsome stranger in his best clothes, walked together to the minister's house, she thought fleetingly, and for the last time, of the way things might have been.

The marriage service was conducted in a small room overlooking the sea, with a glimpse of the graveyard where her father lay beside his wife. To a background of waves crashing on rocks, for it was a stormy day, the minister intoned words and Coll, whose given name, she discovered with a sense of shock, was Colin, took her cold hand in his warm grasp and slipped a plain gold band on to her finger. It was done. She was a married woman.

They walked back past the harbour to the cottage where Annabel, despite her brother's disapproval, was busy organizing the wedding feast. The boat Coll was crewing in was brightly decorated to show that one of its crew was being married – red white and blue flags fluttered and snapped in the late February wind.

Their progress was slow, because everyone they met stopped to congratulate them. Coll was warm enough in his sturdy dark blue coat, but Eden's fringed mantle was meant for decoration rather than warmth. He noticed her shivering, and moved without comment so that his body was between her and the wind.

Beyond the harbour they met John Murray walking with

his wispy, pale-faced sweetheart. As her cousin's pale blue gaze brushed hers Eden flinched back against Coll and felt his hand take hold of her elbow.

'Pay him no heed,' he murmured, and steered her past the couple. She shivered, not because of the wind this time. It was as though John's presence had cast a blight on her wedding and on its future.

Then they were at the cottage, the door was thrown open by Annabel, the interior was warm and filled with well-wishers, and John was forgotten.

It was late before the wedding party broke up. Annabel was one of the last to leave. Her red hair shone like a beacon in the lamplight and her eyes sparkled like sapphires, giving her a youthful beauty.

'I always saw you as a dry sort of stick, but you're a fine-looking woman after all,' Gideon told her, and she twinkled at him.

'I've broken many a heart in my time, let me tell you. One more drink before we go – we'll sail the harbour wi' this ane!' She delivered the local saying with a broad Fife accent that was far removed from her usual genteel Edinburgh speech, and Gideon's deep laugh roared out.

'One more drink and you'll fall into the harbour, lady. I doubt I'll have to walk you home the long way to get you sobered up before the schoolmaster sees you,' he said, and assisted her out into the night.

The two of them, the last guests to depart, disappeared into the darkness. Before Coll closed the door behind them Eden had tied an apron over her wedding finery and was putting the room to rights.

'Leave it till the morning,' he said irritably, but she shook her head. Having something to do kept at bay the sudden shyness she felt now that she was alone with her husband – a man she scarcely knew.

132

'I don't want this mess waiting for me when I waken.'

Coll shrugged and reached for his jacket. 'If you're going to start cleaning I might as well go out along the shore for a bit of fresh air.' He went out of the side door into the passage as she fetched a broom and began her work.

The cottage consisted of a large kitchen at the front with a small bedroom to the back, opening off the main room. The side passage could be reached from the street and also from a door in one corner of the kitchen. It led to the back yard, which held the gallowses where nets and sails could be hung. A wash-house had been built at right angles to the cottage, then came a grassy patch where clothes could be dried. A gate in the low stone wall that bordered the yard led directly on to the rocks. At high tide the sea came in close to the shore cottages; on stormy days spray spattered their back yards.

The big sail loft on the upper floor of the cottage, reached from the side passage, was where Coll's fishing gear was stowed.

Eden finished her work and looked around, satisfied with her new home. Pride of place had been given to Annabel's wedding gift, a small glass-fronted corner cabinet. In it, in solitary splendour, was the Yarmouth plate. Eden lifted it out, one finger tracing the lettering, the bright flowers and berries, the lovely gold edging. Annabel had insisted on giving it back to her.

'It's only right, now you've got your own home. Besides, you need something to put into your new cabinet. Coll can bring more plates when he goes back to England. Imagine, Eden – you'll soon have all the gold edging any woman could want!'

'I will,' Eden promised herself softly as she put it back before going up to the sail loft.

A smile tugged at Coll Galbraith's mouth as he looked round the tidy room some time later.

'It's a change to see a woman's touch about the place.'

He took off his coat and hung it on the nail behind the

133

street door. Eden, her arms full of blankets she had just brought from the big wooden chest under the window, watched as he sauntered towards the bedroom door, loosening the buttons on his yellow waistcoat.

'Where are you going?'

'To my bed. Where else at this time of night?'

She moved fast, getting between him and the door. 'But I'm sleeping in there.'

His eyebrows went up. 'I expected you would be.'

'I've made up a bed for you in the sail loft.'

His brows swooped down again to meet in a frown. 'You've what?'

She stood her ground. 'You agreed – we agreed – that this was more a business arrangement than a marriage.'

'I didn't agree,' said Coll Galbraith levelly, 'to sleep in my own sail loft.'

'You surely don't expect me to sleep there, do you?'

'No.'

'Well then. I'll just take the blankets up. You'll be fine and comfortable – ' She scooped up the blankets and hurried out before he could say any more.

The loft held lobster pots and spare nets, oars and buckets and boxes and buoys, sea-boots and oilskins. The low roof was watertight and the place snug enough despite the wind howling beneath the eaves.

She had already moved everything to one side to make room for the truckle bed. After arranging the blankets she stood back and nodded. It would do for now, but a more permanent arrangement would have to be made.

The kitchen was empty when she went back to it. Coll's coat still hung on the nail at the back of the door, showing that he hadn't gone out. With a sudden feeling that there was trouble ahead Eden opened the bedroom door.

'What do you think you're doing?'

Coll put his hands behind his tousled dark head. His naked chest and shoulders gleamed a smooth bronze in the lamp-light. 'I'm in my bed – and so should you be at this time of night.'

'But – but – we agreed!'

'We agreed to marry, and marriage is marriage.'

He looked so settled, so sure of himself that she could have hit him. 'Because of the boat – that's why we wed. Only because of the boat!'

'If you think I'm going to spend the rest of my days sleeping in a sail loft you're daft,' he said with the air of a man who has just had the last word. 'Now – stop chattering and come to bed.'

'I will not!' She scarcely knew Coll Galbraith; as far as she was concerned this wedding had been contracted for their mutual financial benefit. Nobody, least of all Coll himself, knew that it had also been contracted to spite Euphemia Ross. And Eden had been so taken up with the business of buying and crewing the boat that any thought of the marriage being other than a formal arrangement had been swept aside. She had somehow, foolishly, assumed that he was of the same mind.

'I will not!' she repeated, darting forward and snatching at the blankets that covered him. 'Get out of that b – oh!'

She backed away, hot colour flooding into her face as she saw that he was naked. She threw the blanket over him and fled, his laughter following her through the kitchen and out of the side door. It was still echoing in her head when she reached the sail loft.

She pulled back the blankets on the truckle bed, started to unbutton her fine wedding gown, and realized that her nightgown was in the bedroom, lying over the bottom of the bed in readiness for her. She would have to do without any nightclothes at all, for she refused to sleep in her good embroidered petticoat.

Tears of fury at Coll's insensitivity stood in her eyes as she undressed and tried to find somewhere to hang her fine gown. Lewis wouldn't have humiliated her like this, she

135

thought as she blew out the lamp and climbed into bed. Then honesty forced her to admit that if it had been Lewis's ring on her finger instead of Coll Galbraith's, she wouldn't be sleeping alone.

At first the loft was pitch black, then gradually the single small window showed itself as a dark grey smudge. The wind screamed and moaned on the other side of the wooden wall beside her, a mouse scuttered in a corner. The rough blankets scratched and irritated her skin and Eden lay rigid, wide awake, longing to be back in her own small room in the schoolhouse.

At last she managed to fall into an uneasy sleep, only to waken with a start as the stairs creaked under Coll's weight. She sat up as the lamp in his hand sent weird shadows dancing and scampering for cover.

'What do you want?' She clutched the blankets round her throat, blinking in the light.

He put the lamp safely out of the way on a box. 'My wife,' he said bluntly.

He was still naked; with the lamp behind him she could only see him as an outline in soft gold where the light struck off his skin – broad shoulders and chest tapering to the waist, then flaring to sturdy hips. Lithe sinewy legs and arms, his head a mass of waves shot through with bronze –

Gold round the edges, she thought, and fought back a mad desire to giggle.

'Coll – leave me be!'

In answer he stooped to scoop her up in his arms. She rolled off the truckle bed, away from him, taking the blankets with her and getting tangled up in them when she tried to scramble to her feet.

Coll stepped effortlessly over the low narrow bed and picked her up. 'Behave yourself and come to bed where you belong.'

'I'm not a possession!'

'No, you're a wife,' he said, beginning to descend the

stairs. Eden caught at the flimsy wooden rail and clung to it, using it for support while she levered herself from his grasp. She managed to slide out of the blanket, feeling the harsh rasp of it all along her body as she went, then she was free and scrambling back to the loft, hopping nimbly over a lobster pot, dodging round a wooden chest.

'Damn you, woman – ' Coll Galbraith plunged after her. They faced each other, the lamp between them now. Eden pushed back the long soft hair that curtained her face and shoulders and realized, briefly, that they must both look like heathens, naked as they had been at birth, scowling at each other. A wayward part of her mind had time to register the savage magnificence of his muscular body, highlighted by the soft golden light.

'It was a contract – ' she said again.

'A contract must be sealed.' His eyes moved over her, not with John's frantic hunger and excitement, but with a healthy open approval and desire that tingled a response low in her belly and tautened her breasts. But she had no intention of meekly giving in to his demands now.

'We'll talk about it tomorrow. I'm too tired n – '

He suddenly pounced and she jumped backwards, tripped over something, and landed on a mound of nets in the darkest corner of the loft. In her frantic struggles to get free she only managed to trap herself, the strong netting ensnaring one hand and both feet.

'Get me free!'

He stood over her, laughing, and she flailed at him with her free hand and only succeeded in hurting her knotted fist against his iron leg muscles.

'I never thought to net myself a bride.'

'Coll – !' She made another effort to loose the strands that held her, but only made things worse. Her long hair wound itself into the mesh and her scalp stung when she moved her head, forcing her to lie still and appeal to him for help. 'Please, Coll?'

He knelt beside her and began to untangle the net. His fingers brushed against her breasts and shoulders and thighs, and she heard the breath catch and quicken in his throat. His touch sent tongues of excitement rippling from her skin to somewhere deep in her body, and an increasing desire to hold him, to lie in his arms, took hold of her, weakening her resolve not to yield to his demands.

Coll swore with increasing frustration as the net defied him.

'Why could you not have come to my bed like a proper wife instead of setting my sail loft at odds and ruining my nets?'

'Because we didn't agree to that sort of marriage – ' Her argument was beginning to sound feeble even to her own ears.

'What other kind is there between a healthy man and a woman?' her new husband wanted to know. His eyes moved over her, leaving a trail of fire wherever they went.

'Oh – Eden Galbraith – ' The name sounded strange to her, yet he spoke it as though he had said it a hundred times before. 'You're beautiful. Caught in my net like a – a mermaid sent to draw a man's soul out of him and bewitch him and – '

He gathered her into his arms, net and all, and kissed her, his tongue searching for hers, his mouth claiming and holding her lips, then moving on, travelling over her throat, one shoulder, a pink-tipped breast, the line of her thigh. Eden moaned and twisted and knew what it was like to be a trapped fish.

It took a long impatient time before he managed to untangle the clinging net, and when at last he freed her and carried her to the makeshift bed there was no more talk of contracts and business arrangements.

Coll Galbraith's hard, strong, eager body swept away the memory of John's unnatural lusts and even, Eden thought as she held him, her hopeless yearning for Lewis.

138

When they finally slept, locked in a tangle of naked limbs, dawn had begun to lighten the square of skylight above their heads.

# CHAPTER SEVENTEEN

A week after Eden married Coll Galbraith the papers drawn up by the lawyer were signed.

It had been Eden's plan to call the new company the Murray Joint Stock Company, but Coll put a stop to that.

'Murray and Galbraith,' he said flatly as the three of them pored over the documents Gideon had brought to the cottage. 'Mebbe I've not got silver in the venture, but I'm running your boat for you. Anyway, your own name's Galbraith now.'

Gideon nodded agreement. Eden looked from one man to the other. In seven short months she had fought for the right to call herself Murray. It was hard to have to give up her claim to it so soon. But Coll was right – as Coll was so often right, she thought with a spurt of irritation.

'Very well. The Murray and Galbraith Joint-Stock Company,' she said, and her new husband grinned.

There was further disagreement over the name of the new skaffie. Gideon paid Eden the great compliment of suggesting that the boat should be given her name.

'The *Eden Galbraith* – why not?' he said, but Coll scowled.

'I've had my fill of sailing in a boat with a woman's name,' he said curtly. 'Think of something else.'

They had forgotten that for the past twelve years he had worked in the boat that bore his first wife's name. Gideon had the grace to look embarrassed.

The two of them, settled on either side of the shining range in Eden's and Coll's kitchen, had tossed names back and forth, arguing over each one, until Eden, looking up from her knitting and catching a gleam of light from the Yarmouth plate in its cabinet, said suddenly *'Golden Hope.* She'll be called *Golden Hope.'*

The men looked at her and then at each other, and nodded. It was decided.

Five days later the whole village, with the exception of Euphemia Ross and Caleb and his family, turned out to see the launching of the *Golden Hope,* the new company's first skaffie.

Gleaming in her coat of fresh black paint, gunnels and waterline picked out in white, furled sails clutched to the rich dark brown that marked the Scottish fishing fleet, the boat slid into the water, delivered into her natural element by two dozen strong hands on the ropes while the onlookers clustering the harbour walls chanted the local blessing for a new vessel.

'Frae rocks an' sands, and barren lands, an' ill men's hands, keep free – ' the voices rose to the sky. The skaffie tested the water, lurched, moved forward, dipped, and finally rode the waves as the final line of the blessing roared out triumphantly, 'Weel oot, weel in, wi' a good shot!'

Then there was a cheer that sent the gulls aloft, screaming their disapproval. The men who had assisted at the launch eased the skaffie to the harbour wall and moored her, then went to claim the bread, cheese and whisky they were to receive as their reward.

'It's a good beginning,' Gideon said with satisfaction.

It was. The second skaffie already had its keel and frame in place, and now that the former Ross boat was launched the stocks were available for a third vessel.

Eden's days were filled to overflowing. As a member of the new company she officially took over the boatyard books and carried them home, studying past orders and lists of supplies so that she could develop a more fluent understanding of the work involved. She travelled to nearby ports and found a dealer willing to handle the *Golden Hope*'s catch as well as those of the three other men in the joint-stock company. As soon as Euphemia Ross discovered that they had put their names down for boats built by the joint-stock company she had refused to take the fish they caught, and the three of them had come to Gideon seeking help. Now their boats became part of the Murray and Galbraith fleet.

On the few occasions when she was down at the harbour Euphemia Ross's hard black eyes watched them come in, empty and riding high on the water after offloading their catches at one of the other harbours.

'If they still burned witches that one'd be roasted by this time,' Gideon said, watching Euphemia. Eden followed his gaze.

'She can't do us any harm now. She'll be wondering how well our boats are doing.'

'Och, she'll know that already. Phemie's got her own way of finding out. And she'll know that we're giving a good account of ourselves.' He chuckled. 'No doubt that keeps her awake at nights. Did you hear she's setting your cousin John up as her manager now?'

'I heard.'

John Murray had taken full control of the chandlery and the fisher-lassies. Euphemia was rarely seen in the store or on the harbour, preferring to run the business from her parlour.

'Funny how religion and money can be made to mix for some folk. I'd have said they went together like oil and water. But there's John feathering his nest, and going to marry the lay preacher's lass too. Mind you, he'll find more comfort in counting silver than in bedding that sour-faced besom Teckla Dow,' Gideon said cheerfully, and nodded at the thin black-clad figure on the harbour wall. 'Aye, aye, Phemie – you can look your fill, but we'll get the better of you yet.'

As though she could hear him, Euphemia Ross turned

away. 'No doubt she's racking her brains, wondering how she can best spoil things for us,' Gideon prophesied.

'There's nothing she can do now,' Eden told him confidently, but she was wrong. Euphemia's next move, two weeks later, was to refuse credit in the chandlery to all skippers involved with the Murray and Galbraith Joint-Stock Company.

Eden already bought provisions for the *Golden Hope* in the neighbouring town of Ainster, rather than having to deal with John. When she heard the news she put on her best clothes and went back on her travels round the coast, finally striking a bargain with a supplier who wasn't a part of Euphemia Ross's web. She returned with a promise from him to supply as much meal, salt, tea, and onions as she needed to provision the four boats. It took two carts to bring everything to Buckthorne, and Coll's temper exploded when he came home from sea to find his sail loft crammed and a sack of onions with a box of tea on top of it leaning against the kitchen wall.

'For God's sake, woman – I'm beginning to feel as if I'm living in Gideon Murray's cottage! When a man's at sea most of his days he needs space in his own home.'

'I'd no notion it was going to take up so much room.' She knotted her brows over the problem. 'I'm just going to have to find somewhere to keep it all.'

It was Gideon who discovered that one of the tall narrow houses fronting the harbour was about to be vacated, and Gideon who arranged to rent it. It had three floors, altogether, and the back yard boasted a set of sturdy gallowses and a fair-sized shed.

Eden chewed her lip as she walked round the empty rooms and stood at one of the handsome upstairs windows overlooking the harbour. It was too fine a house for use as a store. An idea was already brewing – one that Coll would almost certainly oppose. Their marriage was by no means an easy union. Coll was used to living alone and didn't take kindly to

143

having decisions made for him, while Eden resented his reminders that compared to him she was little more than a child who needed guidance. She felt that she had a right to her share of respect as a partner while Coll, scarred by his years with Euphemia, resented his young wife's close financial involvement with his livelihood.

In spite of this they had a healthy admiration for each other's abilities, though neither of them would have admitted to it. Their only truly compatible moments were when they shared a bed; physically they were completely suited to each other.

As Eden had expected, Coll refused to agree to her plan for the house at the harbour.

'Not two months wed and you want to move into another house? Have you lost your wits?'

'But we'll have to rent it to store the provisions anyway – '

'You're going to rent it, not me!'

'It's the same thing.'

'No it's not. The money's yours.'

'Isn't that why you insisted on us getting wed – so that we would share everything?'

Coll scooped a dipperful of water from the pail on the table and drank thirstily. His was one of the oldest cottages in Buckthorne and the water had to be carried in from a well further along the road.

'I wed you so that you couldn't throw me out of work the way Phemie did.' He put down the dipper and scrubbed the back of one hand over his mouth. 'But I don't own money unless I work for it. And I don't let my wife pay for the roof over our heads!'

'Listen – ' she took his arm in both hands and shook it. 'The new place is just across from the boatyard. We can live there and store extra gear for the boats in the big shed and use this place for the provisions – '

But he pulled away, storming out into the side passage and up to the loft, where he stayed until the smell of cooking tempted him down to eat.

They argued back and forth for two days. On the third day Coll came in with a pleased twist to his mobile mouth and tossed a bundle of notes on the table before Eden as she sat peeling potatoes for the evening meal.

'There you are.'

She picked up the notes, separating and counting them. 'Where did you get this?'

He stood over her, feet apart and knees locked rigid as though they were still holding his big body steady against the swell of a heavy sea. 'I've sold this place.'

'Sold it?' Eden asked faintly. 'Sold it?'

'Aye. Jamie Livingstone's getting wed soon. He wants somewhere to live. And since you don't want to stay here' – one finger stabbed at the notes on the table – 'that's my share of the rent for the new house. The rest'll come as Jamie earns it.'

'But I was going to use this place as a store for the provisions! I told you that!'

'This is a home, not a store,' he said tightly. 'If we're not going to live in it let someone else have it. You can use some of the rooms in your fine big house as a store!'

And he stamped upstairs to the sail loft, his favourite retreat when he needed to be alone.

A few weeks later they moved from the cottage on the shore road to the tall house at the harbour. One of the two big ground-floor rooms at the front was used to house the boxes and sacks of food for the fleet, the other was set aside for use as their parlour – once the day came when Eden could find the time and money to furnish it. At the rear there were two smaller rooms, one left vacant in case it was needed as further storage space, the other their kitchen and living quarters. Their bedroom was on the next floor, and extra fishing gear was put in the spacious loft.

145

*

As April arrived the herring season ended. The nets were stowed away in lofts and sheds and it was time for line fishing, catching haddock, cod and halibut. Eden hired women to prepare the great lines, each carrying about eight hundred baited hooks.

As always happened at the beginning and end of a season Gideon's yard was busy with repairs. From her front windows Eden watched, fascinated, as the little steam engine hired from a farmer grunted and coughed and chugged, staining the clear air with smoke as it slowly and steadily dragged the great boats up into the shallows, then right out of the water. They came reluctantly, heeling over as they felt sand beneath their keels instead of sea, wooden whales slumped uncomfortably on the pebbles, their seaweed-covered hulls dripping.

She thought contentedly of the busy order book, the good account the *Golden Hope* had given of herself in her first herring season. She went downstairs, her hand trailing lovingly over the fine wood of the banisters, and into the kitchen where the gold edging and lettering of the Yarmouth plate shone softly at her.

She had come a long way since that day, some seven months ago, when she first arrived in Buckthorne. Now she had a fine home, she had married into Euphemia Ross's family in spite of the woman, and she belonged at last.

Life had begun to show the promise of gold around the edges.


It caused a stir in the village when John Murray took up residence in Euphemia Ross's house in May.

'She claims it makes it easier for her to see to business matters, having him near all the time,' Annabel reported on a visit to Eden. 'If you ask me, Phemie's getting a bit wandered in the head. John has a lot of influence with her, and now he's got his foot in the door what'll happen to Lewis's inheritance?'

'I daresay he'll manage, with his fine wife and his clever head,' Eden said coolly. Both John and Lewis belonged to the days before Coll Galbraith put his marriage ring on her finger.

It was Coll himself who told her in June that Lewis's young wife had died giving birth to a stillborn child. 'Phemie went off to Edinburgh first thing this morning, as soon as she got the news.'

A swift memory came unbidden to Eden. A big loft in Yarmouth, the sound and sight of her cousin Charlotte's suffering, Janet taking the tiny motionless body from her hands, wrapping it competently in a piece of cloth, bearing it off somewhere. She wondered briefly if it had been like that for the unknown girl Lewis had taken in marriage. But Charlotte had survived and Lewis's Edinburgh wife had died.

'Poor lass,' Coll said at that moment. 'Not much more than a child herself from what I hear.'

'It's the way of the world.' Eden busied herself about the range, clattering pots and pans.

'That's a hard thing to say.'

She stirred the broth vigorously. 'It's only the truth I'm speaking. Anyway, it's not wise for me to brood about death, not in my condition.'

'Even so – ' he began, then she smiled into the depths of the big soup pot as he halted, then asked cautiously, 'Did you say – '

'For goodness' sake, Coll Galbraith – ' She let go the ladle and turned to him, hiding her own pleasure under mock exasperation. 'You're the one that wanted this marriage to be more than a contract. You have to accept the consequen – '

Then she squeaked as he lifted her clear of the floor and whirled her round, his blue eyes blazing with a naked joy

147

that took years off his age and made her feel as though she had just handed him the entire world on a gold-edged plate.

Eden was determined to prove to Euphemia Ross that sturdy east-coast stock could cope with childbirth more easily than fragile Edinburgh ladies; and indeed, her pregnancy gave her no trouble at all.

She had wondered uneasily if Lewis might come back to Buckthorne with his mother but to her relief Euphemia returned alone from the funeral, her thin lips clamped together, her black eyes like shards of needle-sharp ice.

'She minds me of the turtles I once saw when we sailed the warm seas,' Gideon said thoughtfully. 'It was said that some of them were hundreds of years old. They had just the same old, cold look as Phemie.'

It was rumoured that her business net was spreading, that John Murray was encouraging her to invest large sums of money far afield. More fishermen joined the joint-stock company in a bid to keep out of her grasp.

When a house adjacent to the boatyard fell vacant and Euphemia put in an offer for it, Murray and Galbraith moved to outbid her, thwarting her plans and extending the boatyard in one stroke. They planned to build farlins and a curing shed on the newly acquired land.

Coll looked on uneasily. 'I still say you're both too ambitious. The white fishing's not been good this year; if we get a bad herring season you'll wish you'd kept that money.'

'Man, if we'd let Phemie take over land right by the yard they'd have had us by the throats in a month, her and John,' Gideon told him. 'Don't you fret yourself – Eden knows how to deal with money. You tend to your fishing and I'll tend to my boats, and she'll see to it we don't starve.'

Coll, a man who well knew the necessity of keeping something in reserve against a bad season, grunted.

'I hope you don't live to regret your words.'

148

'I won't.' Gideon knew that the butcher's shop in Eyemouth had been sold, bringing more money to Eden, but he had been sworn to secrecy. The coming baby had brought new serenity to their marriage and she didn't want Coll to be reminded that his wife had money of her own.

In July the second skaffie was launched. A third was half-completed, and within a week of the launching the big oaken keel of another boat took its place on the stocks.

John Murray married Teckla Dow, the lay preacher's daughter, and took his silent, sallow-skinned bride to live with him in Euphemia's house. The two of them were to be seen almost every evening, and three times on Sundays, walking silently together to the meeting house near the school; John, all in black, a step in front of Teckla, who moved as though in a trance, her round brown blank eyes looking unseeingly through everyone she met. Now and then Euphemia accompanied them; on those occasions she and John walked in front, with Teckla sleepwalking behind them. They made up a strange household. Annabel, in her position as the schoolmaster's sister, was one of the few people who were invited in.

'It was always a cheerless house but now there's an air about it that would freeze the marrow in your bones, even on the hottest day,' she told Eden. 'John slides in and out like an eel, and that wife of his sits in the corner of the parlour with her mouth tight shut. I'd the feeling all the time she was saying her prayers. As for Phemie – well, I think the woman's mind's softened. Praise the Lords and hallelujahs dropping into the conversation just when a body least expects it.' She shivered suddenly. 'It was enough to make anyone swear off religion for life. Dear knows what Lewis'll say if he ever finds out what's going on. Whatever it is – it made my flesh creep, I'm telling you!'


Coll refused to hear of Eden going to Yarmouth with him

when September drew to a close.

'You're not a fisher-lassie now. There's nothing for you to do there and I'd only worry about you, with your time coming.'

She turned in bed to glare at him. 'The baby'll not arrive till January!'

'All the same,' he ordered, 'you'll stay here where Annabel can keep an eye on you for me.'

An unexpected stab of jealousy twinged through her. She raised herself on one elbow to peer down at him. The bedroom was shadowy; beyond the square of the window she could hear the boats rubbing against each other in the crowded harbour, and the muffled swish of waves against the rocks beyond.

'Are you going to Louisa?'

'I always lodge there.'

She put a hand on his chest; the skin was smooth and warm, the muscles beneath moved against her palm as he breathed.

'Coll – her child – is he – ?'

His dark head moved on the pillow. 'Mine? If he was I'd be with her now instead of you.'

'But when you lodge with her you – '

'Before I wed you I'd the right to live my own life and do as I pleased,' he cut her short, speaking slowly and firmly. 'Now you're wearing my ring and carrying my child I've no mind to betray you with anyone. Louisa's a friend, and she needs the money I'll pay as her lodger. Go to sleep, Eden.'

And he turned over, refusing to say any more, and went to sleep.

A week later she stood on the wall above the harbour entrance and watched the *Golden Hope* move easily out, her crew bending to the long oars. Once she was clear of the needle-toothed rocks crouching just beyond the entrance the oars were taken inboard and the great dipping lugsail, newly cutched in their back yard, was pulled up the towering mast.

150

The *Golden Hope* turned her bow towards the May Isle lighthouse on the horizon and went skimming over a brisk, white-capped sea to join the other boats that streamed towards the English coast. Coll took time to look back, raising a hand in farewell, his white teeth gleaming in a grin.

She waved back and stood watching until she could no longer make him out properly; moments later the *Golden Hope* merged into the vast fleet of boats from Buckthorne, Pittenweem, Ainster, and other villages up and down the coast.

# CHAPTER EIGHTEEN

Lewis Ross walked across the stone-flagged yard and opened the kitchen door, letting a waft of the cold dark night in with him and frightening the life out of Becky, who was dozing on her chair before the range. She gaped at him, mouth open.

'Aye, it's me, Becky. I've come home. No need to look as if you'd seen a ghost. Is my mother in?'

'She is, but – '

'Good. Put a warming pan in my bed, will you?' Without waiting to hear any more Lewis went on into the hall. He was tired, emotionally as well as physically; running back like a hurt child for comfort to the coast that had bred him. He badly wanted a warm fire, a drink, a bed, and sleep. And he wanted most of all to wake in the morning with the scream of gulls outside his window and good sea air in his lungs.

Three pairs of eyes swept up to meet his own startled gaze as he stopped in the parlour doorway. John Murray sat by the table, reading aloud from a massive Bible. He looked up with a frown as the door opened, and the monotonous drone of his voice stopped in mid-word when he saw who had just arrived. A sallow, plain-faced woman Lewis had never seen before knelt on the hearthrug, hands folded in prayer. But it was his mother Lewis's eyes fixed on – his mother down on her knees, her bony hands clenched, rather than piously clasped, together. Euphemia attended church regularly, but he had never seen her pray at any other time. In the Ross household God was kept for Sundays only.

She caught at the arm of a chair and scrambled awkwardly to her feet. 'Lewis? What are you doing here? What's amiss?'

He came into the room slowly, dropped his travelling bag on the floor. 'Nothing's amiss – with me. I've come home to build boats, that's all.'

'But your position – the office – '

'I've left it all behind me, Mother. I've had enough of it.' He looked away from the dawning anger on her thin face, towards the other two. They were both on their feet now, John closing the Bible, the woman simply looking at Lewis with a queer empty stare that made him shiver.

'We'd best leave you alone,' John Murray said and went to the door, the woman following him. As he passed, Lewis sensed a wave of pure venom, but as he turned to meet it the other man's pale blue eyes slid away, his long pale face carefully blank. The door opened and closed and to Lewis's surprise he heard their footsteps mounting the stairs.

'What's John Murray doing here?' he demanded, rounding on his mother. 'And who's the woman?'

Euphemia drew herself up to her full height. 'Don't speak to me in that way, Lewis.'

But she no longer had any control over him. In the past year Lewis had taken on many roles – a married man, almost a father, a fledgling lawyer, a widower. He had tasted bitterness and loss and frustration and anger.

'I asked you why John Murray was making himself at home in my father's house?'

Air hissed between her teeth. 'This is my house! And John and his wife live here at my invitation.'

'Here? You've allowed that man to settle himself in your own home? Why, for God's sake?'

'Don't blaspheme! He's here because there's always business to see to. Because I need my manager close by. Never you mind about John – what are you doing here?'

'I told you.' He went over to the cupboard, opened it. 'Where's the whisky?'

153

'I'll not have drink under my roof.'

'You sound like Caleb Murray,' he said, puzzled, unable to understand the difference in her.

She brushed the comment aside. 'Answer me! Why are you here and not in Edinburgh where you belong?'

'I don't belong there, Mother. I never did. I'm tired of Edinburgh and tired of being a gentleman. What's it brought me? Nothing but misery. Now I'm going to do what I want.' He ran the back of his hand over his dry lips then stepped back, startled, as she flew at him, pounding her fists on his chest.

'No! You'll not ruin your life in this place the way I've ruined mine!' Her voice cracked with rage. 'I'll not let you!'

He recovered from his surprise, caught her wrists, held her away easily. It was as though she had shrunk during the past year; he didn't remember being so much taller than she was. 'It has nothing to do with you – not any more.'

She pulled away from him. 'Not a penny will you get for boat-building while I've got breath in my body, d'you hear me? Not a penny!'

'I don't need your money, Mother. You always wanted me to marry a rich wife, remember? I've the money Elizabeth inherited on her marriage. And John needn't be afraid that I'll want to put him out of the store – the two of you can keep it.' He picked up his bag, suddenly longing to get away from the woman who had given him life and raised him and was now a stranger. 'I'm away to my bed.'

Becky was hovering apologetically in the hall. 'John's got the front room you used to sleep in. I've made up your bed in the wee room your father had.'

Lewis looked up into the dark silent area at the top of the stairs and nodded.

'That'll do me fine,' he said, and began to ascend, using the banisters, pulling himself up, step by step, like an old man.

In the bleak, sparsely furnished little room where his

154

father had died he went to the window and opened it. Outside there was only silence; the room was at the back, away from the sea that Lewis craved for. He suddenly realized, as he stood there, how Frank, too, must have longed for sight and sound of the waves during his last illness in that room.

He sat down heavily on the bed and put his head in his hands.

It was Annabel who brought the news to Eden, hurrying down the steep cobbled wynd that linked the schoolhouse on the hill to the houses by the harbour.

'I didn't want you to hear from anyone else.'

Eden's blood had stopped moving through her veins when Annabel first blurted out her reason for calling so early; when her pulse got back to work it was fluttering.

'He's probably just here for a few days.'

'They say he's going to stay and build boats. It's what he always wanted to do.'

Eden, sorting clothes for the wash-tub, hurled one of Gideon's shirts on to its allotted pile with unnecessary vigour. 'There's no room for another boat-builder here. If Lewis Ross has any sense he'll find somewhere else. And if you're worrying about me' – she scooped up an armful of clothes and dropped them into the big copper, her face flushed with the heat from the simmering water – 'there's no need. I've made my own life and I'm content with what I've got.'

Gideon confirmed Annabel's story when Eden went over to the boatyard later.

'He was in this morning. He's talking of building one of those new Fifies some of the men further up the coast are sailing now.'

'I hope you told him he can find some other village to build it in.'

'No, I said he could use that empty corner of the yard if he wanted.'

155

'But – there isn't enough work in Buckthorne for two builders!'

Gideon shrugged. 'If you ask me, the lad's in sore need of good friends right now. We're doing well enough – thanks to you. And Lewis wants to build the Fifie and work it himself, he's not looking to do us out of business.'

'We need that corner of the yard ourselves.'

'What for?'

'Another shed – or – ' she floundered. 'There are plenty of uses for it.'

Gideon, leaning as usual on the cottage door-frame, watched the smoke from his pipe frenziedly zig-zagging as the cold November wind took it. 'I'd like fine to see a Fifie being built,' he said thoughtfuly.

'Then build one yourself.'

'He's changed, Lewis has. He's matured, for one thing. And he's not happy, Eden. He's not been as fortunate as you.'

'We all have to find our own road,' she said shortly, determined not to feel sorry for Lewis. He had turned his back on her, chosen to seek his future in Edinburgh with someone else. It was wrong of him to come back now, intruding in the new life that she had made for herself. She had no wish to see him, and she devoutly hoped that he would have the sense to stay away from her.

He did; although for a few days she was nervous every time she turned a corner or went into a shop in case she came face to face with him. Before going to the boatyard she peered from an upstairs window to make sure that he wasn't there. Once or twice she saw him, tall and lean as ever, talking to Gideon or walking round one of the skaffies under construction, touching the planks with a loving hand.

Eden became restive, suddenly impatient for the Yarmouth fishing to be over. She missed Coll's strength, his support – expecially when Gideon Murray collapsed one morning and had to be helped to his bed, grey with pain and gasping for breath.

'It's my lungs again – they get – congested – ' he said when Eden, who had seen him being half-carried into the cottage, when running over, clumsy now that she was only two months away from her baby's birth.

His drawn face and the blue tinge round his mouth frightened her. 'I'll get the doctor.'

'No need – it's happened before – there's a – bottle – ' He gestured to the cupboard by the stone sink and she rummaged frantically among nails and twine and brushes, finally unearthing a small green bottle, half full.

'Give it here – ' he flapped a hand impatiently and she gave up her search for a spoon and handed over the opened bottle, watching as he lifted it to his lips and swallowed. Then he lay back, eyes closed. 'I'll be fine in – a minute – '

'What's in it?' She took the bottle back, corked it, and put it on a table within his reach.

'Something a physician gave me – years ago,' said Gideon weakly, then tried to smile as he saw the fear in her face. 'It'll – put me right.'

He slept most of that day but it was clear that he wasn't fit to get up on the following morning.

'There's work to see to!' he protested, struggling feebly against Eden's restraining hands.

'Walter and me can look after the yard.' She pushed him back on to the pillows, gave him more of his medication and spoon-fed him with gruel, then went through the work book carefully, juggling orders and delivery dates in her head, trying to decide what could be set aside and what had to go ahead.

She slipped the book into her pocket and went out, closing the cottage door against the cold wind, ignoring Gideon's croaked order to leave it open so that he could see what was going on.

She had never had much time for Walter Sheddon, Gideon's right-hand man. Her shrewd eyes had seen how Gideon himself did most of the work while Walter preferred to find some task in a sheltered corner where he wasn't seen and could fritter away an hour or two without any effort. She knew that he was strongly opposed to her role in the new joint-stock company.

'Ach, he's been with me ever since I bought the yard,' Gideon said each time she tried to point out that the man scarcely earned his wages. 'We're used to each other. We get on fine.'

She had to shout several times before Walter's head appeared over the gunnel of the half-finished skaffie looming over her in the stocks.

'You'll have to leave this one for today and get on with making the *Morning Rose* watertight, Walter – '

He cut her short with an abrupt 'Gideon told me to start decking this boat and that's what I'm doing.'

'But the *Morning Rose*'s going to be late if you don't get on with the caulking.'

'Aye?' said Walter, deliberately insolent. 'Let some of the others do it, then.'

'The others are doing work that has to be done. This boat can wait for two days – the *Rose* can't.'

He threw a leg over the gunnel, and began to descend the ladder. 'I'll see what Gideon has to say – '

She blocked his way, anger beginning to burn in her. 'Gideon's ill. It's me that has to decide what needs doing first.'

'Then you see to making the *Rose* watertight,' he suggested, and she heard a subdued snigger from behind her. The three other men had stopped work and were following the battle of wills with open interest. Eden looked from one face to the other, and wished again that Coll was home.

'If you want to be master, lass' – Walter pressed home the attack, aware of his audience – you'll have to serve your apprenticeship. I don't come into your kitchen and tell you how to make a loaf.'

The snigger was heard again, louder this time. Eden's

158

anger boiled over, fuelled by worry about Gideon and frustration over her own inadequacy.

'Are you going to help me to keep this yard going or not?' she snapped at Walter.

'I can see to the yard myself!'

'Then start by getting that boat watertight!'

His eyes narrowed; sure of himself, he moved into open defiance. 'I'll do it when I think fit – and I'll not take orders from a woman!'

For a moment they glared at each other, neither giving ground, then she spun round, pushed past the other men, and marched back into the cottage.

'What's amiss?' Gideon wanted to know immediately.

'Nothing.' Her voice was calm, unworried. 'Why should anything be amiss?' She moved so that her body was between him and the table and he couldn't see what she was doing, then picked up a hammer and waved it at him.

'One of the men's looking for this,' she lied and went back outside, some coins from the battered tin money-box clutched in one fist.

Walter was leaning against the stocks, the other men grouped around him. They edged away as Eden arrived.

She went straight to Walter and held out the money. Uneasiness flickered in his eyes. The tip of his tongue moistened his lips.

'What's this?'

'It's what we owe you. Take it and get out of this yard.'

The man's jaw dropped and hung slack. Eden heard feet shifting on the shingle, mutters from the others, but she kept her eyes on Walter.

'Gideon – ' he began, but she interrupted him.

'Gideon's sick and I'm in charge till he gets better.'

'Now Eden,' he said placatingly, 'you're surely not – '

'Take your money and go. I've no time for wasters!'

Disbelief gave way to pure hatred. He looked behind her at the others, but apparently found no allies, for he snatched

159

the coins from her and stamped off across the shingle.

She turned to the others, two men and a boy.

'Well?' she demanded icily, pulling her shawl about her as protection against the wind. 'D'you want to take your money and follow him, or will you work for a woman?'

Embarrassed, appalled by the scene they had just witnessed, they looked at each other sidelong, then the eldest muttered, 'Come on, lads – there's been enough time-wasting – ' and they all went back to work.

In spite of the cold weather Eden's forehead was damp with perspiration. She pulled the well-thumbed order book from her pocket and checked it again, her heart sinking. The work the other men were busy with had to be done; now that she had sent Walter away there was nobody to see to the *Morning Rose*.

She bit her lip, studying the beached fishing boat. It was one of the smaller open boats used for off-shore work and unsuited for the English season. The caulking between the planks was old and needed to be taken out; once the seams were clear they had to be repacked with oakum then sealed with boiling pitch. The owner was already missing out on the local fishing and anxious to get his boat back into the water.

Eden drew her shawl securely over her head, pulled it across her breasts, and tied the ends behind her back; then she fetched a chisel and hammer, thankful that the *Morning Rose* was small enough for her to work on without having to climb a ladder.

Aware of the men's eyes on her, she put the end of the chisel against the seam between two planks. She had watched Gideon do this so often; now she wished that she had paid more attention. She hit the chisel with the hammer, narrowly missing injury as it slipped, then tried again and saw a piece of the old caulking fly off. She took a deep breath and set to work.

An hour later her spine felt as though it was ready to break

160

and her hands were so chilled they had no sensation in them at all. Her hair straggled out from beneath her shawl, perspiration oozed down her back and between her breasts, and at the same time the cold wind sent tears trickling down her cheeks. But she had managed to work her way along an entire seam.

She straightened to ease her protesting bones and had just returned to her work when feet crunched rapidly over the shingle towards her and a familiar voice snapped, 'For God's sake, woman, what d'you think you're at?'

Lewis, his green eyes stormy beneath knotted brows, wrested the hammer and chisel easily from her numbed, blue-blotched fingers. 'Look at you – you're half frozen. What the hell's Gideon up to, letting you do a man's work in your condition?'

She scrubbed her icy hands across her face to clear the tears the wind had brought to her eyes, and looked up at him, wincing as her back threatened to snap in two. 'Gideon's ill and the work's got to be done.'

'Can't Walter do it? Or is he ill too?'

She lifted her chin. 'He'll not work for a woman so I sent him away.'

A mixture of expressions flitted across his face; surprise, exasperation, amusement, then determination.

'I'll work for a woman. Away and rest before you harm yourself. Go on, now!' he added sharply as she opened her mouth to protest.

'I'll look in on Gideon first – '

'I'll see to him. Go on home and get yourself warm. D'you want Coll to come back to find you've made yourself ill and mebbe lost his child?' he asked with a rough gentleness that was quite unlike the Lewis she had once known.

She went without further argument, knowing well enough that she was too exhausted to snatch the tools back from him and carry on working.

As she hobbled painfully over the shingle she heard the

steady sure chink of hammer on chisel begin behind her, quite unlike the hesitant, erratic rhythm of her own feeble attempts.

# CHAPTER NINETEEN

Lewis appeared at the door later in the afternoon. 'Are you all right?'

'I'm fine.' Her bones were still aching but she was rested and warm now, her hair brushed smoothly back, her nose no longer red with cold.

Normally she would have stepped aside to allow a visitor entry to the house, but she stayed where she was, reluctant to let Lewis Ross over the doorstep and thus into her life.

'I've nearly finished the *Rose*. I'll get on with her tomorrow – and I'll see to the yard for you until Gideon's able.'

'But – ' she began, but he cut her short.

'I'm doing it for Gideon, if that makes you feel any easier. I'll come to you each morning for the day's orders and I'll see to it that the men do as you wish.'

He hesitated, his eyes intent on her face, as though trying to imprint her features on his memory. Then his gaze moved down to where the child, Coll's child, thickened her normally slender waist.

'I'll see you in the morning.'

'Before you go – ' she said, and he swung quickly back to her. 'Could you and the other men bring Gideon over here? That cottage is a cheerless place for a sick man.'

A smile curled the corners of his mouth in a way she well remembered.

'We will – but you'll have to come over and tell him it was your idea, for he'll not like it. After all, it's you that's his partner, not me.'

She fetched her shawl from behind the kitchen door and crossed the road with him, sneaking sidelong glances at him, remembering the very first time they had crossed that road side by side, on their way to the harbour to confront Caleb Murray.

Gideon was right – Lewis had matured. The neat moustache he had had when he came home for his father's funeral was gone; his fair hair was longer, wind-tossed about his head. City life had robbed him of his usual tan and there were fine lines between his eyes and at the corners of his mouth.

He opened the cottage door, stood aside to let her in first. 'Gideon, your partner wants to have a wee word with you,' he said, winking at Eden, wrapping the two of them close in a conspiracy.


When Gideon, protesting all the way, was settled in the big front room that was to be the parlour Lewis lingered at the street door after the other men had gone.

'You'll let me know if there's anything else to be done?'

'I'll manage fine.'

His gaze met hers and held it for a moment. His eyes were the same clear green they had always been, but shadows smudged the fine skin beneath them. He had tasted some of life's bitterness; the tasting had taken the edge off his youthful charm but it had given him a maturity that was just as attractive.

'Don't go trying to take on too much,' he instructed, adding, as she frowned, 'Coll's my kinsman. It's my place to help his wife when he's not here to see to things.'

Then he was gone, swinging along the road without waiting for a reply.

Slowly, she walked back to the room where Gideon was sitting up in bed, his hair standing on end with annoyance.

'Women! I'll be up and about by tomorrow!'

'If you'll not let me get a physician you can just stay there until I decide you're fit to get up,' she told him. 'You can keep an eye on the yard from the window – but that's all you'll do.'

He glowered at her. 'Where's Walter? What have you done with him?' His voice was weak, an echo of its usual deep boom.

She eased him back on to his pillows and drew the coverlet over his shoulders. 'Walter didn't want to take orders from me. So he's gone.'

'Confound it, Eden, you'll have the yard empty and the lot of us in the poors' house if you go on like this – '

His voice tailed off and his eyes closed. She looked down at him, afraid of the future, longing for Coll's reassuring strength by her side.

She slept badly that night and got up early, while most of the houses in the village were still dark and silent. Gideon's snores greeted her when she came downstairs, and rumbled in the background as she lit the kitchen range.

The restlessness that had gripped her for the past week was still there. She thought of Gideon's cluttered cottage, empty now, waiting to be put to rights while its owner was safely out of the way. There was work there to keep her busy until it was time to see to Gideon.

The street was still empty and silent. She picked her way carefully through the boatyard, its shadows fleeing before the glow from the lamp she carried. Lifting the latch on the cottage door she went in and surveyed the room, relishing the hard physical work of the task ahead.

Something rustled and creaked in the recess that held Gideon's bed. Eden stifled a scream, then lifted the lamp high and tiptoed towards the shadowy corner, telling herself firmly as she went that a mouse, even a whole nest of mice, was nothing to be afraid of. There was no mouse; a man lay

165

asleep in the bed, one bare arm thrown above his head, his eyelids fluttering as the light fell on his face.

'Lewis!'

He opened his eyes, peered up at her.

'Wha – ?' he mumbled, then, as she lifted the lamp higher so that it illuminated her face he said with sleepy wonder, 'It's you – ' and stretched his arm out towards her.

She drew back quickly as the tips of his fingers brushed her cheek.

'What are you doing here?' Her voice had more edge to it than she intended. He fought his way clear of the blankets and sat up, blinking sleepily; the lamp reflected gold and green and skin-tints as he moved.

'What time is it?'

'Early yet. What are you doing here?' she repeated, and his eyes were suddenly hooded, his face blank.

'Ach, there's too much Bible talk in my mother's house. I decided I'd get more peace down here, near the boats.'

'Was it something to do with John?'

He ignored the question, shivering and rubbing his bare shoulders. He was naked to the waist and she could see goosepimples rise on his smooth skin as the morning chill struck.

'If you'll throw my clothes over here and turn your back for a minute I'll get dressed.'

She bundled up the clothes that hung over the back of a chair. They were dank to the touch. The range had gone out and the cottage was bitterly cold. 'You'd best come over the road for your breakfast.'

His voice was suddenly formal. 'You've got Gideon to see to. I'd not want to be in the way.'

She stopped at the door, turned to look at him. His hair was rumpled, his face still young and vulnerable with sleep.

'You'll not be in the way,' she lied.

Five minutes later he was in her warm kitchen spooning porridge from the bowl she set before him. He finished it and

166

half-emptied a big mug of scalding hot tea before he said gratefully, 'You know you've just saved my life?'

'I know I might have two invalids on my hands if you sleep in that cold cottage for another night.'

'I'll find a room somewhere.' Then without pausing he asked, 'Are you happy, Eden?'

The question took her by surprise, bringing colour to her face. 'What business is it of yours? You made your own life, I made mine.'

'Aye. But I'd always want you to be happy.'

She turned from the range and their eyes locked, green and dark brown intermingling for a moment before she went back to her work. 'I've done well enough. Coll's a good man.'

'He is that.' Lewis drained the tea and got to his feet. 'I'll get on with the *Morning Rose* now.'

As he was going past her he stopped and put his hands on her shoulders before she could move away.

'Do you know how much I wish I could turn the clock back?' he said intensely.

Eden stared at the buttons on his heavy jacket, avoiding the gaze inches above her head. 'Nobody can ever do that, Lewis. Never.'

His fingers tightened briefly, then released her. 'I'll come over in an hour or so and let you know how the work's going,' he said, and went out.

With hands that trembled slightly she put the crockery he had used aside for washing, and began to make up a thin gruel for Gideon.

When the *Morning Rose* was re-caulked, pitched, and returned to her owner, Lewis turned his attention to the half-finished skaffie. He found a room in one of the shore road cottages, and called at the house each morning to discuss the day's work, returning in the afternoons to give Gideon a report on his progress.

167

With Annabel's help Eden cleared most of the clutter from the cottage to a lean-to in a corner of the yard.

'He'll roar at us when he sees this,' she warned when the two of them stood surveying the tidy kitchen.

'Let him – it's done and it'll take him a good while to undo it again,' the older woman said with satisfaction. 'Let's just be thankful he's well enough to roar, now.'

Gideon was finally judged well enough to return to his cottage on the evening before the boats were due back from Yarmouth. He stood in the doorway, mouth agape.

'Where's everything gone?'

'It's all in the wee shed. Nothing was thrown away,' Eden assured him, adding, 'Nothing that was of any use, anyway.'

'My nails – ' Gideon moaned. 'My hammers – my – ' He made his way to his favourite chair and sat down heavily. 'Woman, d'you want me to have a relapse?' Then he looked up and glowered as Annabel Laird came into the cottage.

'Come to gloat, have you? Come to enjoy the sight of a defenceless man trapped in the midst of all this – this' – he swept an arm out to indicate the neat room – 'this damned housekeeping?'

She raised her eyebrows at Eden, then nodded towards the door. Thankfully, Eden escaped, leaving the older woman to soothe the boat-builder's ruffled feelings.

Annabel closed the door behind her and perched on the edge of the chair on the other side of the range. 'Why should I gloat? I'm here because I've given Robert his supper and I've no wish to sit and listen to him snoring. How are you?'

'Destroyed utterly. How am I to find anything ever again? I could put my hand on the smallest nail if I wanted it, before.'

'Tuts, man, you still can. Everything's in the shed, nice and tidy.'

Then as he winced she added, 'Anyway, it'll be a while yet

before you're properly back to work. Lewis and Eden are managing fine between them – you'd best let them run things till you're more able.'

'I'm perfectly fit. Congestion of the lungs doesn't last.'

'Mebbe not, but heart trouble does. And it gets worse if it's not looked after.'

He stared. 'What are you talking about, woman? There's nothing wrong with my heart!'

'Gideon, there's no need to pretend with me. I saw it looking out of your face. My own mother died of heart trouble.'

'If you say one word of this to Eden or anyone else – '

'What d'you take me for – a tattle? I'm just set on seeing you don't kill yourself.'

'I can do my share of the work. I'm not an invalid.'

'I wasn't talking about the yard. I know you can manage that if you don't take on too much too soon. I'm talking about the women.'

A flush rose to his face. 'Mind your own business!'

'I nursed you through the bronchitis and I'm fond of you, Gideon Murray – though the Lord knows why. Face facts, now' – the schoolmaster's sister leaned over and stabbed at his knee with her forefinger – 'you're getting too old for all that womanizing.'

'Too old? Never!'

She clicked her tongue in exasperation. 'You're fifty-seven! If you were a stud bull they'd have sent you to the slaughter-house long before this.'

'Annabel – ' squawked Gideon, embarrassed.

She refused to be side-tracked. 'You need someone to look after you. And luckily for you I'm willing to take the task on.'

'When I need a nurse you'll be the first to know. Until then – ' he began, and was interrupted.

'As your wife, not your nurse!'

'For someone who's supposed to be guarding me from a heart attack,' said Gideon with none of his usual fire, 'you're

169

showing a great interest in pushing me into one!'

'I'm just offering you a proper home and a proper care in place of the shameful life you've been leading up to now.'

'Sharing bed as well as board?'

'Of course.'

'But a minute ago you said there should be no more of that – ' floundered Gideon.

'Everything's good for you in moderation,' Annabel said serenely.

'You're not serious? What would your brother say to you living with the likes of me?'

'A great deal, no doubt, but I've a mind to live my own life, for a change.'

'And what about your grand china and your bonny furniture? You'd have to leave it behind and settle for this – ' he gestured at the plain table and chairs, the wooden chest and the small dresser.

'Most of it's mine so I can bring it with me. Not here, of course, there's no room. I was thinking of that house you've got at the back.'

'That belongs to the company. Besides, it's to be pulled down to extend the yard.'

'But it's a perfectly good building. My furniture would look fine in it, and you'd be just as near the yard there as you are now. For any favour, Gideon, stop finding excuses and start thinking of the benefits!'

'But – '

She leaned over, took his face in her hands, and kissed him in a way that would have shocked her brother to his toes if he had been there to see her instead of snoring in blissful ignorance by the fire in the schoolhouse parlour.

'I thought I was supposed to be keeping quiet?' Gideon asked shakily when he was finally free to talk. She beamed at him, her blue eyes sparkling and her face flushed.

'A wee bit of stimulation never did anyone any harm,' she said demurely. 'Now – let's talk about the wedding.'

170

*

After she left Annabel and Gideon together in the cottage Eden walked along one arm of the harbour to the spot by the entrance where she would wait for Coll the next day.

The weather had turned mild for early December, ensuring a safe run up the coast for the homecoming boats.

Just outside the harbour, waves broke and creamed round the jagged rocks but further out the sea was in a placid mood, rocking a flock of seagulls that had settled on its surface.

Although it was still daylight the crescent moon could be seen already, a ghost of its usual self. The sky was blue overhead, shading to lemon and pink, then to a soft deep rose along the horizon. She looked inland for a moment, to where lights were beginning to appear in the windows of cottages strung along the shore and the larger houses scattered halfway up the hill.

Eden faced seawards again and lifted her face to the sky, letting the evening's peace soak into her, thinking of Coll and the *Golden Hope* hurrying over the water at that very minute, heading for home.

# CHAPTER TWENTY

The *Golden Hope* had had a good season at Yarmouth; Coll came home in a good mood, bringing with him two small hand-painted china plates to flank the Yarmouth plate in the corner cupboard.

He watched Eden placing her new treasures this way and that, standing back to study the effect each time.

Snowy white china, gilt edging, red and green and blue and purple fruit and flowers glowed at her from behind the glass doors of the cupboard, and impulsively she turned and hugged her husband, breathing in the fresh salty tang of his skin and his hair.

'They're bonny, Coll!'

As they had supper he heard all the village news.

'Walter's working in the chandlery with John now – they're well suited,' she said with a shiver. 'Phemie's hardly ever seen outside the house. And I heard today that Uncle Caleb's talking of giving up his house and taking to the roads as a travelling preacher.'

Coll's deep rich laugh, not often heard, rumbled out. 'God help religion!' Then he raised an eyebrow. 'You've not told me what you think of the best news of all – Lewis coming home.'

'Oh, that.' She took his empty bowl away, replaced it with a dish of herring dipped in oatmeal and fried until it was a crisp golden brown. There had been a warm reunion between the two men when Coll came ashore to find Lewis at the harbour.

'It seems a shame for him to come back here, wasting all that learning he got in Edinburgh,' she said primly.

'You're beginning to sound like his mother. I hear he's lodging with old Sadie Paterson. What went wrong between him and Phemie?'

'How should I know?' I think John made him feel unwelcome. John's well in with Phemie Ross and he's not going to step aside for Lewis. They say he's encouraging her to invest her money in all sorts of schemes.'

Then she asked the question that had been burning in her throat from the moment he walked into the house.

'How's Louisa – and her baby?'

He finished his meal and went to the mantelshelf to look for his pipe. 'Well enough,' he said easily, then turned to look at her. 'What are you scowling for?'

She began to clear the table, clashing plates together. 'I'm not scowling.'

'Eden, look at me. I lodged with her, and that's all. I made vows when I put that ring on your finger.' He reached out and caught hold of her hand, trapping it in his, running his thumb over the broad gold band that encircled her third finger. Then he lifted her hand to his lips, kissed it, and gathered her into his arms.

'And I missed you – ' he whispered, one hand loosening her black hair so that it tumbled down, over her back and shoulders. 'I missed your sharp tongue and your arguments and the feel of you in my arms, and your loving – '


Now that Coll was home Lewis became a regular visitor. He was obsessed with the new fishing boat, the Fifie, that he wanted to build.

'See – ' He sat at Eden's well-scrubbed kitchen table, the crayon in his capable fingers swiftly sketching the outline of a boat. 'This is what she'd be like – '

Despite herself Eden put down her sewing and eased

173

herself out of her seat to stand behind Coll's chair, looking over his shoulder at the sketch. The lines of the new type of boat Lewis proposed building were beautiful, there was no doubt of that. The stem and stern went almost straight down from deck to water with scarcely any of the skaffie's angle.

'She'll not turn as neat as a skaffie – and she'd have less deck room – ' Coll's finger stabbed down on the sketch.

'But she'll move faster than your boat, and she'll have a grand grip on the water with that good big forefoot, you wait and see,' Lewis countered.

Coll nodded slowly. 'Mebbe. I'd like fine to see her take shape.'

It was what Gideon had said earlier. Both men were in favour of giving Lewis room at the boatyard to build his boat, and nothing Eden said would change their minds.

'I can't see why you're so against the idea,' Coll said on the morning after Lewis's visit. The sketch was still lying on the table, and he was studying it as he ate his breakfast.

'We need all the space there is! Especially now Gideon and Annabel need the house and we can't pull it down.'

Coll's thick dark brows drew together. 'Lewis helped you when Gideon was ill and I was down south. It's only right that we should help him now,' he said stubbornly, and so the stocks were set up and the Fifie's keel laid despite Eden's misgivings.

Every minute Lewis could spare was spent on the boat. It was the first of its design to be built in the village, and there was often a small knot of fishermen about it, watching the work in progress, chattering to Lewis, arguing with each other over the merits and failings of the new boat.

Now and then Euphemia Ross descended the steep wynd from the house to stand on the harbour wall, looking at the Fifie. The woman's face was now so gaunt that it was like a skull, lit from within by those piercing black eyes.

Lewis never approached her, and she herself never tried to speak to him, vanishing as suddenly as she arrived; gliding back to the house where Teckla, according to the few who still visited, sat day in and day out in a corner of the parlour with some sewing or a Bible in her hands.

Eden had little spare time to worry about Euphemia or John. The winter herring fishing was due to start and she was busy buying in provisions. The company undertook to supply each of its boats with food, settlement to be made with each skipper at the end of the season.

The rumours about Caleb Murray turned out to be true. Early in January he gave up his house and became a wandering lay preacher, his long-suffering wife following wherever he led. Charlotte, left on her own with nowhere to go, was taken into the Ross household to act as an extra servant.

A week before Eden's baby was due Coll asked Lewis to crew on the *Golden Hope*, replacing a man who was ill.

'It'll be like old times,' he said, and his kinsman grinned at him.

'Aye – and I might as well take another trip on your old bathtub before I sail my own bonny Fifie.'

Eden went down to the harbour to see the boats out. The wind was keen but set fair to blow the fleet quickly to the fishing grounds. In the harbour the wooden vessels lurched and bumped clumsily, the men's oilskins glistening in the light from the masthead lamps.

'It's cold for you,' Coll said as he left her on the harbour wall. 'Don't wait to see the boats out. Get back to the fireside and take good care of young James.'

She glared up at him 'Joshua! If it's a boy at all.'

He grinned, supremely sure of his own masculinity. 'James,' he said smugly, and tossed his provision kist over his shoulder before skimming easily down the iron rungs set in the wall.

The argument had been tossed back and forth between them since they first knew Eden was pregnant – she wanted

175

the child, if it was a boy, to be named after her father, and he insisted that it was to be given his father's name.

'A fine night for the fishing, Eden.' Lewis nodded at her before he disappeared down the ladder in his turn to follow Coll across the slippery heaving decks towards the *Golden Hope,* somewhere in the middle of the crowded harbour.

She lingered to watch the two men. Coll, stepping from boat to boat, sometimes having to leap a gap over the black water, reached his own skaffie and began at once to see that the nets were properly stored so that they could be run out smoothly when they were needed.

Lewis, softened by his time in Edinburgh, was a little clumsier, she noticed with faint amusement. He crossed the deck of the boat beside the *Golden Hope,* stepped up on its gunnels, then for some reason known only to himself he turned to look back at the harbour wall where she stood.

Then the boat that supported him suddenly shied away from the *Golden Hope* like a nervous horse and toppled him, arms flailing the air as he tried to regain his balance, over the side.

Eden's hands flew to her mouth as she saw him disappear. Below him, she knew, was deep water. And there was another danger – if the boat that had toppled him swung back against its neighbour Lewis could be crushed between the two wooden hulls.

'Lewis!' His name ripped out of her throat in an agonized scream and she saw the other women swing round to look at her, then at the confusion of boats within the harbour walls. A pain, more agonizing than she had ever imagined possible, seemed to tear her heart in two. Her own body anticipated the terrible pressure of the two big hulls as they moved in on him, crushing and grinding relentlessly through skin and flesh and bone. 'Lewis!'

And in that terrible instant when she was convinced that he was dying in fear and pain she realized that no matter what he had done to her she still loved Lewis Ross.

Coll reacted with blurred speed. As his half-sister's son clawed at the gunnel he had been standing on only seconds before and managed to catch hold of it, Coll snatched up an oar and pushed it across the gap, wedging it against the other boat's side, throwing all his weight on it to keep the two hulls apart.

Two crewmen on the other boat threw themselves to the deck, reaching over the gunnel to grip Lewis's wrists.

Eden, her throat burning, saw him scramble up on to the deck again, slap his saviours on the back, and skip safely on to the *Golden Hope* to give Coll a friendly punch of gratitude.

Then she turned and fled from the harbour, stumbling as far away from the staring faces as she could, until she had to stop, leaning against a house side, gasping for breath; unable, no matter how far or how fast she went, to run from the knowledge she had tried so hard to deny, even to herself. The truth about her feelings for Lewis.

Another pain doubled her up. This time it was physical, tearing across her back and gripping her stomach muscles. She whimpered, crouching against the wall, afraid to move until it ebbed away and she was able to straighten and walk home.

The baby wasn't due for another week, she reminded herself as she made some tea and poked the fire into a friendly glow. She had been upset by the incident at the harbour earlier, that was all. But just as she was lifting the cup to her lips a second spasm took her and she cried out as the cup fell and shattered on the edge of the range, splattering her with hot liquid. She put her scalded hand to her mouth to lick the tea away, and found herself biting the skin instead as the pain grew stronger and more demanding, taking over her mind as well as her body until a crimson mist danced before her eyes.

It was hard to believe that such a pain could ever pass, but it did, and she made for the stairs to the bedroom, longing to lie down. The third pain took her when she had climbed three

177

steps; as she huddled there, clinging to the banister, she suddenly recalled Charlotte's sufferings in the loft at Great Yarmouth, and the dead baby. She had to get help if she wanted to ensure her own child's safety.

The last of the boats was leaving harbour by the time she managed to crawl to the street door and open it, for the pains were coming almost continuously now and she had to keep stopping until their sharp agony eased.

Some of the women who had waited to see their men's boats out were passing when she half-staggered, half-fell on to the pavement at their feet. They lifted her, helped her up to her bed, ran to heat water and fetch clean cloths, soothed and encouraged her as she twisted and groaned and finally screamed in rage at the agony that refused to let her be.

It was a long birthing. It was light enough to see all the way to the May Isle lighthouse before her squalling, healthy son came into the world.

He had his father's square face and dark blue eyes, and his thick black hair held a suggestion of rich chestnut highlights, rather than the almost-blue sheen of Eden's hair.


'You've a fine bonny lad there,' Annabel said with satisfaction later that day almost as though she had created the baby with her own hands. 'What are you going to call him?'

Eden, tired after her night's travail, intoxicated by motherhood and at peace with the world for the moment, lay on her pillows and watched Coll's face as he looked down at the child in his arms. His eyes were filled with more love than she had ever seen in them before as they lifted to meet hers.

'Joshua – ' he said, offering her the best gift he could think of in return for his son. 'We're going to call him Joshua.'


Whatever happened she must never let Lewis or anyone else know of her discovery the night he had almost died at the harbour, the night young Joshua was born. It was easy enough to keep out of his way; there weren't enough hours in the day now that she had the baby to care for as well as the yard books to keep. And she was busy helping Annabel to plan the wedding that had set the whole village talking.

'It's pleasant to be the subject of gossip,' her friend said contentedly. 'All those years of just being the schoolmaster's sister were wearying.'

Robert Laird, discovering that angry scenes didn't sway his sister one bit, had immediately applied for and obtained a place at a village school miles inland, and was due to leave Buckthorne a few weeks after the wedding.

'It's an ill wind right enough,' was all his sister said when he delivered his news in an accusing tone.

'Tchah!' said Robert, unable to think of anything more crushing.


It didn't occur to Eden that her busy life could be eased by getting some help in the house until Euphemia Ross's maid-servant, Becky, called one day to ask for work.

'In return for my food and a roof over my head. I was brought up in a big family so I could see to the wee one for you – ' Her fingers twisted nervously.

'But I thought you were contented where you were, Becky.'

'It was all right until – until – ' Becky's mouth trembled, then dissolved. Tears filled her eyes. 'Oh, Eden, if you only knew what it's been like since that man came!'

It flooded out, a story that brought back long-buried memories and drew clammy fingers down Eden's spine as she heard it.

John and Teckla, Becky claimed, had never led a normal married life.

'Oh, they share the same bed but she's boasted to me that they've never as much as touched each other, apart from

179

what she called the kiss of commitment at that heathenish wedding her father conducted for them. She says they've joined in the sight of the Lord and pledged themselves to a life of celibacy.' Becky, stronger now that she was able to relieve herself of her burden, sniffed. 'Mebbe she's pledged herself to it, but he's not.'

She shuddered at her memories. 'Night after night he came scratching at my door, whispering to be let in, telling me I was a servant and I had to do as I was bid. I kept a chair tight under the handle always. Some nights I didn't get a wink of sleep, I was so frightened he'd force his way in. And during the day he'd be looking at me with those eyes of his, and I'd know what he was thinking – '

'Did you not tell Mistress Ross?'

'Her?' the girl said contemptuously. 'She'll not hear a word against the man. You'd think he'd bewitched her. It was better when Lewis came home for he was in the next room to mine and he came out on to the landing once when he heard John and frightened him back to his own room. But him and John quarrelled all the time and she'd always take John's side, so Lewis left.'

She hesitated, then said, low-voiced. 'Then Charlotte came. To see to the house, they said – and her a fisher-lassie who knows nothing of housekeeping. Not that that was what she was there for.'

'What do you mean?' But Eden knew well enough, even before Becky spoke in an embarrassed whisper.

'He didn't bother me after she came. She'd Lewis's room, and she didn't refuse him when he went scratching at her door while Mistress Ross was fast asleep. I couldn't put up with it any longer so I told the mistress I was leaving and she put me out there and then and won't give me a reference – '

The tears welled again and Eden put her arms about the girl. 'Don't, Becky. I'll be glad of your help in the house, and with the store too.'

*

180

'Are you soft in the rigging?' Coll wanted to know when he heard the news. 'I'm just a fisherman, not landed gentry! What do we want with a servant?'

'Mebbe you don't need one since you've got a wife instead, but I could do with her help,' she said tartly, and he finally gave in.

'Though you're getting ideas above your station. Next thing you'll be telling me young Joshua'd be wasted as a fisherman, and trying to send him off to university the way Phemie did with Lewis. I'm warning you, Eden, don't start that sort of nonsense when the lad grows up!'

She stood by the cradle. The baby, fed and comfortable, looked up at her with sleepy blue eyes. She put a finger into his curled hand, which immediately closed over it trustingly.

'No – ' she said. 'I'd never do that. Not to him, and not to you.'

# CHAPTER TWENTY-ONE

In February, when Joshua Galbraith was a month old, Annabel married Gideon.

They held a big wedding party in their new house, which was large enough to hold all their guests. Robert Laird declined his invitation.

'Thank the Lord, for the man makes me itchy with his superior way of looking at folk,' Gideon said bluntly, and Annabel, looking young and pretty in her wedding finery, echoed, 'Amen to that!'

It was the first time since her own wedding that Eden had attended a social occasion. Resting after a strenuous dance, watching the others swing and whirl and stamp, she remembered that day almost a year ago, and looked up to see Coll watching her.

'For the sake of Gideon's old bones I hope Annabel doesn't lead him a merry dance in the loft tonight,' he murmured wickedly, reading her own thoughts, and she blushed.

Lewis arrived beside them, a glass in his hand. Almost all his time was spent out of doors and he had begun to take on a tan again. He looked more relaxed these days; the tension that had been so noticeable in his face when he first returned from Edinburgh had been largely smoothed away.

'Coll, you should be dancing with your wife.'

'I've just stopped dancing with her. And my throat's dry.'

'Well, while you're sitting this dance out, and while I've

mind of it – ' Lewis slipped a hand into his pocket, then held it out. 'This is for you, Eden.'

She stared at the fine silver chain, the many-faceted single crystal throwing out a sparkling rainbow from Lewis's palm. 'For me?'

'A wee gift to mark your son's birth. It's all right,' he added lightly as she turned to look up at her husband. 'Coll's already said I can give it to you.'

'I wish I'd thought of something of the sort myself, but Lewis knows more than I do about those wee courtesies. Here – I'll put it on for you – ' Coll took the chain, but his fingers were clumsy and he couldn't get it to fasten at the nape of her neck.

'I'll do it,' Lewis offered. She felt him lifting her hair aside then touching her skin, and tried to control the sudden tremor that ran through her. His hand stilled immediately, then moved again. 'There you are,' he said levelly.

The crystal lay like a glittering teardrop on her creamy skin, just above the curve of her breasts.

'It's bonny,' Coll approved, then went off in search of a drink. Eden closed her fist about the stone, shaking her head.

'I don't want it. Take it back, Lewis.'

'You can't refuse it – not now.' Then he understood. 'It was never Elizabeth's, you needn't fret about that.'

'Then how did you come by it?'

His eyes were suddenly serious. The noisy, laughing crowd at his back seemed to fade away; it was as though the two of them were quite alone.

'I bought it when I went back to Edinburgh just after I met you. It was to have been your New Year gift. Only – '

'Only you never came home.'

'Until now.'

'Until it was too late.'

'Is it, Eden? Dance with me,' he said abruptly and took her into his arms before she could refuse. The tremor racked her again.

183

'Are you cold?'

'No. Why did you not give it to your wife?'

'I don't know,' he said honestly. His face was just above hers, his mouth inches from her own lips. His arms held her lightly but firmly. She looked into his eyes and recognized the turmoil within him; it matched her own.

She locked her trembling muscles into rigid obedience, fastened a bright smile on her face, moved in time to the music, and wondered if there had ever been such a long dance.


He came to the house the following morning when Coll was at sea and Becky was out.

Eden didn't invite him in, but he walked past her and into the kitchen. When she followed him he was standing before the fire, feet apart, chin jutting as though he anticipated trouble.

'Eden, I love you.'

'No!' The word filled the great space between them. 'No –' she repeated, her voice shaking. 'You've no right to say that to me.'

'What difference does that make?' he asked impatiently. 'Since when did loving care about right and wrong?'

'You turned your back on me when I would have followed you to the ends of the earth. You chose Elizabeth – '

'I was a fool! I knew it when I went to the schoolhouse to tell you about her. I looked at you and I knew at once that I'd thrown away all that I held dear. But it was too late – '

'It's still too late, can you not see that? You chose her – ' she went on remorselessly, cruel to him in order to keep her own impulses under control. 'And on that day you gave me up. We've both made our lives and there's nothing more to be said!'

'Listen to me, Eden – '

'I don't want to listen to you! I don't want to be alone with you again!'

'Because you love me as much as I love you.'

'No!'

'Eden –' He took a step towards her, one hand outstretched. It would have been so easy to step forward herself, to walk into his arms. Instead she snatched Joshua from his cradle, holding him close, making a talisman of him. The baby, startled from a sound sleep, began to howl.

'Go away, Lewis! And don't come back into this house unless Coll's here.'

His hand dropped by his side. 'I love you,' he said again, before he went out.

When the street door closed behind him she buried her face against Josh's warm, sweet-smelling little body and wept. His fists, beating the air in furious protest, found her thick black hair and tangled themselves in the tresses.

All through March she and Lewis scarcely saw each other, and she made certain that they were never alone together. She longed for him, but each time she watched Coll with his son she knew that she must deny her innermost feelings.

Coll had put his ring on her finger, given her his name and his child. They were partners, not only in marriage but in business. Their relationship might be stormy at times but he was a good husband and father. She couldn't turn her back on the past year and all it had brought her.

Gradually her reawakened hunger for Lewis was brought under control again, locked away deep beneath her everyday life. The pain dulled to an ache and she knew it would gradually disappear as it had before. At least she'd had the sense to hold her tongue, to resist the longing to look into his clear green eyes and say 'I love you'. At least she had retained her pride and her independence.

The winter herring fishing brought disappointing results; in April, when the white fishing started, Coll decided to take the *Golden Hope* up the coast and fish from Aberdeen for a few weeks in the hope of getting more money for his catches.

Eden stood by the harbour entrance, the baby in her arms, and watched until the vessel's big brown sail was a speck on the horizon.

'You're the man of the house now,' she said to Josh, who gurgled and reached up with a fat fist in a vain attempt to catch one of the gulls floating high overhead.

The weather turned wild the day after Coll sailed. Gale-force winds raced in from the North Sea, carrying sleety showers that swept the village then disappeared again with startling suddenness. Tormented into a frenzy, the sea tossed spray from the tops of racing waves and attacked the shoreline with angry, spitting vehemence. The fishing boats were confined to the harbour and the men gathered in little knots along the foreshore, frustrated and bored.

Eden couldn't sleep that night. She stretched her long legs across the bed, missing Coll's warmth. The wind banged against the front of the house, screaming and raging and rattling at the windows when it was refused admittance. She could hear the boats groaning and creaking at their moorings just across the road; underlining everything else there came the continual deep boom of massive waves hurling themselves again and again on to the rocks.

She wondered what it must be like on the ledge where she and Lewis used to meet. It was probably completely under water now; when the storm went away it would be strewn with clumps of green-brown weed ripped from the seabed by the storm's mighty hand.

Shortly after midnight she got up and dressed, unable to sleep and suddenly unable to breathe. The house was silent; Josh and Becky were asleep despite the noise outside.

She tied a shawl over her head and opened the street door, pushing her way out against the wind, closing the door again and leaving it on the latch so that she could get back in. The wind bowled her across the road and down the ramp, trying to snatch the breath from her lungs. She anchored herself by wrapping her arms about one of the posts used for hanging nets and felt her hair break free of the shawl to whip against her cheeks.

Looking up, she saw ragged clouds scudding madly across the sky, the moon appearing now and then. It was exhilarating to be the only one abroad on a night like this; though she hoped that Coll was safely in harbour and not at sea.

A shadow moved near one of the two boats on Gideon's stocks. As she watched, it moved again, blending with the deep shadow beneath the keel. Thinking that Gideon must be making sure that the boats were safe she let go the post and walked along the harbour, keeping in at the wall, well away from the drop to the water and the restless shifting fleet.

Shingle crunched underfoot as she stepped down at the end of the harbour, then she stood on a large stone, crying out as it turned under her weight, almost toppling her over.

As she righted herself the wind's roar dropped for a few seconds and she heard the thud of something heavy being dropped, then the rattle of small stones beneath hurrying feet.

She lunged forward into the lee of the skaffie. It loomed over her like a great wooden whale, giving her some protection from the gale. She tripped over something – not a rock this time, she saw, but one of the long-handled axes used for trimming and paring planks.

'Got you!' a voice said breathlessly and she dropped the axe and screamed as someone grabbed her shoulder, spinning her round. Then the painful grip loosened.

'Eden?' Lewis peered at her, lowering the fist that had been drawn back to strike. 'For any favour, woman, what are you up to, out on a night like this?'

She clawed hair out of her eyes. 'I heard someone in the yard. Was it you?'

'No. I came to make sure my boat was safe. I thought I heard someone too.'

'Mebbe it was just the wind.'

'Mebbe,' said Lewis, his tone vague, his eyes intent on her. The moon reappeared, casting weird silvery-blue light on the implements about them. The fist that had almost struck her uncurled into fingers that gently stroked the hair back from her face.

'My love,' he said, so quietly that she wasn't sure whether she had heard the words or simply seen his lips shape them. She shook her head, pulling away.

'Let me be, Lewis!'

The wind gusted, slamming a great hand on her back, throwing her against him. There was an odd, low rustling from directly behind her and she saw Lewis's head jerk up and away, looking beyond her. Then he pushed her from him, hard, and she went sprawling, shingle crunching painfully into her cheekbone.

Events seemed to slow down. She took a long time to push herself into a sitting position; the skaffie's bulk seemed to drift on its supports, rather than lurch, sideways towards Lewis. At the same time he stooped, picked up the axe she had tripped over moments before, and jumped forward to wedge its handle in amongst the jumble of logs that made up the stocks.

Then everything snapped back to its normal speed and above the noise of the wind, above the creaking of the great forty-six-foot-long hull as it threatened to topple on to him, she heard Lewis roaring, 'Get help – go on, woman!'

She got to her feet and ran, tripping and falling and picking herself up and running on, up the shingle and on to the road, by-passing Gideon's house because even in her panic and her fear for Lewis she realized that the boat-builder, still weak from his illness, wouldn't be able to help to hold the skaffie's weight.

She pounded on a cottage door, ran to the opposite house,

crashed her fist on its wooden panels, then rushed back across the narrow street to the first door, which was opening.

She never knew whether it took minutes or hours between the time she left Lewis and the time she ran back with four or five sturdy fishermen at her heels. She fully expected to see the skaffie on its side with Lewis pinned underneath, but he was still there, both hands locked round the axe-head in an attempt to hold it in place, feet planted firmly into the shingle for purchase, his back hard against the hull that threatened to slip and smear him on the ground like an insect crushed underfoot. The moon swept a veil of clouds aside at that moment to reveal his face, shiny with perspiration, a grimacing mask of effort, ghastly in the eerie blue light.

Someone pushed her out of the way. The world became a mêlée of feet crunching on pebbles, voices shouting orders, the creak of the stocks as the men she had fetched wedged poles against the pilings and slowly, slowly, eased the threatening skaffie back into place, taking the crushing weight from Lewis. He dropped to his hands and knees, his fair hair flopping to the stones as he drew great gasps of air into his lungs.

'Lewis!' She knelt beside him, hands on his arm, and he lifted his head.

'I'm – all right,' he said, then he was on his feet again, helping with the work.

Gideon appeared, greying hair ruffled, face crumpled with sleep, shouting out crisp instructions that were instantly obeyed. Annabel, wrapped from head to foot in a great cloak, came to stand by Eden.

'What happened?'

'I think someone tried to knock the stocks loose,' she shouted above the howl of the gale.

'John – ' the words were whipped away as they left Annabel's lips, but Eden recognized the shaping of the name.

'Or Walter,' she yelled back. There was little doubt in her

mind – John would doubtless send someone else to do his evil work for him, and Walter, if he had a grievance, was one of the few local men quite capable of destroying a fine boat. Neither of them would have over-concerned themselves if Lewis had died or been maimed by their actions.

The stocks were shored up, the skaffie lashed into place with guy-ropes. One by one, satisfied that there was no more to be done, the men went back to their beds. The moon came out again and in its light she saw that Lewis still looked deathly pale. She took his arm and discovered that he was shaking violently with reaction. Worried about him, she led him across the road and into her kitchen. He went without a word, slumping bonelessly into one of the fireside chairs.

'Here – ' she poured out a mug of ale and gave it to him, then coaxed the range into a deep red glow. 'Did you hurt yourself?'

He drained half the mug before giving her a lopsided smile. 'A few bruises, mebbe, but that's all.'

'Your hand's cut.' She filled a basin from the kettle that was always kept on the range and fetched a clean rag. A thin sleepy wail from upstairs reminded her that it was time to feed Josh.

'Wash the cut and rest here for a minute or two,' she ordered, then hurried upstairs, stopping to look in on Becky, who was a sound sleeper. Indeed, Eden wondered sometimes if the girl was making up for those nights she had lain awake in Euphemia Ross's house, listening to John's pleas and commands through the door-panels.

When the baby was fed and settled back in his crib she loosened her hair and brushed out the untidy tangle the wind had made of it, then went slowly downstairs to make some tea. She had assumed that by that time Lewis would have gone back to his lodgings, but he was still in the kitchen.

Anticipating her longing for a hot drink, he had made tea. He put a mug into her hand and pushed her gently into a chair.

190

'Lewis, how could anyone, even John – ?'

'Hush,' he ordered. 'We can talk about it in the morning.' Then his hand pushed the curtain of shining hair from her face and his eyes narrowed as they examined the long scratches where her cheek had scraped along the shingle when he pushed her clear of the falling hull.

'You've been in the wars yourself.' He emptied out the basin she had prepared for him, refilled it from the big kettle, came to kneel by her chair, dipping the cloth in water, wringing it out, easing it gently over the red, bruised skin.

'I can manage,' she protested, but he ignored her, washing her face and then drying it with a fresh cloth, his eyes intent, his hands as deft and gentle as a woman's.

When he had finished he put the basin aside, then cupped his palm over her cheek.

'Don't –' She put a hand up to push his away, but instead her fingers stayed, holding his hand against her face. The kitchen was very quiet; even the storm seemed to be holding its breath as she looked into his sea-green eyes, struggling then drowning in their depths.

'No – no –' Her mouth formed the words, but her voice was only a half-sigh of sound.

'You sent me away once when I told you I was to marry with Elizabeth, and again when I told you I love you. Don't send me from you again. Please –' His other hand came up to rest on her shoulder. 'Please – ?'

It was more than she could bear, more than she could fight against. She turned her face into his cupped palm, her lips sliding over his skin. He gave a strange cry deep in his throat, half groan, half laugh, then she was in his arms, her black hair over them both, their lips meeting, parting, meeting again in a bruising kiss that spoke only of their wrenching need for each other.

She slid from the chair into his arms and he lowered her gently to the floor to lie with him on the hand-made rag rug. He twined his fingers in her hair, easing her head back so

191

that he could kiss her exposed throat, her shoulders, his hands pushing her shawl and blouse impatiently out of the way, his lips stirring her skin to a new awareness.

She struggled against him, turning her face away from his mouth when it came seeking hers again, wanting only, at that moment, to bury her own lips in the warm hollow of his throat. She moaned a protest when he imprisoned her hand to kiss her fingers when they were impatient to slide inside his open shirt and over the silkiness of his chest.

Coll ceased to exist for her during those insane minutes in Lewis's arms. There was so much they needed from each other, so long a parting to be compensated for. They kissed, touched, murmured wordless things to each other, and at last, when her body was ablaze with desire, he took her, and the world dissolved into such a sensation of pleasure and fulfilment that there was no longer anything in the universe but Lewis and Eden, Eden and Lewis, without end.


Later, after he had dressed to go back to his lodgings, he took her into his arms again.

'I need you, Eden. I want you to come away with me.'

She held him close, her body still tingling and glowing from his loving. 'It's what I want too.'

He kissed her again, a quick hard kiss. 'When?'

'I have to wait until Coll comes back. I have to tell him to his face – tell him how bad I feel that I'm having to do this to him. Tell him how much I need to be with you.'

'Coll – ' Lewis groaned into the softness of her throat. 'God, if only it was anyone but Coll I was robbing like this!'

When he had gone she closed the door behind him, straightened the rug before the fire, and went upstairs. Josh was on his back, a fist lying on either side of his head. His little square face frowned slightly in his sleep. He was so like Coll that her heart turned over.

She got into bed and lay staring at the grey square of the

window. The storm had begun to abate. Her body felt heavy, relaxed, sated. Her mind repeated Lewis's words over and over again.

If only it was anyone but Coll!


'You can see what happened,' Gideon said grimly on the following morning as the four of them – Gideon and Annabel, Lewis and Eden – studied the boat that had almost fallen over in the storm. 'Someone took the axe and tried to hammer away one of the supports.'

His finger jabbed at the fresh scars on one of the pilings. 'No doubt they meant the next gust of wind to send the boat over. She'd have been smashed, the work would have been set back weeks, not to mention the cost of the damage – and we might have thought it was all due to the gale.'

'John's hand was in it, for sure,' Lewis said. He and Eden had scarcely exchanged a glance since they met at the yard fifteen minutes earlier, but she was keenly aware of his presence inches away, his arm almost, but not quite, brushing hers as he stooped to examine the stocks.

'No doubt we'll never be able to prove it.' There was a grim twist to Gideon's mouth. 'It's a bad day for Buckthorne when a man raises his hand against another in this way. It's not our way at all.'

'You didn't see who it was, Lewis?' Annabel asked, and he shook his head.

'I'm certain it was John – or Walter, put up to it by John. But I didn't see his face.'

'I've already put it about the place that from now on the yard's going to be watched day and night. And I let it be known that if anyone was found tampering with company property I'd not bother calling in the militia – I'd see to it myself,' Gideon said, then brightened up. 'Mebbe there's not much we can do without further proof, but at least there was little harm done. It's a blessing you two were around.'

193

'A blessing – ' Annabel agreed. 'What brought you both to the yard in the middle of the night?'

'I couldn't sleep for the storm – ' Eden began, and Lewis finished the sentence smoothly.

'And I was worried about the Fifie, so I came out to check on her.'

'Just as well,' was Annabel's only comment, but her shrewd blue eyes rested first on Lewis, then on Eden, looking at her so penetratingly that she almost wondered if Annabel could see right through her clothes to where her body still throbbed to the memory of Lewis's loving the night before.

'The ledge, in an hour – ' he murmured through rigid lips as Gideon and Annabel moved away.

Now was her chance to stop things before they went any further, to step back inside the safety of her marriage and close the door tightly against temptation.

But Eden felt as helpless as the great piles of seaweed that were being carried in to the shore at that moment, debris from the storm. She had broken faith with Coll, and now she must go wherever the tide of her passion bore her.

# CHAPTER TWENTY-TWO

It was almost impossible to hide their affair from the village; completely impossible to hide it from Annabel.

'You must be out of your mind!' she said flatly to Eden less than a week after the night of the storm. 'Standing talking together when Lewis is supposed to be working on the Fifie, walking together, looking at each other as if you can't bear to look elsewhere – it's all wrong!'

'I know that. But sometimes right and wrong don't seem to matter any more.' Eden realized that she was echoing something Lewis had said to her when she was denying her love, and she smiled faintly to herself.

'You're surely not expecting something to come of this?'

'I'm going with Lewis, once I've had a chance to tell Coll.'

'But what about the company?'

'Coll and Gideon can manage fine on their own.'

Annabel's frizzy hair bounced with impatience. 'You've got a fine man already – a good husband, a provider. What's he ever done to deserve this from you?'

'Don't!' Eden said sharply. She couldn't bear to think of what she was doing to him.

'I must!' Annabel said just as sharply.

'I know he's a good man. I know he deserves better than me. But what I feel for Lewis and what he feels for me – it's something that started when we first set eyes on each other. Something I can't deny – and the Lord knows I tried!'

Annabel's eyes went strangely blank, as though focusing

through Eden on to something beyond her.

'Aye, lassie, I know what you mean,' she said, her voice suddenly quiet. 'I know how it feels.' Then she added heavily, 'All the same I wish Lewis Ross had gone anywhere but Buckthorne when his wife died.'

'So do I,' Eden told her honestly. 'But he came here and I love him still, and now I've to face the consequences.'

She wasn't surprised to find that Annabel had guessed, but it had never occurred to her that Euphemia Ross, now more or less a recluse, would hear about her son's rediscovered love for the former fisher-lassie and come to Eden's door to tackle her about it.

Her heart almost failed her when she saw the crow-like body etched against the sunlit street, but she tried not to show it, inviting Euphemia in calmly, offering her tea, saying pleasantly when it was refused with a tight shake of the head, 'You'll forgive me for asking you into the kitchen, Mistress Ross. We don't have a proper parlour as yet. And you'll excuse me going on with the ironing, for I've a lot to do.'

Euphemia's gaze flicked about the room like a snake's tongue, taking in the gleaming black-leaded range, the freshly baked scones cooling on the window sill, the gold-edged plates in the corner cupboard.

As Euphemia's eyes landed on the baby, babbling contentedly to himself in his crib, Eden had to control an impulse to snatch him up and put her body protectively between him and those cold, fanatic eyes. Then the woman's gaze moved on, completed its swift inventory of the room, came back to Eden's face.

'Not so much to do that you can't spare time for mischief.' Her voice was crow-like too, now; creaky, as if it were scarcely ever used.

'What d'you mean by that?'

'You've taken up with my Lewis again.' Then, as Eden continued to smooth the iron carefully over a skirt, she probed, 'Have you nothing to say for yourself?'

196

'Nothing that need concern you.'

Euphemia's mouth jerked and writhed. 'The whole village is talking! D'you deny he's spending time with you – that you're leading him into damnation?'

'My life's my own concern.'

'It's your man's concern. Or have you forgotten about Coll? My own half-brother, that I raised in a good Christian household, wed to an – an adulteress!'

The word was thrown at Eden like a stone. It struck like a stone, but she would have died on the spot rather than let the older woman know that. She turned the skirt round, ran the iron over it again.

Hatred coarsened Euphemia's voice. 'Curse you, Eden Grey!'

'Watch yourself, Mistress Ross. A curse often turns back into the mouth that makes it. And my name's Eden Galbraith – or Murray, if you can't bring yourself to speak my married name. Not Grey.'

Euphemia began to lose control. 'You've no right to my family name now you've betrayed my brother. And you've no right to Joshua's name either, for your mother was never wedded to him.'

'I'm his daughter for all that.'

The older woman laughed, a mirthless cackle that sent a flicker of doubt over the baby's sunny face and halted his babbling momentarily.

'Nobody can deny that – not now. His daughter, with his evil Satanic ways. His dark eyes and winning smile and offers of the joys of the flesh to trap an innocent soul and drag it down to hell in a burning blazing agony of need – '

The iron slowed, stopped, was set aside.

'He damned me but I'll not let his whelp damn my son, my Lewis – '

Euphemia stopped suddenly, her crazed eyes moving beyond Eden to the door that led out to the back yard, and Eden turned to see that Lewis, who had been cutching the

197

Fifie's sails in the back yard, stood in the doorway, his shirt sleeves rolled up, his bare muscular arms dyed rich brown from the cutch, his face hard.

'Go out of here, Mother,' he said quietly. 'Go back home.'

'Lewis – ' She held out a pleading hand to him. 'Come with me. You don't know what she can do to you.'

'Go home,' he repeated.

'I know – I know, Lewis!' Spittle formed at the corners of Euphemia's mouth. 'She learned it from him – from Joshua. The ways and the wiles, the soft words and the touching – and the loving – '

'That's enough!' His voice cracked across the room at her. Eden felt his breath on her cheek, his body close beside hers. Euphemia looked at the two of them, anguished.

'Come home with me, Lewis – before you're damned!'

'It's you who are damned and warped with your bitterness and your love of money and those two sick people you shelter under your roof!'

Her breath hissed through yellowing teeth. 'No – you mustn't speak about them like that – ' Her eyes darted from side to side as though expecting a bolt of lightning to strike him dead on the spot.

'Get out!' he almost shouted at her. 'Get away from us! You destroyed my father but by God you'll not destroy me!'

Euphemia drew herself up. For a grotesque moment she wore her former cold dignity like a cloak that no longer fitted her thin shoulders.

'No. Joshua's daughter will be the one to destroy you,' she said with a dignified clarity. 'We'll pray for your soul, Lewis. We'll all pray for your soul.'

Then she shrank back into the hollow-eyed crone that she had become and added venomously, 'But not for her!' before stamping out, an angel of doom.

Eden was shaking so much that Lewis had to prise her fingers from the handle of the iron and half carry her to a

198

chair. She buried her face in the hollow between his shoulder and the firm line of his jaw.

'Lewis – the things she said about my father – they must have – she must have – '

'Hush – ' His hand stroked her hair, his lips moved against her forehead. 'Quiet, my darling. She doesn't know what she's saying. She's mad. God help her – John Murray has driven her mad.'

Then he drew back. 'Look what I've done to you!'

She looked down at the brown smears on her blouse where his hands, still wet, had held her, then looked up again to see horror in his eyes as he tried to remedy the damage and only made it worse.

'Oh – Lewis – !' She began to laugh helplessly and after a puzzled moment he joined in, gathering her into his arms, kissing her, holding her, covering them both in the brown dye that was so difficult to get off. She felt her laughter turn to tears and held him close so that he wouldn't see them; burying her face in his shoulder so that he would think that the tremors that shook her were born of mirth, not fear and anguish and a great dread of what the future might hold for them both, and for Coll and Joshua.


Two weeks passed. The weather cleared, summer began early. Josh thrived, and Euphemia Ross left Eden and Lewis alone. The Fifie, almost completed, was a handsome sight, the wonder of the whole village.

The time came for Coll to return from Aberdeen.

'I'll tell him about us,' Lewis said as they sat on their rocky ledge one afternoon watching the sun lay a gold path across the sea.

'No, it's for me to do it.' She shivered in the circle of his arm and his grip tightened.

'The naming time's here.'

She knew it was a ploy to take her mind off her

199

confrontation with Coll, although the naming of a boat was an important thing among the coastal people.

A fishing boat carried its own destiny with it always. The workmanship, the blessing at its launching, the skill of its crew, its name – they all contributed to its well-being or its bad fortune.

'What's it to be?'

He turned from studying the sea and looked down at her with eyes the colour of the waves rolling majestically in to break almost beneath their feet.

'I wanted to name her after you, but I've not that right yet. I'm going to name her *Homecoming*.'

'It's not a usual sort of name.'

'It's in gratitude for being here instead of in Edinburgh, of being with you where I belong.'

He kissed her, his tongue twining with hers. 'I've come home,' he whispered, his voice suddenly thick with love. 'Home to my lovely, lovely lass, after all this long time!'


For only the second time since their marriage Eden wasn't on the harbour wall to see Coll bring in the *Golden Hope* after a trip. Josh was teething and fractious and she had chosen to stay with him until he quietened down.

She laid him in his crib and watched as he irritably battled against sleep, and lost.

'He'll be all right now, Becky. I'll be back as soon as the *Golden Hope* comes in.' She checked the table, set ready for Coll's meal, then moved to the range to lift lids off the pots of potatoes and mutton and broth – all of which were gently simmering. Everything was in order.

Her stomach fluttered as she thought of what she must tell him later, once he had eaten that meal.

'Make sure the potatoes don't boil dry, now. And mind what I said – you're to take the evening off after we've eaten. I'll see to every – '

Iron-studded boots stumbled and lurched along the cobbles outside as though their wearer were drunk. The street door slammed back against the passage-wall.

She had time to think, 'Oh dear God – he knows – ' before the kitchen door flew open in its turn. Josh jumped, murmured a protest, and sank back into exhausted sleep.

Coll swayed in the doorway, gasping for breath as though he had run for miles instead of the few yards from the harbour just across the road. He looked at her with eyes that burned in a grey face, then said to the staring maidservant, 'Get out!'

'Away and visit your sister, Becky – ' Eden said swiftly. 'I can see to the meal – '

White to the lips, the girl obeyed, sliding past Coll as though fearful that he would strike her. When she had gone he kicked the door shut.

'You and – and Lewis.' The words were torn with difficulty from his throat. He dropped the provision box he was carrying.

'I wanted to tell you myself. Who – '

'You shouldn't have made it obvious to the rest of the village, then,' Coll said in a voice soft with rage. 'You should've known that cousin of yours would make sure to be the one to tell me once he knew of it.'

'John!'

'I was scarce on to the harbour wall – looking for you – when he started pouring his poison into my ear. And Lewis didn't trouble to deny it.'

'What did Lewis say?'

'Nothing.' Coll said with a strange satisfaction, rubbing a balled fist in the palm of his other hand. She saw that his knuckles were bloodied. 'Nothing – but when a man stands and takes another man's fist without defending himself it's because he's guilty. So' – he took a step towards her – 'you're too late with your telling. How long has it been going on?'

'Two weeks. Since you went to Aberdeen. We didn't

intend for it to happen, Coll – ' she cried out, destroyed by the pain in his face. 'We didn't want it to happen!'

'Did it have to be Lewis? My own kinsman? You're mine now! What there was between you – it's over! It's by!'

A second pair of booted feet skidded and slipped over the stones outside. The street door banged once more against the wall and Lewis was with them, his eyes wild, blood trickling in slow crimson drops from his chin to his shirt. His mouth was swollen and a massive bruise disfigured his cheek.

'You'll not touch her!' He caught at Coll's sleeve. 'The blame's mine, not hers.'

'Get out of my house!' Coll ordered without taking his eyes from Eden.

'Not until we settle this between us – '

'We'll settle it when I'm ready! And until I'm ready you're not welcome in my house. Get out!' Coll's big hands clenched into fists by his sides.

'Coll – I love him. I have to go with him,' she said quietly.

His face twisted as though she had struck him. 'You can say that after all we've weathered together?'

'I have to – ' she repeated, and went to lift Josh from the cradle.

He was there before her, scooping the child up, holding him close. 'No! If you walk out of here, you go alone! Josh stays with me.'

She stared, her empty arms falling back to her sides. 'But I'm his mother! He's too wee to be without his mother!'

'He's my son,' her husband said stubbornly over the baby's angry yells. He rubbed his chin on the downy little head. 'I'm not going to let you take him. If you go, you go alone!'

She hesitated, looking from one man to the other. Then her shoulders slumped and she said quietly, 'Leave us, Lewis.'

'Leave you here with him, the mood he's in? I'll not do it!'

'I'll be fine.'

202

'Get out of my house,' Coll repeated flatly, his eyes still on Eden. Lewis hesitated.

'I'll come to you, Lewis. But not just now. I can't just now,' she said.

When he had gone she walked over to Coll, arms outstretched towards their son. He let her take Josh without protest, watched as she quieted the baby and laid him down in his crib again. Then he dropped heavily into his usual chair at the table and waited while she silently ladled hot broth into a bowl and set it on the table.

Slowly, methodically, he ate every scrap of the food put before him, while she scarcely touched her own meal. While she cleared the table and washed the dishes he took off his great sea-boots and put them neatly in their usual corner before drawing a chair up to the range.

'We'd a good fishing. I made a fair bargain with the dealers at Aberdeen. I think you and Gideon'll approve.'

It was a grotesque parody of a normal evening.

She finished her work, fetched her knitting wires, and went to her usual chair. Coll had been wronged, it was his place to speak of it first.

At that very moment he said, 'Have I let you down in some way, Eden? Have I not cared for you enough?'

'You've been a good husband – and a good father. But – '

'But I'm not Lewis,' he said bitterly. 'I wish he'd never come back!'

'Wishing changes nothing.'

He got out of his chair to pace the floor with the traditional fisherman's walk – three steps one way, three steps back. Four steps on the deck of a herring boat could take a man over the edge and into the sea.

'You're my wife! And Josh is my son. If you're set on going, you can go without him. I'll not let another man have the raising of my son!'

'I must go to Lewis,' she said softly, insistently. 'And I must keep my baby with me.'

'So – ' His chin jutted in a gesture she knew only too well. 'It's to be a battle of wills, has it? We're a stubborn pair, you and me. We'll see who's the most determined, eh?'

He waited, standing in the middle of the floor, hands hanging empty by his sides. She said nothing, and after a moment he lifted his provision kist and set it in the middle of the floor, unfastening the clasp and throwing back the lid. His big hands lifted out a large brightly coloured ball made of patches of velvet.

'I brought this for the boy.' He tossed it into her lap and she automatically put her knitting down and caught it, fingers sinking into its rich softness.

'And for you – ' From the depths of the chest Coll drew out something protected by several layers of paper. He unwrapped it and held it out, balancing it on the palm of his hand.

Eden caught her breath as she looked at the small china bowl. It was fat-bodied, sensuous, curving from its gold-edged base to a fluted gold rim. Full-blown roses massed richly round the top half, soft pink and deep red alternating, each blossom nestled in a bed of green leaves. It was the most beautiful thing she had ever seen.

'I've been waiting for seven days to see your face when I gave you this,' Coll said. Then as she reached out for the bowl he let his wrist flip over and the beautiful little ornament slipped from his palm to smash against the sharp corner of the kist.

'Coll – !' She jumped up as his stockinged heel, regardless of danger, crushed the delicate shards into the floor.

'No sense in giving you fine things for our fine home now, is there?' he said huskily. 'Let Lewis see to that!'

He lunged towards the corner cupboard, tore the doors open while she stood rooted to the spot, unable to move. The two small plates he had brought back from Great Yarmouth were scooped off their shelf and tossed carelessly behind him to smash; one on the floor, the other flying past Eden to crash against the iron range. Then his fingers closed on the big

Yarmouth plate, the symbol of all her hopes and plans.

'No!' she screamed. She hurled the velvet ball at him, but it merely bounced off his broad chest as he turned to face her, the plate already falling from his open fingers, its gilt paint flashing and its colours glowing at her as it went. The sound of its breaking tore through her head and she flew at Coll.

He stepped forward over the debris to meet her, gripping her shoulders, trying to keep her at arm's length. She balled her fists and punched at his chest, opened her hands and slapped him, clawed her fingers to tear at his face in her rage.

Strong though she was, she was no match for him. One of his hands went to her throat, closed over the crystal that was suspended there on its fine chain.

She felt the chain bite momentarily at the nape of her neck, then it snapped and Coll tossed the stone away. It curved through the air, a tiny blazing star, and fell into a shadowy corner.

His fingers groped at the back of her head. Pins tinkled to the floor and the thick glossy mass of her hair swung down over her shoulders. Strong though the material of her cream blouse was, it ripped like frail lace under his furious onslaught.

'How often, Eden?' he grunted breathlessly as they battled together. 'How often did he see you like this?' Her chemise was torn away, leaving her naked to the waist. 'How often did you give yourself to him?'

There had only been the one occasion, there in the kitchen on the night of the storm. The rest of their meetings had had to be confined to stolen kisses, caresses, talk of what would be, once they were finally together. She set her lips and fought grimly, silently, against her husband.

'Did he touch you like this – ?' Coll's hands were all over her, hurting her, reminding her for a fleeting moment of John. She cringed away, but there was no mercy in him. He caught her to him, dragging her head back with a cruel grip on her hair, crushing his mouth against hers until she tasted

205

blood. Her breasts and stomach were bruised by the buttons on his jacket and the large buckle on his belt. Coll had never been like this before.

'Is this the way he took you?' he panted into her face, forcing her down on to the rug. She writhed wildly against him.

'Coll – no – we'll go upstairs – ' Then, as he ignored her, pinning her wrists above her head with one hand while he tore at his own clothes with the other she gasped, 'Becky might come back and find us – '

He raised himself above her, a wolfish grin distorting his mouth. 'Let her. We're husband and wife, are we not?' he said mockingly, and took her savagely on the very spot where she and Lewis had found each other again.

# CHAPTER TWENTY-THREE

The rose china and the smaller plates were smashed beyond repair but with Annabel's help Eden managed to salvage the Yarmouth plate.

'Dissolve the gum arabic in hot water, make it into a thin paste with plaster of Paris, and it'll hold together until Gabriel blows his horn,' Annabel directed briskly, and the plate was painstakingly put together.

'But it'll never be the same again,' Eden mourned as she replaced it in her cupboard. Once again, it was the only resident.

'A lot of things round here'll never be the same again,' her friend reminded her. 'Eden – you've a good husband in Coll! D'you have to break his heart and turn everything upside down like this?'

Then she looked at Eden's shadowed, unhappy eyes and added with a sigh, 'Aye – I suppose you feel you must.'

The waiting time dragged on, days stretching into weeks. She and Coll went on with their lives, speaking to each other only when they had to, maintaining a formal politeness for the sake of Becky and the baby, lying side by side in bed at night, unsleeping. He made no effort to touch her after that first night on the kitchen floor.

He stayed in the house most of the time, or brooded around the yard, letting the other men take the *Golden Hope* to sea. He and Lewis didn't look at each other if they happened to meet. Eden and Lewis stayed apart, sharing an unspoken agreement, waiting for Coll to make the first move.

Sometimes, when Coll was out of the way, she stood at an upstairs window watching Lewis at work on the nearly-completed Fifie, yearning to be with him, to touch him.

'How long – ?' he always asked on the few occasions when they met accidentally in a shop doorway or at the corner of a street.

'I must wait till Coll agrees to let me take Josh,' she said each time. 'I'll not steal his son away when his back's turned.'

Occasionally she walked out to the end of the harbour wall to try to ease the restlessness in her body. From there the attic windows and roof of the Ross house could be seen. She pictured Euphemia crouched like a witch in her cold, immaculate parlour, casting the spell that held the three of them – Coll, Lewis and herself – in its merciless grip. She had no doubt at all that it was Euphemia who had sent John to tell Coll about her love for Lewis.

The *Homecoming* was finished and launched, and people flocked to the harbour from the neighbouring villages of Ainster and Pittenweem, Crail and St Monans, to see the Fifie that had captured their interest take to the water. Coll and Eden and the four people who lived in the Ross house were the only absentees.

'She rides the water like a gull,' Gideon reported when Eden went to the boatyard the next morning. 'The lad's a boat-builder to the tips of his fingers – Phemie was a fool to ever think he'd be anything else!'

The joint-stock company's farlins weren't ready for the summer fishing season, mainly because Gideon and Annabel were living in the house that should have been taken down to provide extra space, so arrangements were made for the Murray and Galbraith boats to continue unloading at other harbours.

A few weeks before the season began, when the skippers traditionally hired their crews and struck bargains with specific dealers who would provision the boats and undertake to handle their catches, Buckthorne was rocked by the news that Euphemia Ross had broken with her usual dealers in favour of a continental group who would take all the herring from her boats and ship it out to Germany immediately.

'I hear they've pledged her a full twenty-five shillings a cran provided she can deliver a certain number of barrels a week,' Gideon told Eden, shaking his head in disapproval. 'They say she's had to pledge every penny she has and borrow besides to pay the skippers in advance, for they're not happy at all about breaking away from the local dealers.'

Her quick mind was already juggling with figures. 'If it goes the right way she could make a fine profit.'

'Aye – but who's to say how the fish'll run? You can't force the sea to make a fortune for you, it's tempting Providence. They're saying John's behind all this. That's a good reason why she should have stayed with the dealers she knew. John's got no head for anything but prayers and sermons.'

The skippers who were tied for financial reasons to Phemie Ross's apron-strings had indeed grouped together and made her pledge their money in advance. Those who could escape flocked to Murray and Galbraith.

Eden was kept busy setting up agreements with the former Ross men, ordering provisions for a suddenly increased fleet, travelling round the dealers to strike the best bargains she could. She welcomed the extra work. It occupied her mind, and she could forget about her unhappiness and the misery she had brought Coll while she was adding figures, listing supplies, arguing with sharp-eyed dealers. In the end she managed to agree a sliding rate of payment with several companies, and succeeded in pleasing everyone.

'We'll mebbe not make a fortune but we'll come out of it well enough and so will the fishermen, as long as the season's fair,' Gideon complimented her. 'You've a fine head on your shoulders, lass.'

209

He had insisted on bringing *Homecoming* into the fleet, despite Coll's fury.

'Let him work for his mother!'

'And let your head talk to your heart, instead of the other way round!' Gideon snapped. 'The *Homecoming*'s a bonny boat, an asset to any fleet. Man, I'd take on a boat crewed by Phemie and John – and Charlotte and thon strange Teckla Murray too, if it comes to that – if they brought back the herring the way the Fifie will!'


The herring fishing on the Scottish east coast was surrounded by superstitions and beliefs. It was considered unlucky for a fisherman to meet a minister or a red-haired woman on his way to the boat. The mention of various animals brought bad luck. Each season had to be brought in with bloodshed before the boats could safely leave the harbour.

Normally the younger fishermen threw themselves with enthusiasm into a scuffle on the harbour wall while their seniors waited, smoking a final pipe and talking about the weather and the fishing prospects. When the first nose was bloodied the fight stopped at once and everyone went aboard to prepare for the trip.

As the young men were bantering with each other on the first evening of the 1875 summer season in readiness for the blood-letting Coll Galbraith strode down the ramp and through the group and dropped his provision kist on the ground.

'The new skipper should give the first blood,' he said and before anyone realized what he intended to do his fist, with all his weight behind it, crashed against Lewis Ross's jaw.

If he hadn't turned his head at the last second Lewis would have been knocked unconscious by the force of the blow. As it was, he staggered back into the astonished arms of the younger fishermen.

The last time Coll had struck him Lewis had been honour bound to accept the blow. Now, freed from all obligations, he rebounded like a catapult and threw himself at the other man, murder in his green eyes.

It was Coll's turn to stagger back, crashing off the stone wall then twisting out of the way as Lewis threw himself bodily after him. Lewis crashed against the wall and fell, the breath knocked out of his body; Coll pounced on him and the two of them locked together and rolled across the flagstones, booted feet skipping out of their way as they went.

Eden watched from the top of the ramp, unable at first to believe what was happening. Then she thrust the baby into Becky's arms and began to run.

Lewis managed to jack-knife his legs and throw Coll off. By the time he got to his feet Coll, too, was up. They circled each other warily before Coll, with a roar of rage, hurled himself forward, fists swinging. Lewis took a hard blow in the face and his nose exploded into a bloody mess as he grappled with Coll.

The other men crowded round, fishing forgotten as they cheered the two on. Eden, reaching the foot of the ramp, found herself faced with a solid wall of jerseyed backs. She pummelled, elbowed, kicked, screamed at them to let her through, and was almost knocked down as the crowd swayed back to let the fighters have more room.

At last she broke into the centre of the ring and stopped short, horrified by the spectacle of her husband and her lover, both covered with blood.

Lewis was on the ground, Coll on top of him, a great bruise on the side of his face, his fists pounding into Lewis's face. Then Lewis managed to gain the upper hand, his left eye already closing, his fair hair flopping over his forehead, his hands reaching into Coll's thick hair, lifting the other man's head up in order to force it back on to the stones.

'Stop! Stop it! You'll kill him!'

Eden's scream brought Lewis's head jerking round in her

211

direction. He lost his grip on Coll, who seized his advantage and threw the younger man off, rolling away as he did so, coming effortlessly on to his feet and spinning round to grapple with Lewis again.

She hurled herself into the fight, caught at the first flailing arm she reached, hung on like a terrier.

'Leave me be!' Coll roared at her, trying to shake her loose. She clung to him, convinced that one of them would die if they weren't stopped. Then Gideon, dark eyes blazing, burst through the group of fishermen and took Lewis by the shoulders, throwing him aside, putting himself between the two.

'That's enough! You're grown men, not children with no sense in their heads!' he bellowed.

They tried to get to each other again, but Annabel arrived in the arena and stood between them, by her husband, red hair standing on end, the light of battle in her eyes.

'Gideon – don't over-exert yourself,' she ordered, plucking Lewis from her husband's grasp, shaking him, despite the fact that he towered head and shoulders over her. 'As for you two – shame on you, giving yourselves a showing up in front of the whole village! Into the house with you and I'll put some of my arnica lotion on your faces.'

Coll pulled his arm free from Eden, a few drops of blood spraying from his broken lip on to the back of her hand as he did so. For an instant their eyes met and he looked at her as though at a complete stranger; then he pushed his way through the crowd, picked up his kist, and went down the ladder to where the boats waited in the warm June evening.

Lewis ran an arm over his face, smearing his sleeve with blood, then jerked his head at his crew, and followed Coll. The fight was over, the blood-letting done. One by one the others went down the ladder, prepared their boats, got out the great sweeps used to row the boats out of the harbour.

Gideon shook his head as he watched. 'If the old beliefs are right the amount of blood shed tonight'll ensure the best season ever.'

'You think so?' his wife asked. 'It might be that a season begun in bad blood's a bad season. There's different ways to look at it.'

Eden left them and walked to her usual place, above the entrance. The *Homecoming* went out among the first boats; the *Golden Hope*, near the shallow end of the harbour, was one of the last. As the boats went out both skippers lifted their battered faces briefly towards her. Lewis tried to smile, and winced as his bruised mouth protested. Coll merely looked at her the way he had done after the fight.

All night she tried to get away from the memory of that look, and failed.

Early in the morning she rose and dressed and went along to the rocky ledge, huddling there alone, staring out over the sea as dawn began to rise.

Her thoughts were all of Coll, and that final look. Her husband, the man she had married in order to get the best skipper for the *Golden Hope*, the man who had erased the bitterness of John's violence, had taught her the pleasures of physical love, had fathered her child.

She yearned to be with Lewis, but she knew that she would never forgive herself for hurting Coll.


The season started out uneventfully, with the boats bringing in an average number of crans from each trip. The Ross boats came straight back to Buckthorne, where a row of unfamiliar carts waited on the shore road for their cargo. Under John's cold gaze the fisher-lassies worked like slaves, filling barrel after barrel. Instead of being stored in the curing shed to be topped up with pickle most of the barrels went straight on to the carts, to be taken to Leith and shipped abroad from there.

The Murray and Galbraith boats returned later, riding high on the water, their catches already landed at other ports. The figures, reported by each skipper on his return and noted carefully in the ledger by Eden, made satisfactory reading.

'Though Mistress Ross'll have to hope for a better return than this if she's to make money out of the new venture.' She closed the book and put it away in the drawer of the kitchen cabinet. 'I hear she's used her name to borrow a deal of money from the banks.'

'It's John Murray that's behind the whole thing. Phemie was always too sharp to put all her eggs into the one basket,' Coll said, and a ghost of a smile crossed his face when she remarked without thinking, 'You mean all her herring in the one cran.'

'However it's put – it's not like Phemie to take such a chance. Her custom was always to take a little at a time and work her way through the whole banquet. This new way's greedy, and foolhardy. Frank would turn in his grave if he knew what she was about.'

The bruises on his face were fading but the bitterness was still there. She saw it in his eyes each time he looked at her, heard it in his voice if he happened to speak of the future. There was no trust between them any more. She had destroyed it as surely as he had crushed the rose china bowl underfoot.

He was only truly at ease when he was with little Joshua. There was no doubt that he loved his son as much as Eden did. The child bound them together as nothing else could, and she sometimes wondered wearily if she would have to wait until Joshua was grown before she was free to go to Lewis. She would wait that long if she had to, but although she was sure of his love for her, she couldn't see him waiting for years to claim her. He was growing impatient now; trying to persuade her to let him talk to Coll man to man, and when she refused, begging her to go away with him.

'Coll's a good man – he'll take good care of Josh,' he said urgently when he met her briefly at the boatyard. 'I'll give you children, Eden; I'll give you a houseful of them if it'll make you happy.'

214

But she would never be happy away from Joshua; in that respect she understood Coll's anguish more than she accepted Lewis's impatience.

The *Homecoming* was giving a very good account of herself in her first season; having sailed her and found her trustworthy, Lewis offered to sell her to Murray and Galbraith so that he would be free to turn his attention to building a new boat.

There was a stormy meeting when Gideon told the Galbraiths of the offer, adding bluntly, 'We'd be fools not to accept.'

Coll's eyes darkened with anger. 'We can manage fine without his boat.'

'We need it.' There was an edge to Gideon's voice. 'Eden?'

She shifted uncomfortably in her seat. 'I think we should buy it.'

'I'm opposed to putting money into a Fifie. Skaffies are the right boats for this coast!'

'Move with the times, Coll,' Gideon said.

'There's no sense in changing a well-tried design just because it's out of fashion.'

'The Fifie's a better boat.'

'So my vote means nothing?'

'Of course it means something,' Gideon said irritably. 'But Eden agrees with me, and you're outnumbered.'

There was a short silence, then he laughed angrily, looking at Eden. 'So – all at once a fine skaffie like the *Golden Hope* isn't good enough for you?'

'I didn't say that,' she began, but he got up and walked out, leaving the two of them alone.

'Well?' Gideon asked at last.

She sighed. 'We buy the *Homecoming*.'


Coll's anger simmered for two days, then boiled over into an open challenge to Lewis down at the harbour.

'I'll tell you this' – he pushed his way into a group of men

215

standing admiring the *Homecoming*'s fine clean lines — 'a skaffie can get out to the fishing grounds and back with a full hold faster than a Fifie.'

Lewis immediately flew to his boat's defence. 'That's nonsense!'

'Is it? We could put it to the test tomorrow — or are you afraid?'

'I'm afraid of nothing.' Lewis put a hand on the *Homecoming*'s foremast, looking up at Coll on the wall a few feet above. 'I'll even give you my share of the *Homecoming*'s catch if I lose.'

'And I'll wager my share of the *Golden Hope*'s take,' Coll said at once. 'Tomorrow, then.'

The harbour buzzed with interest. The men started laying wagers on the outcome of the contest, the older men backing the skaffie, the younger section putting their money on the new Fifie.

'You've heard?' Lewis put a hand on Eden's arm when they met in the street.

'Aye, I heard. Can you not stop baiting Coll? It makes nothing easier.'

'It was his idea.' His fingers tightened on her arm and she felt her heart flutter as she saw the look in his eyes. 'If I win the wager, will you come to me?' he asked.

'I'll not be dragged into a daft wager between two grown men who ought to know better!'

'I'll not wait much longer, Eden — '

'I must go,' she said, and hurried away.


'It's a daft thing to do, wagering one boat in the same fleet against the other,' she argued early the next morning as she watched Coll pull on his warm woollen shirt and socks and trousers.

'That's my business, not yours,' he said shortly. A pair of 'kersey breeks' made of thick blanket-like cloth went on next,

216

fastening just below the knee to clear the tall sea-boots. Even on a mild August morning like this it was cold out at sea. He reached for the thick blue guernsey and she watched him squirm into it. She had knitted it herself; it bore the zig-zag lines which denoted that its wearer was married, the anchors to represent hope, the ring at the neck to show that he had one child. She wondered who would knit his guernseys when she was gone, and what story the pattern would have to tell then.

He stepped into his boots, pulled on a sealskin cap, picked up his sou'wester and the oilskin dopper she had made by rubbing layer after layer of linseed oil into cotton. The dopper was made in the form of a smock, with no buttons to catch on the nets and carry the wearer overboard.

'Coll – ' she said as he went to the door. 'Don't turn this trip into another fight between you and Lewis.'

He stopped, but didn't look at her. 'I'll do as I think fit. But I'll tell you this – whether he wins or loses, whether or not you go to him when we come back, I'll not let Joshua go. I'll never let you and Lewis take my son from me.'

Then he stepped out into the pearly dawn and joined the men who were clattering down to the harbour.

Almost two hundred boats went out, including the *Golden Hope* and the *Homecoming*. For once, sick at heart over the rivalry between the two men who had once been so close, Eden didn't go to the harbour to see them leave. Instead, she stood at the upper window, watching the masthead lights move one by one out of the harbour and dance across the sea, a cluster of fireflies.

Towards noon the weather took an unexpected turn. The sky began to darken and Becky hurried outside to bring in the washing as the first spots of rain spattered the windows.

'A summer storm,' she said cheerfully as she carried in an armful of damp clothes and began to hang them on the wooden clothes-horse. Eden went to the door. Low clouds hung threateningly in the sky, smoke from the chimneys was blowing horizontally, the sea had turned a sullen grey and the waves were beginning to race.

She put on a cloak and went outside, to be sent reeling by a sudden gust of wind. People were beginning to gather at the harbour, watching the water foam round the off-shore rocks.

'A strange sort of storm for summer,' one old fisherman said, his eyes troubled as they studied the wave formation.

A stack of lobster pots swayed and toppled; the knot of people staring out towards the May Isle jumped as a slate rattled from a roof behind them and smashed on the cobbles.

'I hope the boats had the sense to turn back,' someone said, and another voice suggested, 'They might be sheltering behind the May.'

Another slate shattered; a wave, larger than the rest, rushed the harbour, failed to get in, and broke in a welter of white foam round jagged black rocks.

'God help them if they've not turned back by now,' said the old man, and Eden, feeling a sudden chill of foreboding, began to pray as she had never prayed before for the *Golden Hope* and the *Homecoming*.

# CHAPTER TWENTY-FOUR

There were hundreds of boats spread across the vast fishing grounds. Travelling under full sail, the *Homecoming* reached her destination and began to put down her nets before most of the Buckthorne boats caught up with her.

But Coll's superior seamanship told; the *Golden Hope* arrived shortly afterwards, and shot her nets within sight of the Fifie. Lewis grinned as he settled down to wait. He had no doubt that he would win the wager.

The first sign that the weather was changing came less than an hour later when a moist wind sprang up, bringing with it a sea fog that swirled over the water's surface, blotting out boat after boat.

A heavy swell began to heave beneath the boats; the *Golden Hope*, her raked stern and full body making her vulnerable when the sea was behind her, tossed violently and Lewis saw her lugsail being broken out to keep her head to the wind. A vessel beyond the skaffie began to take its half-empty nets inboard just as the fog crept round it and hid it from sight.

'Are you turning for home?' one of the men wanted to know.

'With a handful of fish in the nets and Coll still fishing? I'll be damned if I will!' said Lewis, his eyes on the *Golden Hope*'s fog-shrouded outline. Let her be the one to turn and run first.

He caught at the mast as an extra-heavy swell ran beneath the keel, lifting the Fifie then dropping it with a corkscrewing motion. The waves were running higher and faster. A boat passed them, dipping sail up, heading for the safety of the shore. Its oilskinned skipper cupped his hands to his mouth.

'Going – be bad – ' The wind snatched away every other word. ' – Turn – home – '

Lewis waved an acknowledgement and turned to peer at the *Golden Hope*. An elated whoop burst from him as he saw the skaffie swing round and head back towards her buoy. 'She's taking in her nets! Coll's going home!'

'Wise man,' someone muttered, but Lewis refused to be panicked. He knew his boat and he knew what she could do. Besides, he was determined to take back a better catch than Coll's.

By the time he judged it wise to start pulling the nets in he had left it too late. Several shadowy boats had passed, fleeing the worsening weather, and for all her crew could see now the *Homecoming* might be the only boat left in the vast fishing grounds. The wind was squalling now, hitting them from one direction then from another, whipping the sea into a boiling cauldron. The helmsman had to work hard to hold the boat steady while the rest of them braced themselves as best they could to haul in the thick slippery nets.

Rain was sluicing down in great sheets now, and it was hard to tell, as the boat plunged and bucked in a world of grey water, which was sky and which was sea. The deck pushed up hard beneath their boot soles then suddenly dropped away, to return with a bone-jarring thump.

A wall of water roared at the boat and took her broadside, lifting her up and then slamming her down into a trough. No sooner had she righted herself, her crew spitting salt water, than the next wave was on them.

It was impossible to bring in the nets under these conditions; Lewis's real concern now must be to get the boat and her crew to shelter.

'Cut the nets!' he roared, sick at heart, watching as the hatchet blade rose and fell, eating its way strand by strand through the thick ropes. White-green water poured over the gunnels, then the *Homecoming* rolled as the ropes parted and her precious nets with their meagre catch came free and disappeared into the tempestuous seas.

The deep forefoot that had fascinated Gideon bit hard into the water, giving the boat a purchase the skaffies lacked in such bad seas. The Fifie's fine spread of canvas carried her forward swftly now that she was free of the restricting nets, but even so the waves broke over her again and again and the crew clung desperately to any handhold they could find to save being torn from the deck and sucked into the sea.

They were forced to put about in order to use the wind to advantage, a move Lewis had hoped to avoid, for it left the Fifie at the mercy of the storm for precious moments, her sails empty and useless.

One of the men shouted, a thin whisper of sound above the storm's screaming, and pointed to a patch of water where the waves were creaming, a sure sign that rocks lay below the surface.

'Get her head round!' Lewis bellowed, working desperately now to save his boat from the mass of hard stone so close to her keel. The dipping lugsail caught the wind and began to belly out. The boat almost lay down on her side, skidding in the water.

Lewis's hold on the mast was broken by a rush of foaming green sea that carried him away, struggling like a fly in a pot of preserve. Something caught both elbows painfully, forcing his arms above his head. His groping fingers encountered a ledge of some sort and he clutched at it, deafened as the water rushed past and away. Then he was able to drag air into his lungs again. There was nothing beneath his feet but water; at first he thought he was in the sea, then his vision cleared and he saw the base of the mast nearby, the sail bellying above his head, and realized the hatch cover had come loose and he had almost been swept into his own hold.

He managed to haul himself up, wedging his elbows over

221

the edge of the hatch, before the boat lurched horribly to one side and a grating grinding vibration almost beneath him told him that the *Homecoming*'s keel had caught on the submerged rock and was slipping down it.

Stark terror gripped Lewis as he visualized the Fifie toppling right over and going to the bottom keel up, with his body trapped for ever within the hold. He thought with fleeting despair about Eden, about the boats he would never be able to build. Then the *Homecoming*'s keel slid off the rock and she managed to get her balance and right herself, the wind gusting in the right direction for once and filling her sails, surging her forward and out of immediate danger. A strong hand gripped the back of Lewis's jacket and helped him to scramble free as the *Homecoming* turned her bow towards safety and fled before the wind.

By mid-afternoon the sky over Buckthorne was as dark as if it were the depths of winter. The freak storm held the whole coastline in its grip; on the top of the cliffs whole fields of grain were flattened and destroyed while down below chimney pots crashed and the sea stormed and raged outside the harbour walls.

The boats on Gideon's stocks had to be lashed down and half of the roof of Euphemia's curing sheds was ripped off by the wind as easily as if it had been made of paper, crashing into some of the barrels inside the shed, toppling them over to burst and spill their load of fish and pickle.

The harbour wall was filled with anxious people now. As the day wore on the boats began to appear one by one, battling their way across the water to safety, only the tops of their brown sails visible each time they slipped down into the trough of a great wave.

Because the harbour mouth was angled away from the open sea the boats had to sail past and turn, then the crews had to furl the sails and row their vessel in, past the rocky

222

outcrops. It was difficult work in any weather, but in a storm it was almost impossible.

As the lucky men came ashore, grey-faced and exhausted by their fight to get home, they were claimed by their families and led away. Eden waited on, the wind whipping her skirts against her legs, the rain chilling her to the bone, her eyes fixed on the horizon.

She caught her breath as she saw a boat with cleaner lines and more canvas than the skaffies, its sails a lighter brown because they were new, and had been cutched only once.

'It's the *Homecoming*,' said a man beside her. 'It's Lewis Ross – he's brought her back!'

Eden watched, her heart in her mouth, as the Fifie came about, her tired crew making one last vital effort, handling the sails with a speed and skill that kept her from being thrown on to the rocks. The sweeps were brought out and a ragged cheer went up from the watchers as the *Homecoming* negotiated the entrance and moved forward into safety.

Lewis's face was radiant when he reached the top of the ladder and saw Eden there. Ignoring everyone else he made straight for her and took her into his arms. She clung to him, scarcely able to believe that he was safe; then she drew back.

'Did you see the *Golden Hope*?'

He stared down at her, surprised, then she saw concern overlying the exhaustion in his face. 'Is she not in? She left the fishing grounds before we did. I was sure she'd reach harbour before us. When I saw you waiting I thought – '

She realized that he had thought that she had let Coll go home alone, had waited to go with Lewis instead.

'How long before you did he take his nets up?'

'It's hard to tell.' Lewis, too, was sick with worry. 'He'll be all right. He's put in at another harbour – or mebbe he had the sense to shelter at the May – '

She broke away from him, ran from one man to the other, asking if anyone had news of the *Golden Hope*. Nobody had.

More boats struggled in, battered by the storm, and still

there was no word of Coll's boat. They waited together for news – Eden and Lewis, Annabel and Gideon.

'Go on home, Eden, you're soaked through,' Annabel urged as the afternoon passed and the sky darkened further. 'You can come back when you've changed into dry clothes and had something to eat.'

But she shook her head, heartsick with fear for Coll. 'I'm staying here until I know he's safe. You go, Lewis – you're worn out.'

'I'm waiting with you.' He put his arm about her and she leaned back against him, grateful for his strength.

Reports had begun to come in from up and down the coast. One village had lost two boats and a dozen men, another had lost three boats, eighteen men and two lads. Debris was being washed in all along the shoreline. Dozens of boats were still unaccounted for, including Coll Galbraith's *Golden Hope*. And still they waited, eyes straining into the gloom while the storm raged about them.

It was Lewis who saw the skaffie first. He shook Eden in his excitement. 'It's Coll!'

She strained to see, but there was nothing but mountainous waves. 'Are you certain?' She was afraid to hope.

'I know by the way she sails. Look!'

This time they all saw the skaffie. She was quite near, tottering on the crest of a great wave, clinging grimly for several seconds before vanishing into a deep trough. Eden dug her teeth into her lip, tasting blood, until the boat reappeared a little nearer than before.

She inched towards the harbour, came about, bow to the harbour mouth; then Lewis's fingers clenched painfully round Eden's as a powerful gust of wind filled the boat's sails and she began to slip sideways towards the waiting rocks.

'Get your sails down, man!' Lewis screamed against the howling storm. 'You're carrying too much canvas! Damn it, what's keeping them?'

'Their hands are too cold to undo the knots,' she said

224

bleakly, her eyes riveted on her husband, sensing and sharing his despair and frustration as his numbed fingers wres-
tled with the ropes.

At the last moment, when it seemed that the boat must be
thrown right on to a rocky outcrop, the dipping lugsail came
down with a rush and a clatter and the *Golden Hope*'s suicidal
skid stopped. The men unshipped the sweeps, manhandled
them into the rowlocks, and began pulling the boat towards
safety. Cold and exhaustion had almost beaten them; they
moved slowly, stiffly, using the last of their strength to force
the boat along until they were almost beneath the watchers'
feet.

Her bows edged between the stone walls towards home
and safety; then a heavy sea raced in behind her like a hound
bringing down a fox and sent the stern spinning seawards so
that she was swung back, bow to the rocks.

Eden's heart seemed to stop as she watched, and she heard
Lewis give a groan of anguish os Coll and his crew fought to
turn the *Golden Hope* again.

'They'll do it – they have to do it!' Gideon said fiercely. 'By
God, they're turning her – '

Then another wave raced in vindictively and forced the
boat's stern outwards towards the reef again.

Eden's knees gave way. She sagged in Lewis's grasp and
he supported her weight. She couldn't bear to watch Coll go
to his death, but she couldn't take her gaze from his struggle
to save his crew and his boat against impossible odds. Then
someone pushed past, going right to the edge of the harbour
wall. As he went by she saw that the man carried a coil of
rope. He leaned right over the edge, almost above the bow,
and threw the looped end to the boat.

Coll scrambled precariously over the heaving deck to
reach it, but the wind snatched it away and it fell short,
almost brushing his numbed fingers before bouncing off the
gunnel and splashing into the water.

The man pulled it back swiftly and threw it again as

225

another wave caught the skaffie. The sweeps flailed helplessly at thin air as she was lifted high and carried side on to the stone walls.

Coll caught the rope noose and made it fast, then the *Golden Hope* slipped down the side of the wave that had caught her, her head coming round as a dozen men jumped to throw their weight on the rope and drag her to safety. Another wave raced in in a final bid to tear her away from the entrance. Held fast by the rope at her bows, she twisted, her stern swinging out to crunch and splinter against the implacable stone wall guarding the harbour.

Eden felt the impact, felt the agonizing shattering and tearing of the hull as though it were happening to her own flesh and bone. Then the *Golden Hope*, crippled and listing, was dragged into the harbour and along the side of the harbour wall until she grounded in shallow water where there was no danger of her foundering.

Her crew had to be helped up the ladder, two or three of them collapsing on the stone flags when they reached the top.

Coll was the last to come up, climbing the ladder unaided, clambering over the top and pulling himself upright slowly, like an old man. Eden went to him, clinging to his arm, unable to believe that he was with her.

His face was blue-grey in the flickering lamps that had been set up on the quay. Deep lines of fatigue and suffering had carved themselves into his features.

'Coll – '

He looked down at her then turned back to look at the *Golden Hope*. 'My boat.' His voice was slow, toneless. 'Did you hear her screaming when her planks stove in?'

'She'll mend, Coll – she'll mend. Gideon'll repair her as good as new.' She put her arms round him, holding him close. 'Come home now – it'll be all right, you'll see. Come home and rest – '

She draped his arm about her shoulders, taking his

weight. As they turned away from the water Lewis stepped into her path, his hands outstretched to help her.

Their eyes met and held then he moved back, his hands falling empty to his sides. She led her husband along the harbour wall and up the ramp, the two of them weaving drunkenly as the wind buffeted them. Coll was almost unconscious on his feet; she had to brace herself to take his weight.

They gained the shore road and she guided him across it towards their home. Tears and rain mingled on her cheeks as she walked away from the harbour and from Lewis.

# CHAPTER TWENTY-FIVE

Eden went out early the next morning, while Coll still slept in the grip of grey-faced exhaustion.

The storm had abated during the night but there was still a sullen swell coming inshore. As she hurried by the harbour she glimpsed the *Golden Hope,* the ugly gash in her side looking worse in the morning light.

Lewis lodged in a house only two doors away from the cottage she had gone to as Coll's bride. The wrinkled old woman who owned the house pursed her lips disapprovingly when she saw who the caller was.

'Lewis,' she shouted over her shoulder, then shuffled away without another word, leaving Eden on the doorstep. He arrived within minutes, pale and unshaven, shadows beneath his green eyes showing that, like Eden, he hadn't slept.

'You – ?' He half opened the door to admit her but she shook her head and he was forced to go out on to the step, pulling the door to behind him.

She couldn't allow herself time to soften the blow. 'I'm staying with Coll.'

His face hardened; a muscle jumped in his jaw. 'Because of last night?'

'He matters as much to me as you do – and mebbe he needs me more.'

'But you gave me your promise – '

'I gave him my promise too – before a minister,' she said,

her heart breaking as she looked into the face she loved so much. 'I must stay. I see that now.'

He glanced up and down the street. On either side women were out on their doorsteps, openly staring at the two of them.

'You pick a fine place to tell me we're finished,' he said, low-voiced, angry. She had chosen that public place just so that he couldn't touch her, couldn't break down her resolution to do what had to be done.

'If you love me, you'll find another place to build your boats. Another woman, another life – '

'And if you love me you'll come with me!'

'I do – but our time's past. Coll would always come between us. I have to stay with him.'

Then, as he said nothing, she added, 'Gideon'll give you the price of the *Homecoming*. Take care of yourself, my love. May God go with you – ' and turned away quickly before he saw the tears flooding her eyes.

'I could do without God if only you'd come with me instead – ' she heard him say as she went down the steps to the road. She had gone only a few paces when he called her name.

'Tell Coll he should take the *Homecoming* while he's waiting for his own boat to be made seaworthy,' he said heavily, and she knew that he had accepted her decision. It made it harder, not easier, to walk away from him.


The tears had been swallowed back by the time Eden got home. She had made her choice, she must abide by it now. She lifted the latch then hesitated and knocked instead. Becky opened the door and gaped at her.

'It was on the latch – could you not get in? Coll's up and wanting to know where you've got to.' She said it all in a hurried whisper, stepping back to let Eden in. For the second time that morning she shook her head and stayed where she was.

'Ask him to come to the door.'

'Eh?' said Becky, bewildered.

'Tell Coll there's someone at the door to speak with him. Go on – ' she added as the girl hesitated. With a look that said she thought her employer had gone quite mad the girl disappeared. Eden nervously paced the pavement outside her own front door, swinging round when Coll spoke her name. He still looked tired, and older than his years.

'Becky says you'll not come in. What game are you playing now?'

She took a deep breath, recalling the scene as though it was yesterday. 'I've come to offer you work.'

It was his turn to say blankly, 'Eh?'

She held fast to her scheme. 'I've bought a new boat – the *Homecoming*. I'm offering you the job as skipper on her.'

His face hardened. 'The *Homecoming* has a skipper.'

'He's going away from Buckthorne – alone.' Then as he stared down at her she added, 'You'll need a boat till your own's repaired.'

'Find someone else. I'll have nothing to do with that Fifie,' he growled, and turned away.

'Wait!' As he turned back to her she said clearly, 'I always want the best in the village to skipper my boats – or have you forgotten that?'

He leaned on the doorway, his eyes intent on her face. 'I've not forgotten.'

'Well? Mebbe I've not got my best bonnet on this time but the offer's the same.' Her heart beat so fast that she was sure he must hear it.

'So's the answer,' Coll said after a long silence. 'I'll take on your boat – if you'll be my wife, to seal the contract.'

She let her breath go in a long sigh, and held her hand out. 'We have an agreement, then?'

He took her hand in his and shook it formally, his blue eyes fixed on hers.

230

'We have an agreement,' he said, and retained her hand, drawing her into the house and closing the door behind them.

# CHAPTER TWENTY-SIX

Lewis Ross left Buckthorne later that day, striding up from the harbour with his belongings in a bag slung over his shoulder and the money paid for the *Homecoming* in his pocket. When he reached the house where he had been raised he stopped and looked down the hill.

Buckthorne had been one of the lucky villages. None of her boats were lost in the great storm, though the *Golden Hope* wasn't the only one to be damaged.

Lewis could see the skaffie in the shallows by the boatyard. The harbour entrance had torn a sizeable hole in her planks and she was lying on her side, weighted down by the water in her hold. The *Homecoming* was moored nearer the street, hidden from his sight by red pantiled roofs. He squared his shoulders and turned his back on the harbour.

It took Charlotte Murray so long to answer the door that he had begun to wonder if the house might be empty before he heard the slow shuffle of feet coming along the hall. The door opened slightly and her small brown eyes peered out at him.

He put the flat of one hand on the panels and pushed the door open so that she was forced to step back. In the hall's gloom her pale face floated within its border of lank brown hair, suddenly reminding Lewis of that long-ago day on the *Rose-Ellen* when the nets brought the drowned seaman from the water.

'Where's my mother?' he asked abruptly, then as the girl

just stared in near-panic he opened the parlour door. Euphemia was in her usual high-backed chair.

'Lewis –' she said without surprise. Something stirred in a shadowy corner and he almost jumped as John Murray's wife Teckla rose from a low chair, her small face with its blank brown eyes and tiny mouth looking grotesquely doll-like.

She said nothing, but slid past him to the door, a large Bible clutched protectively to her thin chest.

Lewis shut the door behind her. Despite the fact that three women lived in the house a thin layer of dust furred the furniture that had once been so carefully looked after.

'I've come to say goodbye.'

'You're going back to university?'

He stared. 'University's long past.'

'Oh – yes,' said Euphemia vaguely. Then her voice sharpened. 'You defied me! You shamed me before the whole village, flaunting yourself with that – that fisher-lassie!'

'I'm going away and I'm going alone. You'll be glad to hear it's all over. You've won after all, Mother. Does that please you?'

Her brows knotted. 'You can't go away – what's to become of the store if you go? I've done it all for you, Lewis –'

'I don't want it, not a penny. And from what they're saying at the harbour you've lost your money thanks to yesterday's storm.' He peered at her, surprised by her lack of response. 'D'you hear me, Mother? It'll be days before the boats can get out again. You've forfeited your contract. You were mad to put every penny you had into such a venture!'

'I know what I'm doing!'

'You used to, but now –' He picked up his bag, hesitated, bent to kiss her cold cheek. 'Goodbye.'

Then he staggered backwards, almost falling against the table, as she suddenly came up out of her chair, clutching at him, her voice high and panic-stricken.

'No – no! Don't go, don't leave me. I can't live without you

233

– I can't stay here with Frank – ' Her hands scrabbled at him, catching hold of his jacket, slipping, grabbing at him again.

Now that she was out of the shadows he saw that her face was old, much older than it had been only weeks before. Her hair was untidy, the hands clawing at him had over-long nails. There was a musty smell about her and the lace at her throat and wrists was limp and dusty-looking.

'Joshua – ' she whimpered, trying to gather him into her arms, 'Joshua, don't leave me here, don't let her take you from me again. My love – '

'Let me be!' He fought free, more terrified than he had been the day before when the sea threatened to drown him in the Fifie's hold. He managed to break her grip and pushed her away violently, not caring if he hurt her. She half-fell into her big chair as the door opened and John Murray came in.

'What are you doing here?' he demanded as if he were the owner of the house and Lewis the intruder.

'Mebbe I should have come back sooner. What's been going on in this house?' Lewis stabbed a finger at Euphemia. 'She's sick – her reason's gone.'

'There's nothing wrong with her!'

'She listened to you and your mad schemes and now you're both ruined – '

John scurried to the fireplace and when he turned Lewis saw that he clutched the heavy poker in his fist.

'Get out!'

'I could take that away from you,' Lewis said with contempt. 'I could break you in two, John Murray, and not one person in the village would criticize me for it. But I'll leave you to find your own damnation.'

He picked up his bag and went out into the hall, fumbling with the door latch, driven on by his mother's panic-stricken cry of 'Lewis – !' from the parlour.

The door opened and he was outside in the daylight again, running up the hill as if something terrible were after him, running from the house where his father had died alone and his mother had lost her mind.

'Let him go – we've more to worry us!' With scant regard for his employer John pushed her into her chair when she tried to follow her son.

'Listen to me! There's three boats badly needing repair, and herring rotting on the floor of the curing shed because the storm burst the barrels.' He paced the floor in a frenzy. 'We'll have to buy up what stock we can from the other dealers if we're to meet the contract – d'you hear me? We need to have all the fish they managed to bring in along the coastline yesterday. I must have more money!'

Euphemia straightened herself in her chair, hands gripping the smooth wooded rests. 'I have no more money,' she said levelly. 'Tell the dealers Euphemia Ross'll see they get paid for their fish.'

He glared. 'The time for that's past! They'll not part with one herring unless they get silver in their hands. You must come with me now to St Andrews, to the bank. Your name's still good for another loan – '

He almost dragged her from her chair in his impatience. She drooped in his hands.

'I'm tired. Lewis has worn me out with his defiance,' she said with a petulance that sat oddly on her. 'I'll give you a note to take to the bank.'

His pale blue eyes stabbed hatred at her, his lips squirmed. 'They'll not deal with me! You have to come yourself – they only trust you!' He threw the door open. 'Charlotte – fetch her best cloak!'

Euphemia felt her way back to her chair like a blind woman and settled herself in it. 'Did you see Lewis when you came in? Did you see he'd no head?'

John's voice died in his throat and he spun round. 'What?' Her voice was matter-of-fact. 'His head was missing. It's

235

that fisher-lassie to blame, if you ask me.' Her own untidy head wagged at him as though they were fellow conspirators. 'They tell me she danced for it so it was given to her. It's a shame, for he had handsome features, my Lewis. Everyone in Edinburgh said so.'

She began to sing tunelessly, a children's Sabbath-school song. John went to her, lifted her head in shaking hands, and saw that her black eyes had turned to clear windows with an empty room behind them. A thin line of spittle gleamed from lips to chin. The song trickled on and on, even when he shook her until she flopped like a rag doll between his hands.

'No! Come back! You can't – you can't!' he raved into her blank face. 'It's only you they'll heed -- you they'll lend money to! Come back – !' he called across the great abyss of Euphemia's mind, but there was no answer.

John Murray heard a great roaring in his ears as his plans and ambitions crashed about him. He released the madwoman and stood in the middle of the Ross parlour, chin sunk on his chest, hands hanging by his sides.

There was a sudden giggle from the doorway, a rusty sound that ran up the scale, stopped abruptly, repeated itself. He lifted his head and looked without interest at Teckla, her strange eyes gleaming dully, her small mouth open and twisted downward in a paroxysm of mirth.

Charlotte stood by her, frightened brown eyes watching John, flicking to the woman who crooned tunelessly in the chair, then back to John.

Then Charlotte grasped the situation and began to smile. She chuckled deep in her throat as Teckla's giggles increased. They held hands, laughed openly at their master, the mirth accelerating until they were helplessly intoxicated with their delight at his downfall.

# CHAPTER TWENTY-SEVEN

It was as though Lewis had taken part of Eden with him when he walked out of Buckthorne. In the long bleak days that followed she wondered if it would have been just the same if she had gone with him – if she would have left a part of herself with Coll.

Although she tried hard to pretend that everything was as it had been before Lewis came back from Edinburgh, she failed. She and Coll were still formal with each other and she moved about her duties in a haze of misery. When he reached out for her in bed she went obediently into his arms, but there was no fire, no loving in her any more, and she knew that he was bitterly aware of it.

He quickly learned how to handle the *Homecoming*, even admitting to liking the new design after all and approving Gideon's plans to start building another Fifie. He took the boat to Aberdeen, and brought back a new plate for Eden's corner cupboard, a magnificent thing ablaze with colour, and with thick gold edging. Beside it the Yarmouth plate with its spider-web of gum arabic looked shabby.

'I'll put this one out – ' she took it from the shelf.

'Leave it,' Coll ordered with the bite that had only come into his voice since he learned of her affair with Lewis.

'But it's spoiled.'

'It belongs,' he said, and she put the plate back, knowing what he meant. It had symbolized her ambitions and dreams, it had given the *Golden Hope* its name; now, shattered

237

and patched together, it remained a pathetic symbol of the marriage she had ruined.

John Murray and his womenfolk had vanished from the village the day Lewis left. A caller had found Euphemia Ross, one-time scourge of Buckthorne, living alone in squalor in her fine house on the hill, chewing stale crusts and quoting great speeches from the Bible.

She was judged unfit to care for herself and quietly removed to an inland institution for the insane. As she was heavily in debt her chief creditor, a big bank, took over the house and put it up for sale.

Gideon had started work on the *Golden Hope*, wrenching off her shattered planks, stripping her back to the oak framework on one side, steaming larch planks until they were pliant then shaping them to the curve of her frame. She would be ready in good time for the English herring season.

'Are you going to take the *Homecoming* to Yarmouth?' Eden asked one evening as Coll got ready for the fishing grounds.

'She's a fine boat – but the *Golden Hope*'s my own. She'll do me.'

'And the Fifie?'

His deep blue eyes studied her face as though searching for something that he didn't find. 'That's up to you. She's yours.'

'She's ours! Murray and Galbraith own her, not just me.'

He shrugged as though her protests didn't matter. 'Then she can go to the next man in line for a new boat.' He stood up. 'I'm going down to the harbour.'

'It's early yet. The tide won't be right till near dawn.'

'There's things to do.'

'Coll – ' she said as he was going out of the door. 'I'm coming to Yarmouth with you.'

'No.'

'But I want to!'

His eyes were hooded, his face blank. 'Your place is here, with Joshua,' he said, and went out, leaving her alone.

She tended to the baby then left Becky in charge of the house and went over to sit with Annabel for a while.

'I wish I could mix a gum arabic paste and mend our lives,' she said drearily as the two of them plied their knitting wires in Annabel's cosy parlour.

'Have you told Coll that?'

'He'd not understand.'

'You don't credit that man of yours with much sense, Eden. He understands more than you know. If he didn't, he'd not be so easy hurt.' Annabel laid her knitting wires down. 'When are the two of you going to stop behaving like strangers towards each other? Make your peace with him before he goes off to Yarmouth. It's not right for a man to go so far away with a troubled heart.'

Eden thought of Coll in the southern port for six weeks, lodging with plump, warm Louisa. The Englishwoman would be a great comfort to a man wedded to a cold wife, she thought, and misery welled up in her.

'I don't think Coll and me will ever make our peace.'

'Because Lewis is still in your heart. You've made your choice, Eden – abide by it and put Lewis aside once and for all.'

Eden bit her lip, stared down at the knitting in her lap. 'It's not that easy,' she said, and Annabel sighed.

'Mebbe I'm too old to know the way of things. All I can say is that I bitterly regret the loveless years I suffered before I found Gideon and rescued him from his own weaknesses. You've already got your man, Eden – don't let the loving go.'


When Eden left Annabel the harbour was a bustle of activity as the crews arrived to prepare their boats for the fishing trip. She should have gone to see the *Homecoming*'s sleek shape pass through the entrance, but instead her feet turned in the other direction, carrying her along the shore road.

It was after midnight. The clear dark sky was awash with

stars and the moonlight gave the cottages an eerie silver-blue light that cast unexpected shadows and softened harsh angles. Windows were still lit here and there, and men's shadowy figures passed Eden, all hurrying towards the harbour.

A child cried fretfully in one cottage as she passed, an old man's wrenching bronchial cough was heard from another.

Just beyond the cottage where she and Coll had begun their married life an alleyway between the house walls led to the sea. She turned down it and made her way along the rocky shore.

The May Isle light winked cheerfully at her, marking the line between sea and sky. Twinkling stars strewn below its beam came from the mastheads of outward-bound boats heading for the fishing grounds. She wondered which light belonged to the *Homecoming*, and what Coll was thinking as he headed away from the shore.

She hadn't scrambled along the rocks for some time but even in the dark her feet and hands found the right crevices instinctively, leading her to the familiar rocky ledge.

Time passed without her noticing it as she stood there, her eyes fixed on the May light, her thoughts absorbed with Lewis and Coll, whirling round and round in a complicated pattern that had no ending and no solution.

The noise of the waves masked the sound of small stones rolling away beneath approaching feet; when a voice spoke her name she spun round with a gasp of surprise, lost her balance, and was briefly in danger of toppling from the ledge. Coll caught her arm and steadied her.

She stared up at him in the moonlight. If it weren't for the grip of his fingers on her flesh she would have thought he had been conjured from her own thoughts by some sort of moon madness.

'You? But you should be at sea!'

'Ach, that fool Lachie Thomson met the wee man in black on the way to the harbour,' he growled. 'He even spoke to him – and the crew refused to take the risk of putting to sea when they heard of it.' He released her and thrust his fists deep into his jacket pockets. 'A night's fishing gone, over the head of that fool!'

It was considered unlucky to meet a minister on the way to the boats, and unluckier still to name his profession or talk to him at such a time.

'Lachie wasn't to know.' Eden rushed to the defence of the newest and youngest member of Coll's crew. She liked the boy's cheery smile and his carroty red curls.

'Mebbe not. I just wish he'd had the sense to hold his tongue about it before the rest of them – or at least waited till we were on our way and it wasn't worth the turning back.'

Then he rounded on her. 'And when I got home there was no sign of you. I searched the whole village before I thought of coming out here. I thought – ' he stopped abruptly.

'You thought what? That I'd gone after Lewis?'

Even by moonlight she could see his jawline tighten so that the muscles stood out like whipcord. 'Can you blame me for thinking it, when I see thoughts of him in your eyes every time I look at you?'

Hurt pride put a sting into her voice. 'I gave you my promise and I'll abide by it!'

He looked down at her, and this time the barriers were gone. She found herself face to face with an open bitterness and misery that appalled her.

'What does a promise mean to you, Eden Galbraith? We went through a marriage ceremony together. We had a child together. Then Lewis came, and now all I'm left with is the empty shell of the woman I took in marriage.'

'Coll – ' She put a hand on his arm but he pulled away sharply.

'What d'you want, Eden? Me? Lewis? Josh? None of us?'

A gust of wind pulled her skirt against her thighs and ruffled his dark hair about his face.

'Lewis is gone! I sent him away – '

241

'He's here as much as ever he was! He's still in your mind, in your heart. He's standing between us every time you look at me. He's even lying in our bed with us in the dark of the night!'

His voice cracked, then recovered itself. 'How can I fight for you now, Eden? How can I use my fists to defeat the shade of a man who's only here because you keep his memory close every minute of the day?'

'That's not true!' She shivered, but whether the chill came from outside or inside she didn't know. 'I'm going home – '

He caught her wrist and pulled her back to face him.

'It's true and you know it. I want my wife back, but on my own terms. If not' – he released her wrist, turned to look out to sea – 'you might as well go to him and leave me and Josh to see to our own lives.'

'What terms?'

'Put him out of your mind for ever. Come back to me.' Then, as she stood helplessly before him, unable to understand what he meant, he said thickly, 'Let me show you how, Eden – '

He tore her shawl free and let the wind take it. It drifted over the ledge and was borne away on a receding wave. Then he dragged her into his arms. They swayed near the edge, locked together, and she was suddenly aware of the waves breaking only inches below.

'We'll fall into the water – !'

'We'll go together then,' he said recklessly into her ear. 'We'll die together or we'll live together, but by God there'll be no more being apart for you and me!'

His hand pulled at her blouse, sending buttons flying. Cloth gave way to his strong fingers and she felt the shock of cold air on her breasts. It was like the night in the kitchen, after he found out about her affair with Lewis, but this time there was a desperate need in place of the terrible cold anger of the coupling.

She struggled to free herself and his grip tightened. 'I love you, Eden – ' he said hoarsely. 'I love you and I need to know you love me – '

His hands were warm on her body, his mouth claimed and held hers. Her struggles slowed as warmth began to invade her heart, radiating through her veins, heating her blood and bringing with it a tingle of desire and excitement she had thought she had lost for ever when she sent Lewis away.

Coll pushed her back on to the rocky ledge, his body covering and warming hers. She tasted salt water on his skin. A great joy seized her and she joined in his loving, her hands fumbling impatiently with his clothes as she murmured his name then said it aloud to the starry night, over and over again, relishing the feel of it on her tongue.

'I love you – ' he said, and she heard herself answer him as the moon filled the sky beyond his dark head and bathed their joined bodies with its light.

'I love you, Coll – ' she said, and knew that it was true. 'I love you!'


'You were made to live and love,' he whispered much later, when passion was spent and they finally lay still together.

He was right. She had to taste and touch and experience life. She had to love and be loved, or there was no meaning to her existence.

Now she knew what it must be like for a man to steer his boat safely through a terrible storm and finally enter a safe familiar harbour. But nobody could stay within the harbour for ever.

The tide was going out. One wave larger than the rest ventured to the foot of the ledge and broke, spattering her arm with chilling spray.

Her husband's tongue licked it from her soft skin and warmed her again.

'Coll, it'll not be an easy life.'

He turned her face to his and kissed her. 'I never looked for

243

life to be easy. But I can take anything it brings if I know you're by me. We'll manage, the two of us. The three of us – and the bairns to come yet,' he added.

The stars had gone and the dawn light was overhead when he helped her up. They gathered their strewn clothes and dressed as best they could. Coll enfolded her in his warm jacket and took her hand in his.

'Time to go home to Josh.'

As they went back along the alleyway and into the street she staggered with fatigue and leaned against his shoulder.

'I must look like a scarecrow!' she suddenly realized, pushing tangled salt-sticky hair back, drawing his jacket together over her half-naked breasts.

'You look beautiful,' Coll told her. There were shadows beneath his blue eyes, yet his face was ablaze with pride and happiness. It awed her to think that she had the power to make another human being look like that.

'I'll take you home, my love.' He scooped her effortlessly into his arms.

'Coll! What'll folk say?'

'What do I care what they say?' he asked, laughter in his voice. 'Let them say what they please.'

Footsteps beat a brisk tattoo over the cobbles and a man turned the corner and came face to face with them. He blinked and stopped in his tracks.

'Morning – ' Coll boomed cheerfully, and began to sing, his deep voice rumbling through his chest and vibrating against Eden's cheek as it rested there.

Some early risers appeared at their windows, rubbing sleep from their eyes, peering to see who sang so loudly at that time of day.

They gaped as they watched Coll Galbraith striding proudly up the middle of the street, carrying his wife home.

244